"YOU DON'T ⬚ ⬚⬚

He sounded ⬚⬚⬚⬚ disappointed. "How about handcuffs?"

Remo was past the bodies now. Nearly upon Roote. "Don't use either. Don't need either."

"That's a cryin' shame. Metal conducts best."

Remo's hand was a foot away from Roote's throat when the private's palms opened up like desert blooms. Remo caught a glimpse of what appeared to be thimbles.

"Surprise," Roote announced. He grinned maniacally.

The power surge lifted Remo off the floor, flinging him back toward the end of the bar.

"Charge is lower than I thought," Roote complained. "Sorry, cowboy. There ain't enough for the full treatment."

Roote lowered only one hand this time. And this time Remo clearly saw the arcs of electrical energy shoot from the private's five fingertips.

Other titles in this series:

Created by
WARREN MURPHY
and RICHARD SAPIR

THE
Destroyer™

KILLER WATTS

A GOLD EAGLE BOOK FROM
WORLDWIDE®

TORONTO • NEW YORK • LONDON
AMSTERDAM • PARIS • SYDNEY • HAMBURG
STOCKHOLM • ATHENS • TOKYO • MILAN
MADRID • WARSAW • BUDAPEST • AUCKLAND

First edition January 2000

ISBN 0-373-63233-9

Special thanks and acknowledgment to
James Mullaney for his contribution to this work.

KILLER WATTS

For John, Erin, Liam, Sean and Molly.

And for the Glorious House of Sinanju,
e-mail housinan@aol.com

1

He couldn't stand up without hitting his head. He couldn't lie down—at least not to stretch out. The way a real human being stretches out to sleep.

Awake, he would sit. Asleep, he would curl in the fetal position on the rubberized floor of the box.

He had been this way for several weeks, isolated in his madness since the experiments had ended in failure.

They kept him like an animal.

An animal. That was what they'd called him when they found out what he'd done. *Animal.* He had heard that countless times. It was a control mechanism, he knew. And that was not all they had said.

"You're going to die, boy," the MPs who arrested him had promised Private Elizu Roote. Hardly a dispassionate statement from a couple of trained professionals. But Private Roote couldn't blame them. They'd seen the body.

She was a girl from town he had picked up in a bar. Barflies were always the best. They never asked many questions and they were hardly ever missed.

This one had allowed him to lead her out behind a U-shaped cinder-block garbage area in the empty parking lot of an abandoned restaurant. It was just on the civilian side of the chain-link fence near the officers' quarters. That had been his first mistake: doing it too close to the base.

The MPs had spotted him as they toured the perimeter of Fort Joy Army Base, near the border of New Mexico and Texas. They caught his frightened-rabbit eyes in the small yellow searchlight mounted on the side of their drab military jeep. Captured in the blaze of lurid, uncompromising light, Elizu did the only thing he could. He bolted.

Mistake number two.

As he fled, the MPs spotted his bloody clothes, then traced his path back to the body.

At the gruesome discovery, alarms had went off immediately.

They caught him, of course. After a helicopter search of nearby Alamogordo.

He'd had too much time to work on this one, which was a mark against him. If he hadn't had so much time, maybe he could have claimed that she was one of those women who liked to be choked when aroused. That it was just some rough sex that had gotten a little out of hand.

But try as he might, Roote knew he could never

make this a sex-related case. No one, but *no one,* liked to have their head cut off while doing it.

It wasn't long after his capture before the authorities began linking him to the other bodies. One in Maine. Three in Oregon. They even suspected him of a few others around his home state of West Virginia, but they could never be sure of those. He didn't decapitate his victims back then.

But even without those confirmed murders, there was enough evidence to convict him of at least one capital offense. Private Elizu Roote was headed for a military discharge, a civilian trial and a likely death sentence. At least that's where he *thought* he was heading.

But at the point when execution seemed inevitable, Private Elizu Roote had found a savior. And it wasn't any of that jailhouse-religion crap. His personal savior appeared before him in an olive-green army uniform with colored bars over his breast pocket and a couple of shining stars on his shoulders.

He was a general, about sixty years old. He carried a gleaming mahogany riding crop with a leather strap at one end. The stick was pressed so far up in his armpit he looked like the victim of an Indian attack in an old western. He weighed three hundred pounds if he weighed an ounce and stood just over six-feet, six-inches tall. His head was as crimson as a sunburn as he stood framed in the cell doorway.

With tiny black eyes that looked to have been chiseled from coal, the general regarded Private Roote. Roote, sprawled on the bare metal bed of the military prison, never moved. The general's eyes darted back to the two men who had trailed after him into the room.

"Dismissed!" he boomed in a gravelly voice.

The soldiers who had been standing guard at the door knew enough not to hesitate. Though it was against their better judgment, they left the general alone with the prisoner.

Once the guards were gone, the general closed the steel cell door gently behind him. He turned back to Roote, a smile cracking his bright red face.

"You're in a bit of trouble, eh, son?" the general asked. He toyed with the leather strap on his riding crop.

From his bunk, Roote shrugged. "Guess so."

Eyes narrowed below the general's close-cut white hair, heavy red lids squeezing a pair of shiny black olives.

"What was that, soldier?"

Roote was at a loss. After the night he had just been through, the last thing on his mind was military protocol. He shrugged his round shoulders again in helpless confusion.

The general seemed to accept Roote's befuddlement for a moment. He stepped farther into the cell, massive chin jutting forward pensively. When he was close enough to Roote he drew his riding crop from beneath his arm with the speed of a striking serpent. It was up, around and down in a shiny blur, striking the private in the meaty part of his thighs. The blow brought the younger man to his feet.

The general grabbed Roote by the front of his pale green T-shirt. "As long as you are in this man's army, you will address a superior officer as 'sir,' is that clear, soldier?"

Roote nodded, the light of understanding suddenly sparking in his sleep-deprived brown eyes. "Yes, *sir!*" he shouted. His legs smarted where they'd been struck. At attention now, he dared not rub them.

"See this hand, soldier?" the general queried. He held the side of his hand—fingers extended crisply—against his huge bobbing Adam's apple.

"Yes, sir!"

"This hand is shit and you're this deep in it."

Roote didn't know what else to say. "Yes, sir!"

The general lowered his hand to his chest. "What would you do to be only this deep, soldier?" he asked slyly. The hand strayed down to his broad paunch. "Or this deep?"

Roote blinked. He wasn't certain what to say, but he dared not remain silent. "Sir?" he asked, confused.

The general sighed impatiently. "I'm offering you a choice, son," he said. "A choice you probably don't deserve, from what I've heard about

your extracurricular activities. How'd you like me
to reach over and yank you right out of that neck-
deep pile of shit, soldier?''

Roote hesitated only a second. The general
could be pulling his leg, but what did he have to
lose?

''Yes, *sir!*'' The words echoed up the dank
cinder-block hallway of the dingy military prison.

General Delbert Xavier Chesterfield smiled
broadly.

''I had an inkling you might say that,'' he said
proudly.

I HAD AN INKLING you might say that.

General Chesterfield's voice echoed in the dark
recesses of Roote's mind, mingling with the other
voices.

He'd been so damned smug. He knew Private
Roote had no other choice. It was either join or
hang.

There were times during the ensuing months
when Roote wished he had allowed the authorities
to prosecute him. The pain was sometimes more
intense than he could bear. And then, when the
surgeries were all over and the scientists had created their miracle, Roote had stepped over the line
once more.

She was just a nurse. No big deal. They were a
dime a dozen. And it wasn't like his keepers
couldn't cover up his crime as they'd done with

the others. But Roote had been stupid. He realized too late that he was merely the prototype, and the scientists could repeat the procedure with others. A rational man might have known that he had become expendable. For Roote, however, that revelation came as a surprise.

After the nurse's charred body had been found, his food was drugged. When he awoke, Roote was trapped in the box.

And here he sat. For weeks on end. No company save the endless, deafening chorus of voices inside his head.

They knew now what they had done.

Roote picked at the corner of the box, where he'd found a weak spot in the caulking that sealed the wall to the floor.

They had created a monster.

The tattered material came loose in chunks.

A monster.

Fingers worked independently of conscious thought as Roote picked at the thin line of flexible caulking. Pick, pick, pick. He rocked back and forth on his naked haunches.

Him. Elizu Roote. A monster.

The caulking came away with ease.

They had confined him here with his demons. Not even granting a merciful death to end his torment.

A yard-long section of caulking pulled up between his fingertips. Roote spun around on the cool rubber floor of the cage. In the darkness he now faced the damaged section of floor. Bracing his knuckles against the rubber matting, he brought the bare soles of his feet down sharply.

Thump!

Muted. It wouldn't even register to their ears.

Thump!

A monster in a cage.

Again! Thump!

He leaned forward, feeling with his fingertips. Dry. Leaned back again, bracing against the cold far wall. Again.

Thump!

He felt once more. Groping fingertips in the darkness. Did that do it?

Yes. *Yes!* He could feel it now. He brought his hand up to his face, touching beneath his nose.

Definitely. It was on his fingertips. Water.

In the pitch-black center of his private rubber cage, Elizu Roote smiled. The chorus of voices screamed with evil joy, all focused on a single, silent thought.

Monsters sometimes escaped.

When he brought his feet down for the last time, a surge of pressurized water flooded the small cage.

THE SENSORS WERE CONNECTED to the feeding and communications tubes at the top of the submerged chamber that housed Elizu Roote. The green light had been lit for so long that Corporal Elber didn't notice right away that it had gone to red. Bored, he had been staring at the blinking lights on a phone on the other side of the monitoring bank when he gazed back at his own station.

The solitary red light flashed like a warning beacon.

The color instantly drained from the Army corporal's face. Grabbing, fumbling, he dragged the nearby long-stemmed microphone to his mouth. His shouts echoed down the sealed hallways of the Special Projects Unit.

"We've got a red light on the board! Repeat! Red light on the board!"

Even as he screamed the words, his chair was toppling over backward. While he ran to the unmarked steel door near his station, he frantically yanked his semiautomatic pistol free from his hip holster. Before he'd even punched in the proper code, civilian men in white coats were swarming in behind him.

Questions were shouted and ignored as Elber's shaking hands entered the final digits into the touch pad. The red light above the door turned green, and the men piled into the inner room, careful to stay behind Elber and his pistol.

The dimly lit inner room was as big as a gymnasium. A huge water-filled tank—large enough for a school of dolphins—rested in a metal-and-concrete base in the center of the floor. Suspended in the tank was the black rubberized box connected umbilically to the surface via a few simple tubes that were lashed together with waterproof tape. Some of the lines from these tubes ran to computerized stations at the periphery of the room.

They hadn't been monitoring in earnest for quite some time. They saw now that they probably should have been.

The seam at the bottom of the box had been broken open.

The pale, naked body of Elizu Roote bobbed at the surface of the tank. From the angle of the men in the room, he was looking down at them. He made not a move as they cautiously approached the tank, bunched up behind the corporal and his gun.

Roote's pinkish eyes were open, staring at nothing. The mouth was an empty black cavern. No bubbles escaped from between the pale, slack lips.

"Is he dead?" asked one of the five civilian scientists.

"He looks it," offered another in a whisper.

"Could I have some quiet, sir?" asked Corporal Elber of the last man who had spoken.

The corporal's breathing came with difficulty. His heart pounded as he crossed over to the side of the tank. A metal ladder scaled the high plastic wall. Gun in hand, Elber began climbing. Below him, the nervous scientists began whispering among themselves once more.

"We should have drugged the water," said one. He bit the already chewed skin around the remnants of his thumbnail.

"I suggested that," said a voice from the rear of the crowd. He was ignored.

"They said he wasn't supposed to get out," challenged yet another. He was referring to the Army Corps of Engineers, who had constructed the tank.

"They didn't even know what we were putting in there."

At this they fell silent.

Corporal Elber was at the top of the ladder by now. High above the floor, he stepped over the upper lip of the tank, placing a boot on the plastic platform connected to the interior wall. One hand trained his semiautomatic pistol squarely between Roote's shoulder blades. The fingertips of the corporal's free hand snaked slowly out to the floating body, brushing the ghostly white back.

The skin was cold and clammy. Like touching a corpse.

"He's dead!" Elber called down to the scientists. Exhaling his anxiety, the corporal holstered his gun.

Reaching, somewhat off balance, he grabbed Roote by the right bicep and tugged the limp body toward the platform.

The relief below was palpable. Two of the scientists scurried up the ladder. They joined Corporal

Elber on the platform just as he was hauling Roote up from the water. He dumped the lifeless body onto its back.

"Are you going to try to revive him?" Elber asked.

The two scientists who had climbed the tank looked at one another. Their hesitation spoke volumes.

Elber paused, as well. Ordinarily he would never have let someone slip away like this without at least attempting mouth-to-mouth, but Elizu Roote was different. Elber had seen with his own two eyes the horrors the private was capable of.

After an awkward moment punctuated only by the lapping water at the edge of the big tank, one of the scientists cleared his throat. "We, um. Ahem. We should think about an autopsy."

"Mechanical failure, you think?" asked the other, as if they were discussing a defective computer sound card and not a human being.

"Could be," said the first man seriously. "I'll have to let the general know. We'll autopsy as soon as we call in the rest of the team."

"Don't I get a say?"

The three men on the platform froze. The voice had come from below them. As one, they looked down.

Elizu Roote's eyes were open, alert. Smiling.

Corporal Elber was first to react. Twisting, he grabbed desperately for his gun. Another hand was already on his holster. He felt the metal pads at the fingertips.

Elber struggled, but he was fighting the strength of a madman. The hand didn't budge.

Roote sat up. "You look shocked," he said, grinning.

As he spoke, Roote swung his other hand around.

More metal pads. Elber saw them recessed into the puckered white flesh at Roote's fingertips. They took the place of fingerprints.

The fight for the gun became more frantic. As Elber struggled to remove Roote's hand from his holster, Roote placed his free hand over the corporal's chest. He looked for all the world like a faith healer at a revival meeting. The image couldn't have been further removed from reality.

As the three terrified men on the platform watched, Elizu Roote's hand jumped. What happened next would have stunned anyone outside that room.

Five blue arcs of electricity launched from each metal fingertip. The surge of raw power punched Corporal Elber solidly in the chest.

His skin had little time to singe as the powerful shock overloaded the soldier's suddenly frail heart. The pumping muscle was jolted into a burst of frenetic activity.

Elber's eyes sprang wide in terror as the gripping pain in his chest intensified. The blue arcs continued to flow from Roote's fingertips until the corporal's heart could no longer take the strain. Bursting all at once, the ragged muscle exploded a river of blood into the soldier's chest cavity.

Roote cut the power.

Eyes already glazing over, a stream of sticky crimson flooding from his mouth, Corporal Elber toppled sideways onto the platform.

It had all happened in a matter of seconds.

Only as the body fell did the reality of the horror seem to sink in for the other two sickly fascinated men on the platform.

The scientists panicked.

One bounded frantically for the ladder, shoving his colleague aside. The trailing scientist lost his balance, tumbling into the tank with a helpless splash.

Roote was across the platform before the man on the ladder had a chance to climb a single rung. Grabbing the scientist by the white coat, he dragged him back onto the platform. With a grunt, he flung the man into the pool.

Up until now, the platform had blocked the view of the men below. But at the appearance of Roote's naked torso, the reaction from the others was immediate. They screamed and ran. They were across the cold floor and out the open door in seconds.

Roote let them go, turning his attention to the men in the tank.

They were splashing madly, like panicked children who had not yet learned how to swim. One had nearly made it back to the platform when he saw Roote's bare legs. In terror, he ducked below the water. Bobbing up, spitting water, he began splashing back in the other direction.

Roote crouched down on his haunches at the edge of the churning pool. Tipping his head, he ran a lazy index finger through the cold water.

The second man had swum blindly up to the edge. He snorted mucus-filled water from his mouth and nose as he scrabbled at the plastic platform. His hand recoiled when he brushed against Elizu Roote's foot.

Skittering sideways, the scientist blinked chlorinated water from his eyes as he looked pleadingly up at the man who had been his test subject. He panted in fear.

"Do you want to beg for your life now?" Roote asked. His soft Southern drawl was mockingly soothing.

Halfway across the tank, the other scientist had made it to the submerged isolation box. He grabbed at the feeding tubes, trying to pull himself from the water. He slipped on the first attempt, splashing back into the big tank.

"Elizu, be reasonable," the nearer scientist begged.

"I don't think I can do that," Roote replied calmly. "That's why you-all picked me. You shoulda kilt me. Shoulda kilt me when you had the chance. That box weren't no way to leave me."

"Think, Elizu, *think. Try.*" Hot tears mingled with cold tank water on the scientist's face. "You were uncontrollable. What would you have done if you were us?"

Roote had to think for only a moment. As he rose to his full height, his eyes clearly registered his conclusion. Without another moment's hesitation, he aimed all ten fingers at the choppy surface of the wide pool.

In the water, the scientist shook his head in horror. *"No!"* the man screamed.

The power surge from Roote's fingers was incredible. It coursed through the water in an instant.

The man across the pool had been halfway out of the water and up the rubberized monitor line. The blue electrical surge seemed to reach up from the surface of the tank and tug him back in. He struck water with a fat splash.

In the tank, both men jumped and crackled like batter-coated fish in a deep fryer.

On the plastic platform, Roote gently closed his eyes, rhapsodic, as the energy poured out of him.

He let it run for a full minute, until he sensed the drain within his hips and shoulders. Only when he knew his internal supply was too low to continue did he cut off the power supply. By then, the men in the pool were long dead.

The crackling continued for a few moments afterward. The pair of white-coated backs bobbed lifelessly on the surface of the churning, steaming water. The material of their lab coats was tinted slightly brown.

Roote left them to bob in the waves. He stepped over the upper lip of the tank and climbed down the ladder.

Walking, not running, he crossed the big room toward the open door. His wet feet left a fading trail of prints on the concrete floor. A moment later, he was gone.

The monster had escaped.

2

His name was Remo and he was fighting gravity. And winning.

Actually, as he strolled along the thin wire eight stories above the dark alley in Providence, Rhode Island, Remo realized that "fight" was not the proper term for what he was doing. Tightrope walkers and trapeze artists fought gravity. Every step or swing they took flouted the simplest law of nature. Remo was no mere circus performer. For him it was not so much a fight as it was a stalemate.

Gravity was there. Remo was there. Both knew it, but each pretty much ignored the other.

The cool breeze brought the scent of the Providence River in from the east. The slight shift in wind would have caught a mountain goat by surprise, flinging it into the black abyss below. Remo merely shifted his weight and he continued to balance delicately as he stepped, one foot casually over the other, toward the distant wall.

To fight gravity would be to lose, Remo knew. One might just as well have tried to wrestle the sun from the heavens. If he taunted nature, he would plummet like Icarus to the hard, unforgiving ground. Instead, Remo became a force of nature unto himself.

Remo was a Master of Sinanju. The latest in a long line of heroes stretching back into the mists of prehistory. To be a Sinanju master was to be in total control of one's physical and mental abilities.

Feats that seemed extraordinary to normal mortals were second nature to the men of Sinanju. Dodging bullets, scaling sheer walls, the ability to lift many times their own weight—all came easy to those in harmony with the forces of the cosmos.

But Sinanju was not just a philosophy. The name derived from the poor North Korean fishing village from which the first master had come more than five millennia ago. Remo was the pupil of the Reigning Master, the last in the original pure bloodline.

Remo had not expected to become a Sinanju master. In fact, Remo—like most people—had never even heard of the most deadly of all the martial arts.

A lifetime before, Remo had been a Newark beat cop. One night a pusher had been found beaten to death, Remo's badge clutched in a hand tight with rigor mortis.

The trial had been incredibly, *suspiciously*, fast. Remo lost. He was executed for a crime he had not committed. When the electric chair didn't work, Remo awoke to find his old life was over and a new one just beginning. Technically dead, but still very much alive, Remo was placed in the skillful hands of the Master of Sinanju. From that moment on, Remo had been taught how to become all that he could be.

"Be all that you can be," Remo sang lightly as he stepped along the clothesline-thick insulated cord.

He wasn't aware he had spoken in more than a whisper until he heard the surprised voice before him.

"Hey! Whoa, hey, what the crap?"

The voice came from the flat roof. When he looked, Remo saw a broad, puzzled face peering from the deep shadows just above the upper roof ledge. It turned quickly away, calling into the darkest shadows in a husky rasp.

"Gino, get over here. You gotta see this."

Another face joined the first. This new face, presumably Gino's, grew as surprised as the first when it spied Remo standing on the impossibly thin wire out in the middle of nothing. The alley below lurked dark and menacing.

The cable swung gently in the breeze. Remo swung with it.

"You know dat guy, Ennio?" Gino asked his partner.

"What, do I look like I know him?" Ennio scoffed. He smacked Gino in the side of the head.

They turned their attention back to the man on the wire, Gino rubbing his smarting head.

Remo was of average height and build. His only unusual features, besides his obvious ability to root to a swaying cable in defiance of gravity, were his abnormally thick wrists. They were as thick around as coffee cans. Though it was cool, he wore a black cotton T-shirt and matching chinos. A pair of expensive Italian loafers were the only things between the wire and the soles of his feet.

"What are you doin' out there?" Ennio demanded.

Remo paused in midstep. "Just out for a quiet little walk." He stuffed his hands in his pockets and glanced around. His dark features grew puzzled. "Hmm. Guess I must have taken a wrong turn in Albuquerque."

"Oh, a smart guy," Ennio mocked. "Hey, we got a smart guy standin' eight friggin' stories in the air."

"How you doin' that?" Gino pressed, ignoring Ennio.

"You boys ever hear of gravity?" Remo questioned.

"What are we, morons?" Ennio demanded. "Dat's what makes things fall."

"Close enough for government work," Remo said. "How about super-conductivity?"

Ennio and Gino looked at one another, each apparently unwilling to admit he didn't know. They looked relieved when the floating stranger let them off the hook.

"No matter," Remo said. "That's a tough one. What I do, see, is I meet the force of gravity with an equal repulsive force. It only *looks* like I'm walking on the wire. In point of fact, I'm a fraction of a millimeter above it."

There was a spark of genuine curiosity in Gino's eyes. He opened his mouth to speak but was suddenly interrupted.

"What the hell is dat?"

A new voice. This one came from behind Remo. He glanced over his shoulder, back to the neighboring building. Three new angry faces peered over at him from just above the spot where the cable snaked into the old brick building.

"He was just tellin' us!" Gino hollered across the alley to his compatriots. "Somethin' about supercondominiums or somethin'!"

Remo rolled his eyes. "Could you yell a little louder? I don't think they can hear you in East Providence."

Gino wasn't paying attention to the others. He was staring at Remo's feet. They seemed anchored to the swaying line as firmly as if it were a broad concrete sidewalk.

"So it's like wit two magnets," Gino ventured.

"Sort of," Remo admitted, tearing his eyes away from the new arrivals. "But the repulsion isn't that intense. It's equal parts repel and attract."

Gino was clearly fascinated. Ennio, less so. With the appearance of the other three men, he had taken on a more authoritarian demeanor.

As Remo watched, a lightweight SMG swung into view, its collapsible skeleton stock already locked in place. Ennio aimed the barrel of the gun at Remo.

"I don't care about no supercondominiums or any of dat gravity bullshit."

At Ennio's lead, the three men opposite raised their weapons. Remo felt the telltale pressure waves of the three barrels aimed at his back. Before him, Gino reluctantly aimed his gun as well. All five of them were a hair away from firing.

In both directions, the men were too far away for Remo to reach before they fired. In the cross fire, with the added difficulty of having to stay balanced on the wire, Remo was at a minor disadvantage. There was only one alternative.

As five hairy fingers tightened against five separate triggers, Remo was already flashing forward. Bending double, he gripped the cable with his right hand, slashing downward with the left.

Bullets sang into the vacant air where his chest had been a split second before. Even as the sheets of hot lead soared in either direction, Remo's hand sliced through the cable. Holding one smoothly cut end, he swung dramatically to the nearest building. For added flair, he let loose his best Tarzan yell as he slapped into the grimy brick facade.

Using a variation on his wire-walking technique, Remo scrambled up and over the side of the building. The gunfire was rattling to a stop even before he crested the wall. He saw why the instant he hit the sheet of black tar.

The gunmen were dead. All *three* of them.

"Oops," said Remo.

Looking away from the bodies that had been mowed down accidentally, he glanced over to the adjacent building—the building he was *supposed* to be on. Ennio's startled face stared back at him. Gino was nowhere to be seen.

"What the frig!" Ennio snarled across the vacant alley space.

"Wrong building," Remo called back sheepishly. "Don't move."

Scampering back over the ledge, Remo climbed, spiderlike, down two stories. As Remo moved, Ennio took frequent potshots at his speeding form. He missed every time.

Puffs of brick and mortar dust burped into the fetid alley air.

Remo found the fire escape. Landing on the rusted upper platform, he raced down the remaining six flights of crisscrossing stairs to the street.

Ennio stopped shooting at him by the time he'd reached the fifth floor. All was silence by the time Remo broke into the alley. He crossed over to the next building and began climbing rapidly up the grimy wall.

He should have gone up this building to begin with. He had used the elevator in the first building so that no one would see him in the second. Now *everyone* had seen him. This was what he thought as he climbed. If his employer wasn't always so damned concerned with security, he would have just gone in, done his job and got out.

Remo had worked up a good head of steam by the time he reached the top of the eight-story building eleven seconds later. He climbed quickly over onto the roof.

As he had expected, Gino lay dead on the black surface. Circles of red kissed his crumpled frame. Killed in the cross fire.

Remo found the stab of weak yellow light from the roof door. He entered the well, climbing down the narrow flight of stairs to the top floor.

The two buildings he'd visited this night, and indeed most of the structures on the block, were owned by the Patriconne crime family of Rhode Island. The eighth floor of this particular apartment building was left vacant for Mob use. The man Remo was looking for was somewhere on this floor.

He stole down the corridor, listening for heartbeats beyond closed doors. He found what he was looking for at the end of the hallway.

Remo kicked in the second to last door. The steel buckled, exploding into the room amid a hail of plaster dust.

Two goons were waiting in ambush. As the ruined door was bouncing atop the sofa and sliding to the floor, they were already firing.

Bullets savaged the wall behind him. Remo moved through the storm of leaden missiles as if they were no more than raindrops in a spring shower.

The anger on both his assailants' faces melted to fear as Remo strode purposefully up to the two men, unfazed by the deafening blast of auto fire. They continued to target their weapons, hoping that a single shot would drop the seemingly unstoppable man before them.

Their fingers continued to tense on their triggers even after Remo had reached them. A tactical error. With a final pirouette, Remo danced between the blazing barrels, slapping both up with either hand.

Bullets ripped through two chins and into two brains, splattering blood and gore on the white plaster ceiling.

Remo spun away from the falling bodies.

There was a closed door at the end of a short hallway that ran off the living room. As Remo was making his way swiftly toward the door, he heard another pop from an autopistol.

He picked up the pace, hitting the door at a run. Remo sailed into the room amid the shattered sections of door.

The body was just slumping to the desk, a single

bullet wound to the side of the head. Ennio stood above the dead man. As Remo strode across the room, the killer swung his pistol in Remo's direction. Remo didn't even look at the weapon.

"Dammit, what did you do that for?" he complained.

"I had my orders," Ennio sneered, the words a challenge.

"So did I," Remo protested. "Did you even stop to think—did you even *care* that someone other than you might have had orders, too?"

"Uh…"

"This is just swell," Remo continued, unmindful of Ennio's dumb expression. "That's Hy Solomon, I presume. Or was."

Ennio had actually begun to feel guilty for a moment. He shook away the sensation.

"Hey, it ain't my fault. I was just doin' like I was told, dat's all." He crossed his arms defiantly, but his gun got in the way. He remembered why he had the gun in the first place and pointed it at Remo.

Remo frowned. "Dammit, dammit, dammit!" he snapped.

His instructions from Upstairs had been explicit. No fuss. Few deaths. Solomon alive. So far, he had a major fuss, bodies up to his armpits and one dead Mob accountant.

"My boss wanted me to get him out alive," Remo griped as he stared angrily at the corpse.

"He was the top accountant or something for the whole Patriconne crime family. He could have brought down everyone in Rhode Island."

"*My* boss told me I should kill him for the same reason," Ennio replied. "Only if there was trouble," he added.

Remo looked at him, face puckering angrily.

"How much do *you* know?" he demanded.

Ennio suddenly appeared horrified. "I don't know nuthin'," he admitted.

"You'd better get an education fast," Remo warned. "Because you're going to turn state's evidence."

"No way," Ennio insisted. "I do what I'm told and I don't rat out nobody. Ain't you never heard of *omertà?*"

As he spoke, he waggled a finger at Remo. It rattled. Remembering his gun once more, he again aimed it at Remo.

Remo wasn't up for an argument. Things had gone horribly wrong on this assignment. He had no choice but to improvise.

He plucked the gun away. Ennio was left grasping at air. Grabbing Ennio by the scruff of the neck, Remo dragged the big man back up to the roof, where he dropped the thug to his back. He pressed a foot against Ennio's chest to keep him from scurrying away. As the mafioso wiggled beneath his loafer, Remo reached over the building's side and pulled up the nearest section of wire he'd severed.

Remo lashed the wire around one of Ennio's fat ankles. He rolled the man to the edge of the building. Remo paused, holding the man in place at the edge of the precipice. The soft wind toyed at the gangster's dark hair.

"One last chance," Remo offered. "Testify or fly?"

Ennio looked at Remo. He glanced down at the darkness below. His breathing was ragged. Sweat glistened across his face, accompanied by a nervous reddish rash.

"Screw you," Ennio panted.

Remo shrugged. "Bombs away."

He gave Ennio's belly what seemed like a gentle push. The Mob killer rocketed out into the alley like a startled pigeon.

He hung there impossibly for a moment, suspended in air directly across from Remo. All at once the bottom seemed to drop out from beneath him. He dropped.

Ennio fell only two stories before the wire dug into his ankle.

"Ouch! Ouch! Son of a bitch! Ouch! Dammit!"

His head bounced half a dozen times against the wall.

Above, Remo leaned his chin on one hand. He jiggled the wire, causing the mobster's thick head to bounce a few extra times. In all, he was suspended above the alley for no more than sixty seconds. But they were the most horrifying sixty seconds of Ennio's life. He was upside down. Blood rushing to his head. Swinging, bouncing. Six stories of nothing between him and the too-solid alley far below.

When Remo dragged him up over the edge of the building a minute later, the Mafia killer looked to be coated in sweat. Much of what seemed like perspiration was actually the wetness of his released bladder, which had run up and around his greasy hair while he was dangling in space.

"Enjoy your flight?" Remo asked sweetly as he dumped Ennio back to the rooftop.

"Oh, man... Oh, man..." Ennio panted. On hands and knees, he attempted to kiss the roof's surface. Something was in the way. He kissed anyway.

"Get off my shoes, you idiot," Remo complained, kicking Ennio away from his loafers. "Change your mind?"

Crawling, the gangster peered into the terrifyingly deep shadows of the alley. When he looked back into Remo's eyes, he saw that they were far darker and much more menacing.

"*Shit*, yeah," Ennio gasped. Still on his knees, he nodded so hard gravel from the roof became embedded in his chin.

"Good," Remo said. "I'm holding you to that. Remember. You go back on your word—" he pointed to the space between the buildings "—next flight you take is one-way."

As Ennio Ticardi began vomiting his last meal onto the surface of the roof, Remo slipped back over the side. He was gone before the first spurt of linguine hit the cold black tar.

3

Chiun, Reigning Master of the House of Sinanju, awesome custodian of five thousand years of accumulated secrets of the most feared and respected assassins ever to tread the dirt of the earth, was content.

It was a feeling with which he had little experience. Chiun savored the rare sensation.

He was a wizened Asian with skin like ancient parchment. A brilliant gold brocade kimono decorated his frail frame. Two white-turning-to-yellow tufts of hair clung in impossibly delicate clusters to the taut tan skin above each ear. A third thread of hair jutted from his bony jaw. The wisp of hair at his chin quivered as the old Korean repeated the lines of his favorite Ung poem.

> "'O spider spinning web, in strands.
> O insect snared, flutter flitter.
> Spider, insect.
> Insect, spider.
> Consume in Nature's endless Beauty Cycle.'"

A single, perfect tear appeared at the corner of one deceptively young hazel eye as the Master of Sinanju pictured the spider twirling endlessly in its web of Life. The tear rolled down his parchment cheek as he continued to repeat these same lines over and over. In the best Ung, whole sections were repeated as many as six thousand times in order to achieve the desired result of perfect unity between poem and soul. Chiun was on his four thousand and fifty-first repetition of this same beautiful verse.

As he recited, suffused in the beauty of the words intoned, the front door of his condominium opened.

"Chiun, I'm back!"

Remo. In a state of bliss, the Master of Sinanju ignored his pupil's braying voice.

"'...insect snared, flutter flitter...'"

A moment later, Remo stuck his head around the door. He was puzzled to see Chiun sitting immobile on his reed mat in the center of the living-room floor. "Didn't you hear me?" he asked, stepping into the room. "I'm home."

Chiun did not look his way. He continued reciting his poetry undaunted.

"Are you crying?" Remo asked, suddenly worried. When Chiun still didn't respond, Remo listened for a moment. The light finally dawned. "Pee-yew," he said once he'd caught a few words.

"I'd cry, too, if I had to listen to that Ung crapola. What are you up to, the millionth verse?"

"'...Nature's endless Beauty Cycle.' Visigoth!"

The last word didn't seem to be part of the poem. Remo had heard the spider poem more times than he cared to remember and he didn't once remember any references to Visigoths. He asked Chiun about this.

"'...spider spinning, web in strands.' Heathen!

'O insect snared, flutter flitter.' Vulgarian!

'Spider, insect,' barbarian!

'Insect, spider,' oaf!

Hater of beauty who ruins even the most elegant of lyrics with his fat, stomping white feet and his stupid, loudmouthed, loutish interruptions!"

Picking himself up on bony knuckles, Chiun spun away from Remo. He dropped back down facing away from his pupil. Staring at the wall, the old Korean continued to recite his poem.

Remo got the message. "If you wanted privacy, you should have used the meditation tower," he grumbled.

Backing from the room, he left the tiny Asian alone. He wandered back to the kitchen for something to eat.

In the back room, he found the wall phone off the hook. Chiun must have taken it off before he had started on his Ung. Expecting a call from Upstairs, Remo replaced the phone delicately in the cradle, figuring that when it rang he could snare it before the noise bothered Chiun.

He had no sooner hung up the phone when it rang sharply.

Remo snatched the receiver back up. Down the hall, the Master of Sinanju's angry mumbling grew louder.

"Hi, Smitty," Remo whispered.

"Remo?" asked the puzzled lemony voice on the other end of the line. The tart voice belonged to Dr. Harold W. Smith, Remo's employer and director of the supersecret organization known only as CURE.

"Yeah." Remo turned away from the open kitchen door. He used his body to muffle his voice.

"Is there something wrong? You sound odd."

"You've got a lot of nerve for a guy who sounds like his voice box was soaked in grapefruit juice," Remo commented.

Smith didn't press the issue. Instead, he went straight to the subject at hand. "Remo, what the devil happened in Providence?"

"What do you mean?" Remo asked, his tone one of absolute innocence.

"You knew the assignment, did you not?"

"Yes, I knew the assignment," Remo sighed,

annoyed. "It's just things didn't work quite right once I got there."

"I should say not. The accountant you were supposed to deliver into federal hands is dead, and with him goes our hope of sending Bernardo Patriconne to prison."

"*Your* hope," Remo stressed. "I'd just as soon go in and separate that rat bastard's head from his neck."

Smith sighed. "Need I remind you that this is not a one-man war against the Mafia?" he explained patiently. "The Mob is dying as a criminal force in the United States. We must continue to allow it to seem as if the system is taking care of society's worst elements."

Remo guffawed at this. "Maybe you're the last guy to hear this, but the system is not working, Smitty. For every Mob boss the Feds spoon out, an ocean of scum floods back in to take his place. Cubans, Jamaicans, South Americans, Russian Mafia, Yakuza, Indonesians and about a billion donless Guidos are all running like madmen through the streets. Let alone the Crips, the Bloods, the Gangsta Disciples and all the other homegrown junior skunks."

"I am not going to argue the issue with you," Smith said tartly. "We are discussing last night's debacle. According to my information, Hy Solomon knew enough to sink much of the Patriconne syndicate. Now he is dead."

"I got a replacement," Remo said defensively.

"Yes," Smith said, voice thin. The drum of rapid typing filtered through the receiver as Smith pulled up a file on his computer. "Ennio Ticardi. A low-level Mob functionary with no real knowledge of anything remotely connected to Bernardo Patriconne. It is even questionable if he has ever even *met* the Rhode Island don."

"Not a problem. If you want I can get him to swear he did," Remo offered slyly.

The ten seconds of ensuing dead air spoke volumes. "Let us put this disaster behind us," Smith droned eventually.

"Fine with me," Remo replied jovially.

It seemed a chore for the CURE director to forge ahead.

"There has been an incident near the White Sands Missile Range in New Mexico," Smith began. "Two charred bodies were discovered in the desert this morning."

"And?" Remo asked. "What, a couple joy-riding teenagers broke down in the desert and fried in the sun?"

"Hardly. These two were not alone. Similarly burned bodies have appeared in and around Alamogordo. Clearly they are linked murder victims."

"A serial killer who gets his jollies dousing people with gasoline," Remo speculated.

"Perhaps," Smith admitted. "Local authorities have reported a number of deaths. In fact, members

of some of the surrounding police forces have succumbed, as well.''

"Succumbed?" Remo asked, puzzled. "Don't
they believe in guns?"

Smith sounded puzzled. "I am not entirely certain what is going on. But so far, by all accounts
only one man *seems* involved."

"Wait a minute, Smitty," Remo said. "They
know who the guy is who's doing this?"

"As I said, I do not know for sure. The accounts
are sketchy. From what I have been able to learn,
however, it could very well be one man. A man
known to authorities."

"So what do you need me for? Why the hell
don't they just arrest him?"

"They have tried," Smith explained. "So far
with no success. General Chesterfield of nearby
Fort Joy has offered assistance to the remaining
local authorities. They have taken him up on his
offer, but as yet the individual or individuals remain at large."

"This is screwy." Remo frowned. "How much
trouble could one guy be?"

"I know you meant that rhetorically," Smith
said dryly. "But you know as well as I the answer
to that question."

"Oh. Right. Well, whoever he is, he's *not* Sinanju."

Chiun chose that moment to pad into the

kitchen. His leather face was stern as he crossed to the refrigerator.

Remo hadn't noticed until now that his voice had gotten louder as his conversation with Smith had proceeded. He had been speaking at his normal level for a few minutes. At Chiun's appearance, he lowered his voice. Pointless now, since he was sure he was going to get reamed for interrupting the elderly Asian's recitation.

"Book me on a flight to New Mexico," Remo said softly. "I'll check out whatever's going on."

"There is a U.Sky flight to Alamogordo leaving from Logan in two hours. I have already made the arrangements."

Remo frowned with his entire face. "What the hell is U.Sky?"

"It is a new shuttle service. I have found their rates to be quite reasonable."

"By *reasonable*, I assume you mean cheap."

"It is no-frills," Smith admitted.

"Just as long as I don't have to flap my arms out the windows," Remo said as he hung up the phone.

When he turned, he found Chiun sitting at the low kitchen table. The Master of Sinanju had a bowl of cold leftover rice sitting before him. He picked at the white clumps with a pair of wooden chopsticks.

"Smith has another assignment for me," Remo ventured.

"The neighbors and I heard," Chiun replied icily.

"Yeah. Anyway, I don't know how long I'll be."

"Mmm," Chiun grunted as he chewed a mouthful of rice to paste.

"Look," Remo sighed. "I'm sorry I interrupted your little poetry recital. Once I'm gone, you'll be able to go through all twenty-four hours' worth of 'spider eating bug' in peace, okay? Are we friends again?"

Chiun glanced up from his bowl. Hazel eyes glinted. "No," he said flatly. "I am your teacher and you are my tin-eared pupil. I am your adoptive father and you are my thankless foundling. We are victims of fate who have been thrown together. We are not, nor have we ever been, friends."

The somber tone he used was obviously forced. The truth was, Chiun was still in a happy mood, in spite of Remo's interruptions. What's more, thanks to the glimmer in the Korean's eyes, they both knew it.

"You're breaking my heart." Remo grinned, clutching his chest.

"You have no heart," Chiun sniffed in reply. "Nor a soul. If you did, you would not feel as you do about beautiful Ung."

"Beautiful Ung is an oxymoron," Remo pointed out. "Even Robert Frost laughs at Ung."

"I do not know who that is," the Master of Sinanju said. "But if he does not appreciate Ung, then he is no poet." He raised a finger. The nail was long and wickedly sharp. "You would be advised to keep on my good side, Remo Williams. I will soon be in a position to grant you the celebrity you crave."

"Michelle Pfeiffer?" Remo deadpanned.

"She, as well, if that is your wish," Chiun admitted. "But what I was referring to was your own big break, as such happenstances are termed in the Industry. Perhaps I might someday get you your own star on the Hollywood Walk of Fame," he added coyly.

Remo felt the lightness go heavy. He was beginning to get a sinking feeling. Chiun was talking movie talk again. Something he hadn't done in months.

On assignment in Hollywood eight months ago, the Master of Sinanju had conned a pair of slimy producers into reading a top secret movie script he had written. If Chiun's early boasting was accurate, his film was going to be produced. He had been in touch with the West Coast as late as last fall, but since then the Master of Sinanju had grown silent on the subject. Remo assumed the deal had fallen through and thought it wise not to press the point. But here it was, resurfacing again.

"Don't tell me you've been on the phone with Bindle and Marmelstein?" Remo asked.

Chiun's thin lips formed a wrinkled smile. "Play ball with me and I will make you a star."

That was all the answer he needed.

"Oy vey," Remo muttered.

"However," Chiun warned, "interrupt my Ung again, and I will refuse your telephone entreaties, your name will be stricken from my Rolodex, and I will see to it that you are excluded from the most important social affairs. You will never assassinate in this town again, Remo Williams."

"You don't own a Rolodex," Remo pointed out. The old man's knowing smile told a different story. Remo shook his head. Chiun's movie was something he didn't have the energy to deal with right now. "I've got to get going," he muttered.

Chiun happily returned to his rice.

In the doorway Remo paused, a twinkle visible once more in the back of his deep-set eyes. "Do you really think we're not friends?" he asked.

The Master of Sinanju did not even look at him.

"This I have said," Chiun replied, chewing softly.

"I still like *you*, Little Father," Remo challenged, a broad smile spreading across his face.

Chiun continued to chew. "I will like you better when you are gone," he replied blandly.

"Absence does make the heart grow fonder," Remo said with a nod as he stepped into the hallway.

"Leave for ten years and I will love you," Chiun called after him.

4

Alamogordo was one of the many cities in the modern West that had grown weary of trying to dispel the myth of the typical small border town. It was a pointless battle. The Hollywood image of New Mexico had been pounded into the consciousness of most Americans since birth.

Even though there were no tumbleweeds rolling down a lonely main street lined with a few wind-battered wooden buildings, the small towns out beyond the larger city managed to fulfill the preconceived notion nicely—much to the chagrin of the more urban-minded local community leaders.

Conforming perfectly to the maddening stereotype was the Last Chance Saloon, a parched watering hole that sat on a desert road on the far side of Lincoln National Forest near the town of Pinon.

The saloon had been built in the early 1970s by a pair of enterprising young business partners who had hoped to capitalize on the very image the people of nearby Alamogordo wanted to eradicate. The problem was, they were too successful in recapturing the feel of a lonely desert saloon. They stuck their bar out near the flat black strip of Route 24. If there was an actual Nowhere, the Last Chance was dead center of it. The two men went broke in a year.

The Last Chance went through a number of owners in the ensuing two decades, all the while settling farther and farther into the desert sand.

Buckled almost like staves on a pickle barrel, many of the sand-ravaged wooden clapboards on the street side of the battered old building looked as if they were ready to fall off. The MPs noted this as they slowed their jeep to a stop before the dust-covered porch.

Corporals Fisher and Hamill were following up a lead. So far, five such leads had failed to pan out. Of course, it would have been helpful to know precisely *what* they were dealing with.

Old Ironbutt Chesterfield—the name affectionately used when referring to their base commander—had turned many of the men under his command over to the local authorities. All anyone really knew was that they were looking for an AWOL private who had been involved in some kind of crazy spree the past couple of days. Word was there'd been a few deaths.

Acutely aware of this fact, the two MPs unholstered their side arms as they climbed out of their jeep.

"My mouth tastes like a mud pie," Fisher, the driver, complained as he rounded the front of the

Army vehicle. Windblown sand pelted his aviator sunglasses.

"Maybe Ironbutt'll buy you a drink after the arrest," Corporal Hamill said dryly.

"Right," Corporal Fisher mocked. "Chesterfield's like a Vogon. The only way to get a drink out of him is to stick your finger down his throat."

Thinking longingly of the water-filled canteen in the rear of the jeep, Fisher glanced around.

There was a gas station near the Last Chance that looked as if it had been abandoned some time in the 1950s. Farther down, a small hardware store squatted in the baking sun. A few other tiny shacks lined the dust-caked road. Telephone poles listed morosely into the simmering distance.

Desolation was as palpable as the windblown sand. Fisher's throat was filled with desert dust.

"Let's get this over with," he muttered.

Walking abreast, guns aimed before them, the MPs mounted the two squeaking steps to the saloon's broad front porch.

ELIZU ROOTE had been hunched at the long, dust-covered mahogany bar since the previous midnight.

He'd used the same glass straight through to dawn. A few empty bottles lay on their sides on the bar's surface. One had rolled off at some point during his hours-long bender, shattering near the greenish brass foot rail at the end of the bar near the men's room.

His shot glass was empty now. Roote tapped the metal pad of one index finger endlessly against the lip of the thick glass.

The pads were gold. Even though they didn't look it. Very expensive. At one time, Roote had been impressed. No longer. Now the metal pad on his index finger was just something that made noise against a bar glass.

The staccato tapping had been going on for hours.

He had gotten away.

At first when he'd made it off the base, he had allowed himself a moment of happiness. It quickly died.

There was no way Chesterfield would want a blot the size of Elizu Roote on his record.

He would be hunted. They'd want him dead or alive. With the trail of bodies he'd left after his escape, most likely they'd prefer dead.

Roote was soon proved right. The Alamogordo police had been on the lookout for him much sooner than he had expected. Obviously, however, good old General Chesterfield had neglected to tell them exactly what they were dealing with. When he'd left town, Roote was five and zero with the local police.

After a day of stumbling and blind killing, he had made it out here. Even though the Last Chance

Saloon sat in the middle of nowhere, it was only a matter of time before they found him. And killed him.

As his finger continued to tap repeatedly against his glass, Roote heard a squeak on the porch somewhere behind him. His finger froze.

Cocking an ear, he listened intently.

Footfalls. More than one set. Someone sneaking in.

They'd found him. Quicker than he'd expected.

Hunching further, he resumed his tapping.

The louvered saloon doors creaked open a moment later. The soft footsteps grew louder as the men behind him walked carefully across the floor.

Not one word. Just steady, certain footfalls.

They had made him. Not only that, their guns were most likely drawn. Hunched over the bar, Roote smiled at the thought.

The men had gotten only halfway across the floor before they stopped suddenly.

"My God," gasped a voice.

Roote cleared a wad of phlegmy dust from his throat. "I see you've met Tommy." He didn't turn. He just continued to tap relentlessly at the rim of his glass.

The two MPs had paused near the dusty tables arranged around the bar floor.

Corporal Fisher glanced at his partner. Hamill was staring, horrified, into the dancing dust.

A charred corpse had been propped up in a chair

in the shadow of one of the thick wooden support columns.

There was no hair. Only a few black remnants of clothing remained. His eyes had exploded, cooking like eggs in the sockets. Lips shriveled away, exposing skeletal rows of teeth. The man's lower fillings were clearly visible through the strands of grisly black that had been his cheeks.

"This guy looks like he's been cooked," Hamill hissed. His voice sounded sick.

"He was the bartender here," Roote explained from the bar. "Think he might've owned the place, too." Roote tipped his head pensively. "Never did get 'round to askin' him. Too late now, I suppose."

The two MPs steeled themselves. They left the body, stepping over to Elizu Roote.

He matched the description they'd been given. Thin, just under six feet tall. Ghostly pale skin. Hair blond enough to be almost white. The kid was a freaking albino. With a nod, they confirmed it was the man whose photograph they had been given. They hadn't been told his name.

"Get up," Fisher commanded.

Roote continued tapping. "No."

That was enough for Corporal Hamill. "Let's go," he ordered bluntly, grabbing Roote under the armpit.

Corporal Fisher followed his partner's lead. They yanked Roote to his feet. The private's bar stool clattered over. Corporal Hamill immediately began patting down his clothes for weapons.

"How'd you escape from the stockade?" asked the MP as he worked.

"That what they told you?" Roote smiled. He held up his arms halfway, allowing the man to pat his shirt.

"He's clean," Hamill told his partner.

Roote was blinking lazily, weaving in his slightly drunken haze as the men spoke. He didn't lower his arms. "Don't matter that I escaped," he drawled. "Nothin' to escape to."

"Should we cuff him?" Hamill asked.

"Hell yeah."

The handcuffs were brought out. As Fisher flipped one bracelet open, he noticed something clutched in Roote's hand. The cuffs were instantly dropped. Fisher's gun flew up once more.

"Open your hands," the MP ordered.

"I don't think you really want me to," Roote confided.

"Open your hands!" Fisher commanded. By this point Hamill had raised his gun, as well. For safety's sake they'd moved a few feet away from the AWOL private.

Roote's giggle came out as a drunken snort.

He held his hands up near his ears, elbows deeply bent. Until now, his fingertips had been pressed against his palms.

Slowly, with deliberate ceremony, Roote unfolded his fingers, exposing the rows of curved metal pads at the tips.

"What the hell are those?" Corporal Fisher asked, more of his partner than of Roote.

His question was answered in the most horrible way imaginable.

Ten tiny blue sparks appeared to ignite all at once on the tip of every one of Elizu Roote's pale fingers. It was as if some strange internal switch had been flicked.

As the men watched in growing concern, the sparks erupted into ten uneven lightning jolts. The surge of electricity hopped from Roote to the men, attracted to the nearest metallic source. In this case, their guns.

The electricity surged through weapons and up arms, jolting hearts, firing up spinal cords, frying brain synapses. They were dead in an instant.

Roote didn't stop.

Electricity continued to pour from him. The men cooked and smoked and finally dropped, their skin a leathery black. The power surged from the fingers of Elizu Roote until the MPs were fried beyond recognition.

Long before his internal supply was used up, Roote cut the power. Woozy, he fell back against the bar.

Sickly sweet smoke from burning flesh filled the stagnant air of the dusty saloon. It rose from the shriveled corpses, searing Roote's eyes.

He leaned, panting, for a long time.

Finally, he stooped over, righting his stool. Turning his back on the dead men, he took his place at the bar.

"Don't tussle with the monster," he murmured to the bodies of Corporals Fisher and Hamill.

Pulling his empty glass toward him, Roote resumed his maddening, incessant tapping.

REMO FOUND that he didn't actually have to flap his arms out the window of the U.Sky flight, but the condition of the old DC-10 was such that he wouldn't have been surprised if he and the other passengers had been asked to.

The frills of the bargain airline's "no frills" policy apparently extended beyond the customary drinks, food and magazines to include carpeting, an intact fuselage, stewardesses and a pilot.

The last two items on the list were probably technically untrue. While boarding, Remo had seen two middle-aged women in hats who were with either the airline or the Salvation Army. But if they were stewardesses, he and the other passengers never found out. The women had made themselves scarce long before the plane had even left the runway.

As far as a pilot was concerned, Remo realized that there most likely was one. He merely had either an equilibrium or drinking problem. Remo was of the opinion that it was a combination of both.

When they finally landed in New Mexico, Remo was amazed that the rickety plane didn't erupt in flames and rattle apart as it bumped down the steaming runway of Alamogordo-White Sands Regional Airport.

As the engines chugged and smoked to silence, the uniformed dowagers reappeared in order to snarl at the passengers as they deplaned. Remo was the first off.

He followed the drably painted corridor from the plane to the main terminal building, taking an escalator down to the entry level. The automatic doors slid open at his approach, giving him his first full blast of New Mexico air.

It was hot in the precise way air should not be. Remo felt the heat permeate his cotton clothes as he stepped out onto the sidewalk. He glanced around for a taxi.

His search was interrupted by a young man in a bedraggled white T-shirt and calf-length short pants. Some sort of bizarre image adorned the filthy shirtfront. Though Remo couldn't quite make it out, it looked vaguely familiar.

"They're here!" the youth announced, jumping in front of Remo. He had a wild look in his dirt-rimmed eyes.

"Bully for them," Remo said, looking past the

man. What kind of airport didn't have cabs lined up waiting?

"They landed here years ago," the young man insisted. "Crashed." He pointed. "Out there. In the desert. The Army knows about it. Big government cover-up. The A-bomb tests they claim they had here? Part of the cover-up. They don't want the truth to get out."

"Of course not," Remo agreed.

He thought he spied a few cabs parked in the shade of the terminal's overhang. He began walking toward them. The young man dogged his steps.

"They've taken me up dozens of times," he insisted. "Ever since I was a kid." All at once, he jammed a finger up his nose. "You know what's up here?" he asked.

"I have a sneaking suspicion," Remo replied.

"Microprobe," the young man intoned. "Miniaturized processor. Location coordinator. The works."

"What do you know," Remo said absently. "I was wrong."

They *were* cabs. The drivers were staying out of the oppressive heat. Remo couldn't blame them. He steered toward the parked cars.

"Are you a believer?" the young man enthused. He was used to having people either punching him or running away by this point. Since this new arrival had yet to deck him, he assumed him to be a fellow traveler.

Remo stopped dead. He looked down at the man's shirt, a sudden realization dawning on him.

"That's one of those alien composites, isn't it?" he asked.

The picture on the T-shirt was as he had seen it on television, albeit a lot filthier. The head was like a grayish lightbulb. The mouth was a crushed O. Two lemon-shaped eyes stared out from the bulbous cranial section.

It was the picture drawn by many who claimed to have been abducted by aliens.

The young man beamed proudly. Perfect white teeth that must have set his parents back tens of thousands of dollars gleamed in the desert sunlight. If those same parents knew what their offspring was up to right now, they were probably burying their heads in the backyard in shame.

"Have you had an otherworldly experience, too?" the youth asked earnestly.

Remo placed a paternal hand on the young man's shoulder. "Kid, let me tell you something that I hope will change your life." As he spoke, he kept his voice perfectly level. "There are no such things as aliens. There are no alien visitations. There are no spaceships. Get used to it. We're alone."

The kid backed away from Remo's hand, shocked.

"They *got* to you!" he gasped.

Without another word, Remo resumed walking.

He ducked under the overhang, pulling open the door of the nearest cab.

"You're from the government!" the young man accused. He shouted from the sidewalk a few yards behind Remo. "I bet you're part of the conspiracy!" He turned to a female passerby. "He's part of the conspiracy!" he yelled to the startled woman.

"Kid, you don't know how true that is." Remo nodded. He slammed the door as the taxi pulled away from the curb.

HE WOULD ADMIT they had made a huge miscalculation.

Huge? No. Wouldn't fly. Ass-is-grass time if he came clean on the magnitude of the screw-up.

Better scratch that.

In the private sanctuary of his battlefield command nucleus, General Delbert Chesterfield crossed out the simple four-letter word. It was not the first such blot.

Chesterfield frowned deeply. What had begun as a clean white sheet of paper was now a hodgepodge of thick black graphite marks.

Huge...not huge...

Minor? Certainly not. He doubted even he could get away with that.

No, don't characterize it by its greater dimensions. And anyway, anyone looking at it would know it was huge and not small. Couch it in mathematical terms. That usually worked to confuse the less focused of his superiors.

"Arithmetic."

The word flowed off the end of his pencil as if drawn unbeckoned from deep in his subconscious. Yes, that would work. He smiled, growing more excited as he stared down at the single word.

Yes. Absolutely. Arithmetic. He made an extra little graphite loop around the ten magic letters.

An arithmetic miscalculation.

The general frowned once more.

Could it even be characterized as a miscalculation?

Softer terminology. That's what was required here.

Put *retrospective* in there somewhere. After all, everything looked better in hindsight.

It was nearly 11:00 a.m.—a full three hours since the latest batch of Fort Joy MPs had gone missing—by the time Chesterfield settled on the proper terminology.

"An arithmetic retrospective postcircumstantial error."

He crossed out *error* and replaced it with *event*.

Whipping the paper off his desk, he examined the words in the bright sunlight that flowed in through his closed office window. He liked what he saw.

"Damn good bit of soldiering. Damn good," he boasted to the empty room.

In the wide, dusty courtyard beyond the window, the flurry of activity that had been going on for the past three days continued unabated. Chesterfield hadn't seen that many soldiers preparing for battle since the Gulf War.

Of course, his own physical self had not actually personally participated in the Mother of All Battles, it being stateside at the time. But he had watched Dan Rather's coverage almost every night. On his twenty-seven-inch screen, it looked like there were a lot of soldiers in that war. He found as he peered through the open blinds of his office window that, in real life and without the limitations of his TV screen, fewer soldiers looked like even more.

There were men marching. Sergeants barking orders. Jeeps tearing this way and that, sending up awesome plumes of desert dust in their wakes. To Chesterfield, it looked for all the world like a real goddamn army.

Even though he understood the concept of mob mentality, he could easily have been whipped into the kind of military fervor that had taken hold of his men if only he didn't know the reason behind all the action.

But he knew all too well. And it'd be the end of his whole damn career if anyone else found out.

Chesterfield tore his eyes away from his troops, settling back on the paper in his big hand. Now that he had the proper terminology, the rest would flow like crap through a goose. He placed the paper to one side of his desk.

Gathering up his swagger stick, General Chesterfield marched out of his office, past his aide's desk and out into the unforgiving New Mexico sunlight.

Rows of soldiers were being marched by a drill instructor past Chesterfield's HQ. The general nodded his approval as the men—some seemingly barely out of diapers—trudged in lockstep past their commanding officer.

Chesterfield towered over all the men. He was a huge bear who looked as if he could squash a man with a single press of one large thumb.

As the last rows of soldiers were marching by, the general noticed something beyond them. It was coming toward him from the main gate in a cloud of dust.

Squinting at the intruder, Chesterfield swept his riding crop out from under his great arm. He slapped it to the chest of the nearest soldier in the last row of marchers.

The man stopped dead in his tracks. As if he'd walked into a solid wall.

"Soldier, what the hell is that?" Chesterfield boomed. He swung the swagger stick out like a pointer.

The baby-faced recruit seemed terrified to be addressed by Ironbutt Chesterfield. The leather riding crop was directly beneath his nose. He followed it to the end, peering off in the direction of the main gate. He immediately saw what had caught the base commander's eye.

"Taxi, *sir!*" the soldier yelled.

Chesterfield frowned deeply. A great mass of skin gathered at his fleshy jowls. "Join your unit," he said.

"Thank you, sir!" the soldier shouted. After exchanging salutes, the recruit ran to catch up with the last row of men.

The general watched as the taxi approached. Outwardly he displayed mild suspicion. Inwardly, it was a whole other story. His apprehension level was great as the cab slowed to a stop several feet from his highly polished boots.

As a lone man got out of the back, the general's apprehension faded. The suspicious expression turned to one of disgust.

Typical civilian. The guy wore a pair of tan pants and a white T-shirt. Though thin, he seemed to be in pretty good physical shape. Still, Chesterfield could tell that the guy wouldn't last a single day in the United States Army.

He tried to give the new arrival a condescending glare. Trouble was, the fellow was looking at the general as if *he* were the one that should be condescended to.

"How's it hanging, Eisenhower?" Remo commented, after sizing up the military man. Not waiting for a reply, he turned his attention to the cab-driver.

Chesterfield's radish-red face took on shades of beet-purple.

"This is a United States military base," Chesterfield's booming voice announced as Remo dug through his pockets.

"I didn't think it was the Alamogordo Y," Remo replied blandly. He handed a few bills over to the cabbie. "Thanks," he said, smacking the roof. The taxi drove off in a cloud of dust.

As the cab headed down the road to the main gate, Remo turned back to the general. He had taken only two steps before Chesterfield propped his walking stick against Remo's chest.

"Hold it right there, civilian," Chesterfield commanded.

"The name is Remo. And before this conversation ends with that cane sticking out of your ass, I was sent here from Washington."

Shocked, Chesterfield quickly removed the riding crop.

"Washington?" the general asked, feigning surprise. He pulled himself up to his full height. He towered over Remo like a small mountain. "What's this all about?"

Remo sighed. "Serial killer. Burned corpses. Army soldier." Even as Chesterfield's jowly mouth opened to deny the last accusation, Remo cut in. "Don't bother," he said. "I asked in Alamogordo. He's one of yours."

Chesterfield was already doing some rapid calculations in his head. He didn't want to admit to anything that could come back to bite him later on. After weighing the options for a split second, he decided that there probably wasn't much harm admitting that Elizu Roote was from his base.

The general nodded crisply. "He's one of my boys." He quickly added, "That is to say, one of the *Army's* boys. They just send me the crates. I don't know how many rotten apples are sitting in them."

"So there *is* only one man."

"One United States Army soldier, yes," Chesterfield replied haughtily.

"General Chesterfield!" The excited voice came from near one of the single-story barracks-type command structures.

They turned to see a lieutenant, who appeared to be too young for a razor, running across the dusty yard. He barely avoided bumping into dozens of men in his haste to cross over to Chesterfield.

"We think we've got him, General," panted the excited lieutenant as he reached Chesterfield. He nodded crisply to Remo. "One of the MP units failed to report in. Chopper spotted their jeep at a saloon beyond the forest."

Chesterfield's eyes had gone wide. With facial

tics as subtle as a baseball bat to the back of the head, he tried to warn the lieutenant not to speak in front of Remo. The officer didn't get the hint.

"You think he killed them?" Remo asked, surprised.

"It wouldn't be his first, sir," the lieutenant replied.

Remo wheeled on Chesterfield.

Chesterfield's face froze mid-tic. He pretended it was an itch. He scratched at it with his riding crop.

"How many has he killed so far?" Remo demanded.

"Ohh, let's see now...."

The lieutenant answered for his commander. "Eight MPs confirmed, two now suspected."

Chesterfield started to signal anew.

"He's killed *ten* MPs?" Remo asked, stunned.

"And a dozen civilians," the lieutenant offered.

Chesterfield gave up trying to signal altogether.

"Lieutenant!" the general interjected.

The younger man snapped away from Remo. "Sir!"

"I'm sure you didn't join this man's Army to chatter away like a member of my dear sweet departed mother's quilting circle, God rest her soul," Chesterfield menaced.

"Sir, no, sir!"

"Then kindly stow the hearsay until we've got some damn solid facts!" The general screamed so loudly his beefy head looked ready to explode like a tomato with a firecracker packed inside.

"Yes, *sir!*" the lieutenant shouted back.

"Why hasn't this made national news?" Remo asked, baffled. He spoke more to himself than to the others.

"We've been keeping a lid on things so far," Chesterfield offered. "Don't want to alarm the populace."

"What about warning them that a maniac is on the loose?" Remo commented, annoyed. "Who is this guy? Has he had some kind of special training or something?"

"That is Army business," Chesterfield announced in a superior tone. He wheeled his great girth to the lieutenant. "Ready my chopper. I want everything we've got thrown at him. Is that understood?"

"Yes, sir!" The man spun to go.

"Wait a minute," Remo said, grabbing the lieutenant by the arm. "You're doing all this for one man?" he asked Chesterfield, his voice betraying his complete bewilderment.

"One *Army* man, yes," Chesterfield replied impatiently.

"As opposed to one *Spider* man," Remo said aridly.

"He's not under my command," the general retorted, his ruddy face clouding.

"Forget it," Remo said. "And while you're at

it, forget sending any more of your men in. I'll go."

"Alone?"

"That's the general idea."

Chesterfield snorted loudly. "You? Against Roote? The desert sun's getting to you, boy."

Remo's face was deadly serious. "Humor me."

When he saw that Remo was not joking, the general's laugh slowly petered out.

His keen military mind instantly went to work. He began weighing the idea of sending all the troops under his entire command after Roote against the prospect of sending Remo in alone. For him to go along with the outlandish scheme, there would have to be a mighty big benefit for Delbert Xavier Chesterfield. The plus side of the scenario immediately presented itself.

"You've got authority to override me?" he asked.

Remo shrugged. "I suppose," he said. "If it's necessary, I can go right to the top."

Chesterfield's eyes narrowed. "Washington takes the blame for any screw-ups?" the general asked cagily.

"Yeah, sure, whatever," Remo said indifferently.

General Chesterfield happily slapped his swagger stick against one massive thigh. His smile was as wide as the New Mexico desert. "Son, I think you and I can come to what my grandpappy used to call an understanding."

5

The drab, brownish-green U.S. Army Apache advanced attack helicopter swept across the sunbaked landscape like a lone, angry wasp. It soared northeast, just skirting the periphery of Lincoln National Forest as it raced on toward the likeliest location of Private Elizu Roote.

General Chesterfield sat in the gunner's seat behind the pilot. Remo was crammed in beside the general's bulk.

"It would have been easier to drive," Remo complained into the slender microphone that was connected to his thick headset. Although he didn't require the protection the earphones offered, Chesterfield wouldn't have been able to hear him without them.

"Easier, but not quicker," the general replied loudly. Grinning, he turned to Remo. Large parts of his anatomy spilled over into Remo's seat. "What's the matter, boy? Don't like the company?"

"Not particularly," Remo answered.

Chesterfield laughed. "You're lucky you're not under my command with a mouth like that, boy."

"Speaking of mouths, does every word that comes out of yours have to be shouted?"

"That's the way they taught us to command respect in general school," the officer bellowed.

Remo had heard a great many military men in his life—both in his personal experience and on television. Although he could easily picture Norman Schwarzkopf shouting, he couldn't remember hearing him doing so even once on TV. Rather than hear a shouted further explanation, he decided not to press the issue.

They swept across the desert for a few long minutes, the muted, constant noise of the rotor blades the only sound in the cabin.

As the helicopter soared toward their rendezvous, the general glanced surreptitiously at Remo several times. Curiosity finally got the better of him.

"You CIA, boy?" Chesterfield boomed into his mouthpiece.

Remo stared out the curving windshield to the endless desert below. "Maybe," he replied without much interest.

"You don't look like CIA. NSC?"

Remo sighed. "You know, a *good* general would have asked to see my ID before schlepping me out into the middle of nowhere like this."

"I take umbrage at that, sir. I *am* a good general.'' Chesterfield stabbed a large finger at the two stars on his right shoulder board. "You know what I got these for?" he demanded in a booming voice.

Remo shrugged. "Base pie-eating contest?"

"They were awarded to me for being a very good general. What do you think of that?"

"I think it's a telling comment on the all-volunteer Army," Remo replied.

"I don't much like your tone," Chesterfield announced.

"Double," Remo replied, bored.

"I'm not even sure you're CIA."

"That's good, 'cause I'm not." He was still staring out the window. The desert wasn't very pretty.

"Let me see your identification," the general demanded.

"No."

"I will set down this helicopter right now and put you out in the desert if you do not comply."

"And I'll let you take the blame for the body count your man has accumulated."

General Chesterfield thought long and hard over this prospect. He finally settled into a sullen, reluctant silence.

It was several minutes more before the chopper came upon the road that led to Roote's last suspected location. Huge plumes of sand and dust were thrown up by the swirling rotor blades as the Apache helicopter settled on the soft shoulder to one side of the strip of baking asphalt.

"What happened there?" Remo asked.

He pointed past the pilot's shoulder out through one of the front bubbled windshields.

A sorry line of telephone poles sulked along the side of the road. Until quite recently, the nearest had apparently had an old-fashioned goose-neck light attached high atop it.

But now the metal was black and peeled back in large strips where the streetlight had exploded. What's more, the pole itself looked to have suffered in the blast. The top was cracked apart like a viciously stubbed-out cigar.

Through the haze of swirling dust, it was apparent that two more poles down the road had suffered a similar fate.

"Lightning storm," the general explained hastily. "We get them in the desert from time to time. Can be pretty nasty when they hit."

It was obvious to Remo that Chesterfield was lying. By the look of the operation he was running down here, Remo wouldn't have been surprised if the general's men had shelled the poles by mistake during mortar practice.

Truth be told, Remo wasn't that interested in an explanation. He just wanted to get this over with.

"That way?" he asked, slipping off his headset.

"Follow the road. It's the first small town you hit."

Remo popped the door. "It would have helped if you'd landed a little closer," he complained.

"Any good military man will tell you surprise is half the battle, boy," Chesterfield shouted.

"Find me a good military man so I can confirm that."

Remo climbed out the helicopter and down to the desert sand, slamming the door back into place. The open expanse of desert was a welcome relief to sharing a seat with Ironbutt Chesterfield.

Inside the helicopter, Chesterfield wondered if he shouldn't warn Remo about Roote. In the moment it took the general to consider, the helicopter lifted off once more, stranding Remo on the ground.

Inwardly, Chesterfield was relieved. If it came to an inquest after Remo's charred body was discovered, he'd blame the pilot for beating a too-hasty retreat.

The matter of a scapegoat settled, General Chesterfield sat back into the gunner's seat.

The Apache tore back toward Fort Joy, leaving the lone black shape of Remo Williams to be consumed by the swirl of desert sand.

THE FIRST HOUSE on the way into town was no more than a toolshed with a half-rotted carport. A mangy dog lay in the shade of a rusted 1947 Studebaker, which sat on rocks beside the shack. Clumps of desert brush grew up around both dog and car.

Next came a pair of larger homes, sand-ravaged

wooden structures roughly the size of small house trailers. They sat across from one another on the flat roadway. Tin mailboxes perched like sentries before their short, hard-packed driveways.

Remo saw no sign of any police activity whatsoever as he walked up the long stretch of highway.

Chesterfield had dumped him farther out in the desert than he had let on. It had been a five-mile trek beneath the scorching sun to the first lonely buildings.

Several times on their flight from Fort Joy, the general had expressed concern that the Apache might be heard, but it was caution taken to the extreme for him to drop Remo so far away from the AWOL private's location.

As he wandered down the road between the pair of larger houses, Remo wondered what on earth the general thought one man could do to defend against a heavily armed piece of military hardware like the Apache. He chalked the extreme caution up to Chesterfield's apparent general incompetence.

As he walked down the desolate desert road, Remo sensed eyes following him.

A dark figure was peering from behind a set of ancient gauzy curtains in the ramshackle home to his right.

Up ahead was the Last Chance Saloon. Remo

ignored his audience of one as he pressed on toward the bar.

He got no more than a few more paces on the gummy road when the black shape slipped from the window. A moment later, the screen door opened at the side of the house. A short man in dungarees and a grimy, untucked T-shirt gestured frantically to Remo.

"Señor!" he rasped. Snapping his attention up the road to the bar, he dropped his voice lower. "Please!" he begged, beckoning Remo over.

Remo didn't want a detour right now, but if the desperate old man decided to hound him all the way to the bar, he might alert Roote to Remo's presence. And if the private bolted, it could extend Remo's time in this desolate town by minutes. Annoyed, Remo left the road, hurrying through tufts of brittle brush to the old man.

"What's wrong?" Remo asked once he'd reached the stranger.

"You do not want to go there," the man whispered. He had a bristly white mustache and a three-day growth of black stubble across his dark cheeks.

Remo followed his gaze to the bar. "You a friend of Bill W.?"

It was as if the man didn't hear him. "The Army has already come for him," he pleaded. "It has done no good. I see them go in hours ago. They did not come back out."

Remo looked again to the Last Chance Saloon.

From this angle, he spied a military jeep beside the battered wooden structure.

"You know who I'm looking for?"

The old man nodded desperately. "He come during the night. I see him kill Tommy. He own the bar." The man's eyes were wild with fear. "He use his hands." He threw his own hands out before him like a witch casting a spell. "He *kill* Tommy with his hands. I don't know why he no kill me. He want a drink, I think." He jabbed his hands in the air in a dramatic and inexplicable re-creation of the bartender's last moments alive.

Remo couldn't figure out the man's pantomime. But judging by his breath, he'd been drinking pretty steadily since his encounter with Elizu Roote.

"Relax," Remo assured him. "He's probably passed out by now. Just do me a favor and keep the yelling to a minimum the next few minutes, okay?"

He turned to go. The old man bullied in front of him.

"He is *el Diablo,*" the man insisted, grabbing his shirt. His rheumy eyes were pleading.

"In that case, I've got a date with the devil," Remo said evenly. He pulled away from the surprisingly powerful grip.

As he headed up the road toward the saloon, the old man made a rapid sign of the cross. Afterward, he hurried back to the safety of his ramshackle home. To drink. And pray.

ROOTE'S HEAD WAS BOWED over the bar, fists clasped at his temples.

Some of his shot glass lay in fragments before him. The endless tapping had eventually grown in ferocity until the thick glass shattered beneath the metal pad of his index finger. He'd swept most of the fragments to the floor.

His charge was low. He'd been taught to recognize the signs. He felt drained. Physically and mentally.

He had loosed too much juice on the pair of MPs. The baked corpses lying on the floor of the saloon were a grisly testament to the horrible power of the force within him. He thought he had held back, but drunkenness and insanity had impaired his judgment. If there ever came a day when he finally climbed off his stool, he'd have to recharge.

An intense silence gripped the desert beyond the bar's clapboard walls. He thought he'd heard the distant sound of a helicopter more than an hour before, but it had been swallowed up in the desert wind. No matter. Even though they hadn't found him yet, they were still looking.

Only a matter of time…

Recharge. Had to recharge.

Sniffling, Roote lifted his head from his hands.

Only then did he see the reflection in the bottles behind the bar.

Stomach knotting, Roote whirled on his stool.

He wasn't alone.

The stranger had somehow gotten inside the saloon without the creak of a single floorboard or the squeak of the half-rusted door hinges.

The intruder had a look of death in his dark eyes. Roote had seen the same expression countless times in the past. Virtually every time he looked in the mirror.

"You're Roote, I assume?" the stranger asked.

"Yes, sir," Roote replied. He wore his eyes at half-mast. His Southern drawl was slurred.

His charge was still low.

Dang! He shouldn't have let it drain so far. It was easy enough to recharge. It was only a matter of finding the nearest electrical source. The outlet behind the bar would have been sufficient. But he had sat morosely at the bar for hours, not even caring that they were looking for him. Now he regretted his apathy.

As the stranger closed in, Roote hoped the limited energy stored in his capacitors would be enough.

Bracing his back against the bar, Roote rubbed his thumbs against his fingertips. Weak blue sparks began to pop inside his palms.

He wouldn't take any chances. He couldn't afford to miss. Roote would let this latest intruder get in close. Then he'd fry him like an egg.

ACROSS THE BIG BAR FLOOR, Remo was trying to figure out what Elizu Roote thought he was doing with his hands.

As he watched the pale man raise his hands up beside his shoulders, images of the old Mexican man's impersonation of the Army private popped unbeckoned into his mind.

And strangest of all, it appeared as if Roote's conjuring was working. There was a sporadic blue flash coming from between his curled fingers. It illuminated the bones in his hands like some weird, palm-size X ray.

Probably palming a couple of joy buzzers. His unique serial killer's stamp.

That Roote was insane, Remo had little doubt. The bodies of two of the men he had killed still lay on the floor, charred beyond any hope of identification short of dental records. The private must have soaked them in gasoline and burned them alive.

Remo wondered why he would have brought them inside afterward. Obviously they hadn't been killed in the bar. The saloon's bone-dry wood would have gone up like a struck matchstick if he had done it in here.

The two pairs of boot marks were the only evidence Remo did see of any kind of fire residue.

The boot prints were burned into the wood floor. As he walked toward them, the prints seemed almost like a brief map to some macabre dance step.

When he looked up, he saw that Roote was smiling proudly. He nodded to the footprints.

"They died with their boots on," he said. He was still leaning against the bar, rubbing his fingertips on his palms.

Remo kept coming.

There was a strange tingle of electricity in the air. It seemed to be coming from Roote's direction, though Remo couldn't determine the source.

"It ain't really my fault," Roote speculated. "The Army's what made me a monster."

That was enough for Remo. Roote was just another kook who wanted to blame his training for everything wrong in his life. Not my fault. The Army told me to kill. The devil made me do it. An old argument.

"You-all are here to arrest me, I suppose," Roote said as Remo closed in.

Eyes flat, Remo shook his head. "We're way beyond that. Just for the record, how many people have you killed?"

"Today or all told?" Roote asked with a proud smile.

Remo's dead expression didn't change. "Does the term 'you just sealed your fate' have any meaning to you?"

Roote began slapping his fingertips in unison

against his palms. The soft clapping sound was accompanied by an increased sparking.

"You don't have no gun," Elizu Roote said. He sounded a little disappointed. "How about handcuffs?"

Remo was past the bodies now. Nearly upon Roote. "Don't use either. Don't need either."

"That's a cryin' shame. Metal conducts best."

It was a puzzling thing to say. And between the kid at the airport and General Chesterfield, Remo had already wasted enough time on nutcases today. It was justice time. He let the remark pass, reaching out a thick-wristed hand to Roote.

He'd do it quick and easy and be on the first flight out of town before the body was even found.

Or so he thought.

His hand was a foot away from Roote's throat when the private's palms opened like desert blooms.

Remo caught a brief glimpse of what appeared to be thimbles. But for some reason, they looked as if they were buried at the end of Elizu Roote's fingers. It was also obvious that they were the source of the mysterious sparking.

"Surprise," Roote announced. He grinned maniacally.

There was a pop of light like a flashbulb going off.

The sudden brightness took Remo by surprise. Even as the light was registering on his retinas,

Remo felt the shock of electricity grab him in the chest.

The short power surge lifted him off the floor, flinging him back toward the end of the bar. Stools toppled out of his path, spilling over, crashing and rolling against tables.

Pain gripped his chest like fingers of flame. His heart began racing, pounding in spastic bursts.

Lying on his back on the floor, Remo had no idea what had just happened. Whatever it was, it had stopped. He rolled over weakly, looking up at Roote. His heart still thudded angrily in his chest.

Roote seemed disappointed. He was leaning against the bar with one hand as he looked at the recessed metal pads of the other.

"Charge is lower than I thought," he complained. "Sorry, cowboy. There ain't enough for the full treatment."

Roote lowered only one hand this time. And this time, Remo clearly saw the arcs of electrical energy shoot from the private's five fingertips.

His system had been practically overloaded the first time. When the second burst came, Remo wasn't even strong enough to roll out of its deadly path.

The next blast caught him in the chest. His heart immediately began to fibrillate wildly. The electricity surged through his body, flying up his finely tuned spinal cord and racing out to his overloaded extremities. Every nerve in his body screamed in pain.

As the power flowed, Roote stepped forward, eyes gleeful.

Not even a body trained to the perfection that was Sinanju could withstand such a direct assault against its nervous system. Remo had seconds to live.

Flailing on the floor, he grabbed out blindly, desperately seizing something cool and cylindrical at his side. The brass footrest that ran the length of the bar.

The pain that racked his body was unbearable. Yet some distant, lucid part of Remo's mind told him to clutch on to the footrest. To fight for life.

He grasped the metal tube with one shaking hand. The electricity instantly coursed through his body and out into the long brass pipe. Dissipating its force. Throwing it from his own ravaged body.

He didn't know if he'd grabbed the rail soon enough. His body had already taken a beating. Still, he held on for dear life, feeling the current disperse along the footrest even as a cloak of darkness began to pull across the sparking field of blazing synapses that was his mind.

As Remo lost consciousness, the last vision he beheld was that of Elizu Roote standing above him—eyes crazed, death pouring like hellfire from his fingertips.

For a moment locked in time, Remo hoped more

than anything that a demented Army private with supernatural powers would not be the last thing he would see in life. And then he ceased to care at all.

The darkness of eternity consumed all conscious thought, and Remo Williams became one with the nothingness.

6

Behind the locked door of the administrative director's office of Folcroft Sanitarium in Rye, New York, Dr. Harold W. Smith sat nestled in the well-worn seat of his cracked leather chair.

The chair had been a gift from his wife on the occasion of their fifteenth wedding anniversary.

At the time of the gift close to forty years ago, Smith had just retired from the CIA. He had assumed his duties as the director of Folcroft, and Maude Smith had wanted more than anything to show her husband how grateful she was that he was out of the dangerous espionage business. The chair had been just the thing.

When his beaming wife had presented the gift to Smith, he promptly tried to return it. Parsimonious in the extreme, Smith had told his wife that there were more than enough chairs at Folcroft already. One more would be redundant.

But in the few short weeks from the time she had bought the chair and stored it at her sister's house in Connecticut to the time Smith attempted to bring it back, the office-furniture store had gone out of business. With no hope of getting back his thirty-five dollars and ninety-nine cents, plus tax, Smith had grudgingly accepted the gift.

Though it bothered him at first, over time he had actually come around. After more than fifteen hours of sitting per day, seven days a week, the chair he hadn't wanted now fit him like a comfortable old shoe. The chair was as much a fixture in the Spartan room as Harold Smith himself. They had grown old together.

Smith had been a relatively young man when he assumed his post at Folcroft. Now, as he typed at the high-tech keyboard buried at the lip of his gleaming onyx desk, the reflection that looked back up at him from the shining surface was eerily reminiscent of his father.

The unflattering image accurately reflected its subject.

Smith's bland spirit tinted his entire gaunt being in washed-out, virtually colorless shades of gray. Indeed, the only inaccuracy in the reflection was its failure to properly reflect Smith's green-striped Dartmouth tie. The visual error was forgivable. The green was swallowed up by all-consuming gray.

It was not the daily work of Folcroft that had kept Smith here so late into the autumn of his life. If sanitarium business had been the only reason for Smith's tenure behind the ivy-covered walls of the venerable institution, he would have packed up his chair when he'd reached sixty-five and headed off into well-earned retirement.

No, the thing that kept Smith toiling in his waning years could be summed up in a single word: America.

Smith was the product of a time when being an American meant something. Before coarseness and flagrant lying took the place of public discourse; before depravity and cheap titillation took hold of the popular culture; before America began its slippery slide into narcissism and hedonism, Smith had learned right from wrong.

It was his black-and-white grip on reality as much as his keen analytical mind that brought Smith to the attention of a young President years before.

A new agency was being formed. Its mission was to safeguard the Constitution by flouting the very laws that existed in that monumental document. That agency—called CURE—needed a director. It was Harold W. Smith's unflagging love of country that had been the deciding factor in the clandestine contest for agency head.

His "retirement" from the CIA was a pretense for the work that would consume the rest of his life. Director of CURE.

Over the years, CURE's mission had changed. It had branched out from domestic threats to address international challenges. The greatest change came when the agency was sanctioned to use assassination as a tool to achieve its ends. But the two things that seemed never to have changed completely were Smith and his beloved chair.

As Smith typed at the capacitor-style keyboard, he scanned the information on the monitor.

He had been checking on the New Mexico situation for the past ten minutes. It now seemed more problematic than he had originally thought.

The news was leaking out. It seemed almost as if the military had been strong-arming the local authorities to downplay the number of deaths. For people who had lost loved ones, this could only work for so long. It appeared as if the dam had broke.

An Alamogordo newspaper had carried the headline story that morning. The names accompanied the text.

Smith scanned the list of confirmed dead. There were twelve names in all, alphabetized as they would be for a telephone directory.

Twelve people dead.

It could have been any number of things. Although authorities were suggesting a lone killer, the paper speculated that he might have accomplices. They further theorized involvement of a cult or gang. In New Mexico no one would be surprised if the deaths were drug related.

When he had been dispatched to the area, Remo hadn't been concerned. Smith did not share the casual attitude of CURE's enforcement arm. The names on Smith's computer screen belonged to innocent Americans. It was his duty to see to it that whatever was behind their murders did not become a menace to the nation at large.

Smith left the news story with its accompanying roster of murder victims and shifted his attention to the electronic files of nearby Fort Joy.

Although the base appeared to be heavily involved in the search for the lone suspect in the murders—at least according to what he had been able to glean from local police sources—very little information was being transferred via its computers. To Smith, this was suspicious. It was almost as if a computer blackout had been initiated at the base. Why would they not enter data into their computer network? Did they fear that their quarry was computer literate and might access the database from a remote source? If this were the case, would it not be wiser to enter false information, thus steering the suspect into a trap?

It was all quite puzzling.

As he reentered the base computer system, Smith was surprised to find some information posted.

Those in authority must have realized that the facts had begun to leak out to the public. It was pointless not to list that which was already known.

He scanned the lines, finding only the driest details that had already been covered in both the local police files and the Alamogordo press. There was nothing new.

Smith was about to exit the file when something out of the corner of his eye caught his attention.

He turned his attention back to the screen.

There was something not quite right.

The list of names was there, as it had been in the newspaper. But it seemed longer on the base computer.

As he passed over the lines, his attention was unerringly drawn to one name in particular.

Smith froze.

It was an add-on. The twelve-name list was now up to thirteen. The new name had not appeared in the papers.

As his flat, gray eyes passed slowly over the name, Smith felt his mouth go dry as desert sand.

Remo Halper.

The cover identity Remo was using while in New Mexico.

His mind raced. A million thoughts vied for supremacy as he read and reread the name.

Was it even possible? Had Remo fallen victim to the same unknown force that was killing innocent people near Fort Joy?

Smith managed to pull himself back together after a moment of dull inactivity. No. It was no use speculating until he had all the facts.

He cleared the cobwebs from his brain, looking down at the ten characters with new eyes. It was only then that he saw the asterisk at the far end of the column. A quick scan proved that Remo's was the only name so noted.

Hands shaking, Smith hit the page-down key. He found the asterisk again, this one followed by a few brief lines of sanitized text.

Government agent. Suspected CIA. Great interest expressed in Shock Troops project. First victim to survive encounter with subject Roote. Complicity? Agent taken to Ft. Joy infirmary. Condition: critical.

There were initials typed at the bottom of the report. ''Gen. DXC.''

Smith already knew that General Chesterfield was the base commander. But there was much in the report that he did not comprehend—the references to the Shock Troops and subject Roote, as well as the alarming and erroneous suggestion that Remo was connected with the Central Intelligence Agency.

Smith forced self-control. Adjusting the rimless glasses that were perched in perpetuity atop his patrician nose, he took a steadying breath.

Anything he might venture about either Remo's condition or the goings-on at Fort Joy would be academic. There was only one way to find out for certain what was happening there.

The time of hospitalization listed beside Remo's

name was 11:45 a.m., Mountain Daylight Time. He had been alive then. Smith had no reason to believe his condition had changed.

The Master of Sinanju would have to be informed.

As one arthritis-gnarled hand snaked toward the blue contact phone, the nimble fingers of Smith's free hand were already booking passage on two flights to New Mexico. One ticket was for Chiun. The other, for Harold W. Smith.

THE MASTER OF SINANJU had just completed the four thousand nine-hundred and ninety-ninth verse of his second favorite Ung poem. Rarely was he given the opportunity to go through one entire Ung without interruption, but with Remo away he had not only completed the classic spider poem in peace but had moved on to the near-classic melting-snowflake poem.

Through the recitation of both poems, he had achieved a level of joy unparalleled in the years he had spent in the wasteland of America.

Chiun was basking in the afterglow. He sat in full lotus position on his simple reed mat, eyes closed, face relaxed. The many wrinkles of his parchment skin were drawn into lines of pure rapture. There was almost an angelic cast to his wizened features.

The air of this heathen land had never smelled

sweeter to his delicate nose. The sounds of traffic in the street outside were almost soothing.

He was completely at peace.

Even the bray of the telephone which had been going on for the past ten minutes, was not enough to disturb his placid mood.

Remo had left the phone on the hook after talking to Smith. Typical thoughtlessness. It no longer mattered, however. Aside from the current incessant jangling, the phone had not rung during the entire time he had spent reciting.

To Chiun, the ringing phone was almost a sign to not become too at peace in this godforsaken land.

Chiun rose from the floor like a puff of steam. He padded down the hall to the kitchen. He had not yet opened his eyes as he pressed the receiver to a shell-like ear.

"Though unworthy even to hear my voice, you have reached Chiun. Speak, but do not annoy."

"Master Chiun, there has been an incident in New Mexico," Smith's voice blurted.

Chiun's eyes remained closed. "Knowing of the severe case of Anglophilia that grips this land, I understand the reason for the upstart provinces of Hampshire and York. But I have been to Mexico, Emperor Smith. Why would you wish to evoke the image of such a squalid land within your borders?"

"That is irrelevant," Smith insisted. "Remo has gone on assignment to New Mexico."

At Smith's sharp tone, Chiun opened his eyes. "This I know," he said evenly.

"According to what I have learned, he has been injured. He has been taken to the hospital."

While Smith spoke, the sound of his rapid typing sounded in the background. Chiun did not comment on this rudeness.

"I have just accessed the computers of the Fort Joy infirmary," Smith continued. "They have not entered details of his condition. However, it appears that they have put him in the intensive-care unit."

Chiun let Smith prattle until he sounded as if he was through. Only then did the Master of Sinanju interject.

"I appreciate your concern, O Emperor, but I assure you that Remo is in good health. We both remain robust of heart and stout of soul, the better to serve your regal self."

"It *is* Remo," Smith insisted. "Something has gone terribly wrong. I have booked you on a flight out of Logan. A cab will be there to collect you shortly. My flight leaves Newark airport before yours. We will rendezvous near the U.Sky terminal in Roswell."

"Forgive me, Emperor—"

Chiun was not given time to complete his

thought. The coarse hum of a dial tone grated on his delicate eardrum.

Slowly, he replaced the phone.

Smith had sounded agitated. More so than usual.

Chiun was not unused to this level of disquiet in his employer. Indeed, it seemed to be his lot in life to deal with the vicissitudes of Mad Harold.

Of course, there was nothing wrong with Remo. During the course of his last assignment, Remo had been wounded by a uniquely dangerous foe. Because of this, Smith must have now decided that every hoodlum with a boom stick could injure the Apprentice Reigning Master of Sinanju.

It was doubtless some other lout with Remo's name who had been injured. But that explanation would never work for Smith. To try to give a reasonable rationale to an unreasonable mind was to invite further madness. If he had attempted to explain the reality of the situation to Smith—that nothing was nor *could* go wrong with Remo—surely some of Smith's insidious madness would escape into Chiun in the process. In the end, for all his futile efforts, Chiun would wind up as crazed as Smith.

No, the old Korean knew from experience that it would be best to satisfy this latest insane whim of his Emperor.

Alone in his kitchen, he frowned. He would not need to bring all fourteen of his steamer trunks with him. Two would be sufficient. After all, he would undoubtedly dispense with this crazy white errand in short order.

That decided, Chiun left the kitchen to pack the few things he would need for his trip to Upstart Mexico.

7

General Delbert Xavier Chesterfield was doing the
one thing that put him head and shoulders above
all the other military men he had ever met—passing the buck.

"I can see where you're a-comin' from on that,
sir, I really can," he said into the phone.

He fell silent during the five-minute reply from
the other end of the line.

Chesterfield sat behind his desk in his Fort Joy
command barracks. His red moon face had begun
to take on shades of sickly orange not long after
the beginning of the call. Drops of sweat as big as
dimes collected on his forehead. They rolled down
in icy rivulets to his bull neck, soaking his starched
uniform collar a darker shade of green.

"*Absolutely* it was them, sir," Chesterfield said
when a break finally came in the monologue. "I
don't have the actual physical proof yet, but one
of their own agents is flat on his back in my infirmary right now."

In his huge mitt, his desk phone was like a min-
iature toy prize from a supermarket candy dis-

penser. He held it in only two fingers as he nodded vigorously.

"Yes, sir. I'd say CIA, sir. Or some other shadow element of the civilian government." After a pause he added, "Not under my nose, sir. I wouldn't categorize it as that. It's more likely a White Sands spillover thing. You know the stuff they've cooked up over there since the first nuke. Them superquiet planes and choppers, smart tanks and missiles. Hell, they've even got some of them Star Wars-type lasers on the burner, too. I only feel half-safe living next door and they're on *our* side."

Whatever his superior said to him did not seem to soothe Ironbutt Chesterfield's agitated mood. After a few harshly delivered words, the connection was severed. The general's big hand slowly lowered the receiver to its cradle.

He stared at the drab gray wall. His eyes were bloodshot saucers buried in his massive red face. The yard beyond the window to his right was still a hive of activity. He hardly noticed.

His sickly eyes went dry as he stared blankly. After a long, long time Chesterfield blinked. His great neck wobbled as he swallowed a lump of heavy saliva.

"Dag-nabbit," he murmured.

This was horrible. Terrible. Almost the worst thing that could have happened.

The brass knew that Roote was one of his. He never should have let the name remain under his command. He should have expunged the base records.

Even as he thought it, he knew it wouldn't have been possible. The damn Pentagon had to keep everyone on active military duty on file. Hell, they even had genetic records of Roote, as well as every other soldier in the United States. It would have been impossible to erase the psycho private's entire history.

In retrospect, Chesterfield realized that there was another alternative. He could have faked the private's death. Heck, he could have claimed the fella went AWOL. Who'd have known?

But he hadn't. Roote was his. The civilian authorities knew it. Washington knew it. *Everyone* knew it.

It was time for some serious CYA duty.

General Chesterfield dropped a finger as big as a turkey drumstick onto his intercom.

"That spook patient," he boomed into the microphone. "What's his condition?"

"Unchanged, General."

"Keep checking," he commanded, releasing the button.

That was a blessing. The government guy had been out like a light when they found him. Some kind of coma due to neural overload or some such malarkey. Base doctors had never seen a case like it before. They wanted to ship him off to one of the better equipped facilities off the base. Chesterfield had put the kibosh on that idea.

The spook was Chesterfield's ace in the hole. If things went to hell any more than they already had, he was the one who was going to shoulder the blame for old Ironbutt. He might not know it—he might not ever come out of his coma—but the whole Roote debacle would *still* be his fault.

Chesterfield hoped that when the time came he could make it stick.

As the general was considering the potential bleakness of his future, there came a sharp rap at the door.

"Come!" he yelled.

The same lieutenant who had spoken to him on the parade grounds the day before marched into the room. Crossing over to the general's desk, the much younger man saluted crisply, standing at full attention. Chesterfield returned the salute with very little conviction.

"At ease," the general grumbled.

"Thank you, sir," the lieutenant replied, though he did not seem to relax to any discernible degree. "Searches have come up negative, General. Private Roote is nowhere to be found, sir."

"That's not good enough, Lieutenant," Chesterfield barked. "Everybody's got to be somewhere. You just haven't recovered him yet."

"No, sir," the lieutenant replied.

Chesterfield closed his eyes. Ordinarily he liked

the way everyone around him was always agreeing with him. But under the circumstances, being surrounded by yes-men was not particularly heartening.

"Last known sighting?" the general asked.

"A local saw him leaving the saloon after his assault on the civilian."

"The *CIA* agent," Chesterfield corrected. He had been planting that seed for the past twenty-four hours. A little positive reinforcement never hurt.

"Yes, sir," the lieutenant agreed. "He took off into the desert in the jeep of the two MPs he killed. Our men attempted to follow, but the wind overnight wiped the trail clean. We haven't been able to pick up his tracks since first light. The local— he's Mexican in origin—he says that before Private Roote attacked the bartender, he said something about coming back after you next."

"I know all that, Lieutenant," Chesterfield complained. He frowned as he stared out his window.

Before his desk, the lieutenant stood uncomfortably. The officer wasn't certain whether he should say something.

His agitation was apparent to his commanding officer. After a few moments, General Chesterfield scowled.

"Dismissed," the general said.

"*Sir!*" the lieutenant announced. He threw a snappy salute before hustling from the room.

The general's frown deepened after the man had gone.

Chesterfield stared out the window, deep in thought.

The whole base was on a toboggan ride straight to hell. But if he had anything to say about it, General Delbert Xavier Chesterfield would still be standing in the snow at the top of the hill as the rest of them raced headlong into the devil's own court martial.

ROSWELL, NEW MEXICO, sat beneath the blazing sun approximately ninety miles northeast of Alamogordo. In the airport of this desert city sat a man who was arguably the most powerful individual on the face of the planet.

Dr. Harold W. Smith was waiting.

No one looked twice at the gray man in the gray suit with the gray disposition.

Smith's battered leather briefcase was open on his lap, balanced atop his bony knees. The keyboard to the portable laptop computer that connected via satellite uplink with the CURE mainframes back at Folcroft clacked remorselessly beneath his drumming fingers.

In his near paranoid desire for security, Smith had opted not to fly into the same city Remo had flown to.

Never mind the fact that, even if some airport employee had seen the both of them, it would have been on two separate days and that no one would have remotely connected the two men. Smith's zeal for security had suited CURE well in its four-decade existence. And he considered Alamogordo to be too much of a risk. Especially with all of the activity that had been going on there the past few days.

The airport in Roswell would preserve his precious anonymity. At least that was what Harold Smith had thought. Originally. For the past few minutes he had been having second thoughts.

The longer Smith sat in the uncomfortable plastic airport seat, the more agitated he became. Chiun was late. The U.Sky flight that he was supposed to be on had landed in Roswell three hours ago. The Master of Sinanju had failed to deplane.

Checking the computer records, Smith found that the old Korean had gotten a seat on a later flight. It was not U.Sky but one of the more expensive commercial airlines. First class.

To kill time while he waited, Smith had been working.

There was no new information concerning Remo's condition. The updates only listed him as "critical."

The CURE director had also refocused his attention on the Fort Joy computer system. Specifically, he had checked on the two things that had most puzzled him earlier. But as he searched, he found no other Shock Troops reference beyond the one connected with Remo's alias. And Roote was a twenty-one-year-old private on the base, originally from West Virginia. Private Roote had not done much to distinguish himself in the United States Army.

Smith had hit a wall.

Since exiting the Fort Joy system, the CURE director had busied himself with other matters, attempting to keep his mind off Chiun's tardiness, as well as Remo's condition. He had been working for quite some time before he began to get the creeping realization that someone was watching him.

Smith had no idea what triggered his sixth sense. He only knew that his old CIA training had kicked in, alerting him to potential danger.

He continued to type as if unconcerned. But even as his hands swept purposefully across his plastic keyboard, his eyes shifted upward.

It was just a moment's glimpse. But it was enough.

Peering over the bifocals of his rimless glasses, Smith instantly spied the man sitting across the terminal.

He was in his thirties or forties. His flat, owlish glasses were similar to Smith's. A week-old beard sprouted in scruffy patches from his sunburned face. A green nylon knapsack sat between his worn hiking boots. His faded jeans were torn at the knees. In spite of the heat outside, he wore a khaki

Army field jacket. Sitting, he seemed very lanky. He was certainly several inches above six feet.

He was also staring directly at Smith.

Shocked, the CURE director focused back on his computer. His mind reeled even as his fingers typed nonsense strings of letters.

Look casual. Do not appear obvious.

Smith tried to pull himself together. It could be that the man just happened to be looking at Smith at the same time Smith happened to be looking at him.

Coincidence. That *had* to be it. Convinced that this must be the case, Smith cautiously looked up.

His eyes again locked with those of the stranger. Worse, the man stood, collecting his knapsack.

Heart thudding, Smith looked back down at his computer.

The man was leaving. That was it. The only real explanation. The stranger would step outside, and afterward Harold Smith would get on the first plane back to New York. Chiun could deal with the Remo situation. It was foolish for Smith to have come out here in the first place. The very idea was a security risk.

Staring at his laptop, Smith waited for the stranger to step past him and continue toward the exit.

But the man did not go. As Smith felt his bowels clench in sick fear, the khaki jacket slid into the seat beside him.

''The truth is out there,'' the man said cryptically.

Smith continued to type. His mind swam. Fingers pressed blindly against keys.

''Trust no one,'' the man said. His voice was hushed.

''Excuse me,'' Smith said, not looking up from his computer. ''I am trying to work.''

There was silence for a moment. Smith felt the man hovering somewhere to his left.

''Is that some kind of code?'' the stranger said suddenly.

With a start, Smith glanced up from the jumbled letters of his bar screen. The strange man was leaning back in his seat, peering at the CURE director's hidden laptop.

In a surprisingly swift move, Smith slammed the lid on his battered leather briefcase, shutting the lid on the laptop in the same move. He didn't even care if the device was broken.

''That is none of your business,'' Smith snapped.

''Relax, old-timer,'' the man said. ''Arthur Ford,'' he held out a hand, smiling broadly.

Smith didn't know what else to do. To refuse the gesture would have been to draw more attention to himself. Feeling the life drain from him, he shook the man's hand.

''You're a believer. I can tell,'' Ford said cheerily. ''You dress the part.''

Smith shook his head, baffled. "Part?"

"You know," Ford insisted. "The *C-Files*. We get a lot of your kind around here. I'm more a *Star Trek* man myself, but to each his own."

"I am sorry," Smith admitted. "I am at a loss."

"Sure you are." Ford laughed. "I suppose you're going to tell me you don't know what happened here in Roswell?"

Smith was beginning to relax slightly. He had obviously caught the eye of a local nut. Still, he had no desire to engage the man in conversation.

"I am busy," he said. "If you would not mind."

"Aliens," Ford insisted. "They crashed in the desert. Everyone knows about it. There's been a big government cover-up of the whole thing. The military is using reverse engineering to figure out how their ship works. Where do you think stealth technology came from?"

"From years of hard work," Smith replied.

"Yeah, picking apart *alien* technology."

Smith had had enough. Uttering a firm "Excuse me," he got up, shifting down a few seats. Arthur Ford followed.

"You really aren't a believer?" he asked, surprised.

"I believe in reality," Smith said, exasperated.

"But the spaceship? I mean, come on," Ford insisted.

Smith's expression soured. "Young man, the only thing of great historical significance to happen in Roswell were the experiments of Robert Goddard. Perhaps it is his research into rocketry that led you to believe something more fantastic has occurred here, but I assure you that it has not.'' Smith was greatly relieved at that moment to spy the Master of Sinanju coming through the gate far down the terminal. He had been so unnerved by his unwanted visitor that he hadn't noticed the arrival of Chiun's flight on the electronic board. ''Excuse me,'' Smith said firmly to Ford.

Rising, he walked briskly away from the obviously deluded man. He and Chiun met up in the middle of the terminal.

The Master of Sinanju wore a silver kimono that shimmered in the light. Behind the old Korean, a helpful stewardess was pulling the Master of Sinanju's two lacquered steamer trunks on a wheeled dolly.

''Greetings, Emperor Smith, Preserver of the Eagle Throne, Guardian of the Constitution,'' Chiun intoned, bowing formally.

''We should go,'' Smith said in crisp response.

Without a word of thanks, he took control of the cart away from the flight attendant. Chiun fell in beside Smith.

''I would have arrived sooner, but the craft on which I was to journey was unacceptable,'' Chiun announced.

''I understand,'' Smith whispered, hustling to the door.

''They would have been better advised to affix paper wings to a sow's back and launch it from a catapult than to attempt flight in that death apparatus.''

This time Smith did not even respond. Gray face pinched, he hurried through the automated terminal doors and out into the bright New Mexico sunlight. The Master of Sinanju followed close behind, his silver kimono sparkling in the brilliant desert light.

At the row of plastic seats near the closing doors, Arthur Ford viewed Smith and Chiun with intense suspicion. As he watched them hurry down the sidewalk through the tall glass windows at the front of the terminal, he seemed to reach some internal decision.

Gathering up his nylon knapsack, Ford pulled himself up on his long legs. He hurried out the door in the wake of the two strange men.

8

Major Arnold Grant had been a U.S. Army doctor for more than ten years but had never seen a case like this one.

The patient had been warehoused in a secure wing of the Fort Joy infirmary. "Warehouse" was the best term Grant could come up with to describe the treatment of Remo Halper.

Lying in a private room at the end of a guarded corridor, the patient was doing little more than breathing. There was neural activity, but it was low, as if the man were a computer running some kind of self-diagnostic program. Occasionally a finger or leg would twitch, clearly indicating that there was no paralysis. At one point during that long first night, Halper's hand had snapped upward with such ferocity that it launched an orderly out into the hallway. But the patient remained in a coma.

He should have been dead. The patient had absorbed a massive amount of electrical energy. Major Grant had sat in on the autopsies of two of the other victims. Their skin had been like that of burned barbecued chicken.

Even if he had accepted less voltage, the man—who General Chesterfield insisted was a CIA spy to all who would listen—should not have survived. Somehow he had.

Grant had a sneaking suspicion why, though he dared not speak it to anyone.

The agent's nervous system was what had fascinated Major Grant the most, as well as given him the most concern. It was far more complex than that of any human being Grant had ever seen. For a brief time while studying the X rays, Major Grant had allowed the possibility that some of the crazies who hung around in the desert outside the base were right. This man's nervous system was complicated enough to be extraterrestrial in origin. Even as the thought occurred to him, the doctor dismissed it with an uncomfortable laugh. What he was looking at was an aberration. A naturally occurring, very human aberration.

Grant was walking down the infirmary hallway toward the special wing. Even though he hadn't mentioned his fleeting suspicion to a soul, the ludicrous thought that the patient might be an alien embarrassed him as he passed the two soldiers on guard duty.

He pushed through the double doors and walked down the silent end of the corridor to the patient's room.

Halper was still in bed. No surprise there. Grant doubted he'd be going anywhere for a long time.

Beside the agent's supine form, an EKG monitor beeped relentlessly. Grant saw that the heart rate was still slightly irregular. Probably due to the electrical shock. Something like that might never correct itself. Even if he did come around, the arrhythmia might be permanent.

He watched for a few long minutes as the sheet rose and fell with the patient's steady breathing.

There was nothing Major Grant could do for him. The Army was ill equipped to handle such a unique case. The man would have been better off at one of the civilian medical units.

As soon as he was brought in, the doctor had argued for sending the man either to Alamogordo or to one of the even more advanced facilities over in Texas. He had been shot down, overruled by Ironbutt Chesterfield.

So here Remo Halper lay. And until the general changed his mind, here he would remain.

As he stood contemplating the inexplicable decision of his base commander, Major Grant was surprised to find that he had begun to breathe in the same deep manner as his patient. It was so hypnotic, so relaxing, he hadn't realized he'd been doing so.

The doctor shook himself from his reverie, turning away from the government agent.

Without even realizing it, his breathing returned

to normal. On his way out of the room, Major Arnold Grant snapped off the lights.

HIS STOMACH SINKING, Smith noticed the car trailing them while they were still in Roswell. Once they had driven out into the desert, his suspicions were confirmed.

"We are being followed," he said. His gnarled fingers gripped the steering wheel tightly.

"I know," Chiun replied simply.

The Master of Sinanju was sitting in the passenger's seat of Smith's rental car. He watched, bored, as the few spotty houses faded into endless miles of desert.

Smith was taking nervous, furtive glances in the rearview mirror.

"I believe it is the man who accosted me at the airport," he said, voice taut.

"It is," Chiun said, clearly not interested. "If you recall, *I* recommended that you let me remove him while we were still at the airport."

"I thought we had lost him after the rental agency," Smith replied. "He must have gone to get his own car."

"If you wish, I could eliminate him now," the Master of Sinanju offered blandly. "Stop this vehicle and he will be but an unpleasant memory."

"I prefer another alternative, Master Chiun," Smith said, his lemony tone anxious. "He is obviously deranged. I do not believe he has any interest in CURE."

"He may join the club," Chiun muttered, using one of his new Hollywood expressions. More loudly, he said, "Take the next path off this concourse, Emperor. I will deal with our pursuer."

Smith did as he was told. At the next off-ramp, he steered off the highway. The vehicle behind them continued to follow. Smith saw now that it was an ordinary jeep.

There were only a few buildings scattered in a wide area around the lonely roads. A few homes, a gas station, as well as a tourist information stop.

When they had driven past the only signs of habitation and were only a few miles out into the desert, Chiun raised one sandaled foot from the well beneath his seat. Twisting, he slammed it down atop one of Smith's black cordovan dress shoes. To the CURE director's dismay, it was the shoe that had been pressing carefully against the gas pedal.

With a squeal of tires, the car lurched forward like an F-14 launched from the deck of an aircraft carrier.

Even as the car soared up the road, Chiun was checking the side mirror. As expected, the jeep behind them had accelerated in pursuit.

"What are you doing?" Smith demanded, breathless. The black strip of road flew away behind them.

"You did not wish him dead," Chiun replied, as if speaking to an imbecile.

"I did not wish myself dead, either," Smith reminded him.

Chiun didn't reply. He continued to monitor the jeep as it closed the gap between them.

Smith gripped the wheel so tightly he thought it would melt and squish up between his fingers.

The speedometer needle had fired up to eighty at the initial pressure of Chiun's sandal. As Smith watched, it crept steadily up to the hundred-mile-per-hour mark.

Smith's one consolation as the desolate scenery whipped by was that he was partially in command of his fate. He still controlled where the car was going. But even as this thought passed through his mind, he saw a bony hand snake up between his wrists.

Chiun grabbed the wheel tightly. He turned sharply, and the rental car dumped off the asphalt strip in an angry squeal of tires. The roof seemed to come crashing down on Smith as he bounced wildly in his seat.

Desert brush flew past the windows at alarming speed.

Chiun's eyes narrowed as he checked to see that they were still being followed.

The jeep remained behind them. It was speeding through the desert, barely visible in the cloud of dust that rose behind the rental sedan.

"Perhaps you should hold on, Emperor," Chiun suggested once they were only a few hundred yards from the road.

Smith thought he already had been. With a sinking feeling, he released the steering wheel, grabbing on to the seat with each hand.

Using both hands now, Chiun steered the car into a screaming arc. A huge cloud of dust rose from the desert floor. Cutting sharply back in the opposite direction, he gunned the engine. Another enormous plume of dust and sand joined the first.

Weaving back and forth several times in a serpentine manner, the Master of Sinanju created a massive cloud of impenetrable dust. He spun the wheel one last time, twirling the car around 180-degrees. His foot instantly slammed down on the brake.

As they jolted to a stop, Smith felt himself being flung forward. A hand flew up, pressing against his chest, guiding him delicately back into his seat.

As he released Smith, Chiun's keen hazel eyes studied the cloud that swirled around them.

Smith was still in the process of trying to catch his breath when he saw the murky contours of the jeep fly past, inches from the nose of their car.

As soon as the jeep had passed, Chiun clomped his foot on the accelerator. The car lurched forward in the direction from which they had come, bouncing back up onto the highway a minute later.

Chiun kept the gas pedal to the floor as they

zoomed back down toward the highway on-ramp. In the driver's seat, Smith was like a passenger. Only when they were back on the main road did the Master of Sinanju relinquish control of the vehicle to the CURE director.

Briefly as they raced toward Alamogordo, Smith caught sight of the lonely jeep tearing away across the desert. He turned his attention back to the highway. His heart still thudded madly.

Beside him, the Master of Sinanju tipped his head. "You are shaking, Emperor Smith," Chiun mentioned, wrinkled face a pucker of concern. "Do you wish me to drive?"

"No!" Harold W. Smith insisted.

Shrugging, Chiun settled contentedly back into his seat. The rest of their trip to Fort Joy was uneventful.

WHEN HE SPOTTED the dust-caked car driving up from the main gate, General Delbert Chesterfield was in front of his whitewashed headquarters checking on the truck that would be his mobile command post.

The general frowned deeply as the civilian vehicle closed in. He tapped his boot with his swagger stick.

"Find out who the hell this is," he called up to a radioman sitting in a swivel seat in the back of the truck.

A moment later, the radioman had the reply.

"Top security clearance out of Washington according to the gate, sir," the soldier replied. "An FBI special agent and some kind of consultant."

Chesterfield's black eyes registered shadowy concern as the car pulled abreast of his command truck. All around, a kind of organized chaos gripped the base. The soldiers swarming around the courtyard appeared to be gearing up for a major offensive. The nearest men broke away from the opening doors of the sedan.

If the general could have frowned any more deeply, he would have done so upon seeing the two men who climbed from the vehicle.

One was old as hell. The other was even older. The slightly less old one had spook written all over him. Forget the ID he had shown at the gate—he was CIA, not FBI. Chesterfield would have staked his career on it.

The younger old man wore a three-piece gray suit. The briefcase he carried looked as if it had been in his hand the day he was born. The older old one wore a brilliant silver kimono with gold accents. It seemed like a stiff breeze would have launched him halfway to Arizona.

Despite their apparent frailty, both men walked with an erect purposefulness that would have put an average mall-dwelling seventeen-year-old to shame. They strode over to Chesterfield. He turned away as they came, absorbed once more in the soldiers working in the rear of the truck.

"General Chesterfield," Harold Smith said. It was not a question, but a statement of fact.

"You've got him," Chesterfield replied, not looking at the CIA man.

"You have a patient on this base. A man by the name of Halper. We wish to see him."

"One of your secret agents, huh?" Chesterfield asked.

It was an effort for Smith to hide his surprise. Immediately images of Remo speaking while under sedation came unbeckoned to mind. It was CURE's worst-case scenario.

"We would like to see him," Smith pressed.

Chesterfield finally turned a baleful eye on Smith. The general towered over the CURE director. He outweighed Smith by almost 150 pounds.

"I *bet* you would," Chesterfield menaced. He shook his head, disgustedly. "You spook bastards really stuck everyone's ass in the fire this time. I hope you know that."

"I am certain I do not know what you are talking about," Smith retorted, with forced blandness.

Chesterfield snorted loudly. "Of course you don't." He turned away again. As he did so, he jerked a big thumb over his meaty shoulder. "The infirmary. He's still out like a light. Don't think you're taking him anywhere, 'cause you're not. He stays put until *I* say so."

Smith didn't push further. He left the general to his work. Hoping that Chesterfield did not know anything about the secret organization, the CURE director hurried across the crowded grounds toward the infirmary, Chiun in tow.

"That centurion was very rude," Chiun sniffed as they walked.

"Something is going on here," Smith replied. "It looks as if they are preparing for an invasion."

"A war is not an excuse for discourtesy," the Master of Sinanju insisted. "When Tamerlane sacked Damascus, he was very polite about it. And the people practically thanked Lucius Cornelius Sulla for conquering Rome, he was so mannerly. Civility does not necessarily fly out the window during times of war."

Smith didn't bother to point out to Chiun that both rulers he mentioned as pillars of courtesy were described as bloodthirsty madmen in every historical text he had ever seen.

"There is no war," Smith insisted. "Whatever he is up to, he is doing it without authorization."

Chiun glanced back across the grounds to Chesterfield. The general was yelling at another officer.

"Perhaps he is raising an army to march against the bloated puppet President. Do you wish me to remove the lummox?" he asked slyly.

"Not yet," Smith said, his voice hushed.

Smith's stomach was acid-fueled water. The fact was, if Remo had spoken any of the true nature of CURE while unconscious, General Chesterfield was as good as dead. And if too many people had heard either Remo or the general to keep this crisis contained, so too was Harold W. Smith.

Acutely aware of his own mortality, Smith quickened his brisk pace.

MAJOR GRANT WAS LISTENING to his mysterious patient's irregular heartbeat when the two men stepped into the room.

Chiun's eyes instantly went wide in shock. He had not prepared himself for the possibility that it actually could be Remo who had been injured. Crying out as if in pain, the old Korean raced over to the bed, swatting the doctor away.

Major Grant quickly removed his stethoscope from Remo's bare chest. "What is the meaning of this?" he demanded, stepping backward.

"If you do not want this one dead, Smith, remove him from my son's bedside," the Master of Sinanju threatened. Even as he spoke, he was probing Remo's rib cage with his fingers.

Smith instantly steered Major Grant to one side of the room, away from the Master of Sinanju.

"Son?" Grant asked. "Is he this man's father?" He looked at Smith for an explanation.

"In a manner of speaking," Smith said uncomfortably. His own anxious eyes were trained on Remo. "What is the patient's condition?"

Grant glanced at Remo's pale form as he spoke. "Unchanged since admittance."

"He is comatose?"

"He's in a profound unconscious state, so he fits the definition. But it's a coma like I've never seen. I really can't find anything wrong with him beyond his unexplained low neural responses. With the condition he's in, he *should* be awake. Or dead. Somehow he's in between."

"Have you done any CAT scans or an MRI?"

"We're not set up for either on base," Grant complained. "I'd like to try a PET scan, but we don't have the facilities here for that, either. Not that it matters. I doubt we'd be able to give him the necessary injection."

"What do you mean?"

Grant seemed uncomfortable. "You tell me," he countered, crossing his arms. "Does this man have some kind of special training? Something that I should know in order to better treat him?"

"Not that I know of," Smith lied.

Grant studied the CURE director's face. He didn't seem convinced by Smith's words.

"Whenever we tried to take blood, his muscles tensed," Grant explained. "It was like the skin above was stretched to its limit every time we tried to insert the needle. I'd have had better luck injecting it into solid concrete. This was all on an unconscious level, obviously."

"It sounds quite fantastic," Smith said, doubtfully.

"Yes, it does," Grant admitted.

They both were looking at Chiun. The Master

of Sinanju had completed his initial inspection. He was now tapping each of Remo's ribs in turn. He started from the bottom of one side and worked up to the clavicle. Shifting to the other side, he began to work his way down.

"Did you land in Alamogordo?" the doctor asked abruptly, shifting his gaze to Smith.

"No," Smith replied. He didn't elaborate.

Major Grant could see he didn't wish to speak.

"Roswell is worse, if that's where you came in," the doctor said, turning away. "The desert all around here is crawling with UFO nuts." Chiun caught his attention once more. "What is he doing now?" he asked Smith.

The Master of Sinanju had placed one cupped hand to the left of Remo's sternum. The other hand was placed atop it. He began a slow up-and-down massage of the area over Remo's heart, his hands acting as suction.

"He has knowledge of some unusual healing techniques."

"Acupressure?"

Chiun snorted.

"Something like that," Smith said. "Doctor, if you would not mind—"

Grant turned from Chiun, interrupting. "The reason I mentioned the UFO nuts is because they'll have a field day if they find out about your friend here."

Smith blinked. "What do you mean?"

"In case you haven't heard, there's some lunatic out there who's frying people alive. Mr. Halper is the first one to meet him and come out alive."

"Yes," Smith said evenly. "There have been a number of deaths, as I understand it. The killer or killers are setting people alight."

Major Grant shook his head. "They've been fried, yes, but they haven't been set on fire. The killer uses electricity. And from what I've heard around base, there's only one man."

"One man?" Smith asked, surprised. He thought of the "subject Roote" reference picked up by the CURE computers. The story jibed with the initial reports.

"That's right," Grant said. "And your friend met him. He took a powerful hit of electricity. Somehow he survived. If you lump that in with his strange muscular contractions and his supercomplex nervous system, the UFO people could begin to think that he's not quite human."

"That is ludicrous," Smith sniffed dismissively.

Major Grant nodded agreement. "I'm just telling you the spin people put on reality around here. The latest rumor I heard was that the killer is an alien who's come back to look for some ship that supposedly crash-landed here years ago."

Smith was ready to tell the doctor how foolish he sounded but was distracted by a noise from across the room. A low moan had issued from Remo.

Major Grant turned in surprise. He was stunned to see his patient's eyes open. They rolled around, unseeing, in their sockets for a few seconds. Then, as he moaned once more, Remo's eyelids fluttered shut.

"Amazing," the doctor hissed, stepping toward the bed.

Smith quickly restrained him. He took the major firmly by one arm, leading him swiftly to the door.

"Your assistance has been appreciated, Doctor," Smith announced efficiently. "We will assume control of this patient's care now."

"But what about—"

"Thank you very much," Smith said as he shut the door in the doctor's startled face. Quickly he joined Chiun at Remo's bedside. "Will he recover?" he asked worriedly.

"I do not know," Chiun replied, his face a mask of tight concern. "The witch doctor did speak some truth. Remo has been exposed to a great deal of electricity. It has affected the parts of his body controlled by such impulses."

"Do you think he spoke while he was under?" Smith asked, addressing his greatest concern.

"It is not likely," Chiun replied, annoyed by the question. "His body has concentrated all of its energies on restoring itself to health. He would not expend resources on anything as unnecessary as speech."

Smith felt the tension drain from his shoulders.

"That is a relief," he sighed.

"Would that I shared your opinion," Chiun responded, his singsong voice hollow. He waved a bony hand. "Leave us now," he insisted. "Remo's heart beats incorrectly. I must minister to him without interruption."

Smith did as he was asked. At the door he paused, glancing back at CURE's—and America's—two greatest weapons.

One lay on his back, unconscious, while the other seemed very old and frail as he toiled to save him.

This was supposed to have been a simple assignment. Now Remo's health and possibly his life were in danger. And the force that had felled him was still out there. Loose.

The nature of his work had long ago made Smith surrender any vestiges of the religious ideals of his distant childhood. Still, as he closed the door on the two Masters of Sinanju, Harold Winston Smith said a silent prayer. For all of them.

9

His quarry had disappeared.

For a time, Arthur Ford considered the possibility that the mysterious G-man and his strange Asian companion had been beamed up to a circling spaceship, Hertz car and all. But then he found the tracks in the dirt that led back out to the desolate road. Ford was pretty certain spaceships didn't use Goodyear radials.

They'd outsmarted him.

Annoyed, he got back on the highway. He was still in a funk when he arrived at the desert surrounding the military base just outside the White Sands Missile Range.

Ford tried to purge the thoughts of the government agent from his mind as he drove out into the vast expanse of burning flat desert beyond Fort Joy.

He planned to make the big trip this time out; he would circle down around Joy National Cemetery where it extended into Texas, and swooping up through El Paso, he'd come around White Sands from the west.

He had brought along enough food and gasoline for the several days he would spend in the desert. As he bounced along the rough terrain, Ford sipped from one of the bottles of Lubec Springs water he had packed in two insulated cases in the rear of the jeep.

The sun was dropping lower in the late-afternoon sky. Night would soon follow. It was best at night. Sometimes they would come out in the daytime, but at night the show was always better.

At times there would be a single ship. Flying high above the endless desert. At other times there would be multiple craft. These occasionally would fly in formation above the desert watchers, multi-colored running lights blinking cheerfully at the planet inhabitants below. The lights would break formation all at once, darting up into the heavens.

Ford had never seen any of the smaller, grouped spacecraft. He had seen many of the larger ones in his life. He even used to report them years before, but the sinister forces in the United States government were always one step ahead of him. Their stooges always got to the local police or airport or FBI or civil-defense offices first, passing out the old "landing airplane" cover story. Ford was so upset at the blatant cover-up that he was nearly ready to stop calling anyway when the cease-and-desist order was issued.

This was part of the reason he had been so anxious to follow the G-man from the airport. If the guy wasn't a ufologist, then he was the enemy. Especially dressed like that. Arthur Ford might have been able to expose the whole conspiracy if he'd been able to tail the guy.

Too bad for Ford. Everyone knew the government was always involved in all sorts of cover-ups. He would have been a hero if he'd been able to expose the mother of them all—the great Roswell UFO conspiracy.

One thing was sure—if he *had* exposed the truth, his family would finally stop snickering whenever his name was mentioned. Except for his mother. She'd stop crying.

Though he had tried since losing the G-man's car outside of Roswell, as Ford drove through the ATV furrows and around clumps of desert scrub, he could not help but think of the opportunity that had slipped through his fingers. Tonight, dammit, the universe *owed* him a spaceship.

He steered his jeep down into a well-worn trail that led down into a dried-out riverbed. He followed the contours of the old river for fifty yards, driving up the angled path that led up the far side.

Bouncing, the jeep crested the hill.

It was as he was leveling the jouncing vehicle off for the short trip down the rocky incline at the far side of the old riverbank that Arthur Ford saw the spaceship.

It was directly ahead of him in the gathering

redness of the afternoon desert sky. A tiny black dot moving swiftly toward him.

Ford was so shocked it took him a moment to realize he'd slammed on the brakes. A cloud of dust kicked up from beneath the skidding wheels.

"Shazbot!" Ford complained as the cloud crept swiftly forward, enveloping the jeep and blocking his view.

He tossed his water bottle onto the floor, quickly gathering up his camera from the passenger's seat.

Hopping down from the jeep, he ran out beyond the thin periphery of the cloud.

He saw the ship instantly. It was closer than it had been, zooming in from the west.

The brilliance of the sun in the western sky was too great to distinguish the craft clearly. Hands shaking with excitement, Ford brought the expensive camera up to his eye.

Desert vista flew by as he swept the horizon for the enlarging dot. He found it quickly.

As he adjusted the lens focus, the thrill of discovery collapsed into deep disappointment.

It was not an intergalactic spacecraft at all; it was a helicopter. A single, stupid, common U.S. Army helicopter.

No. Check that. *Two* stupid Army helicopters. The other was much farther back and could only be seen through his magnifying camera lens. It, too, was flying this way.

Ford trudged bitterly back to his jeep. He tossed

the camera onto a rear seat as he climbed behind the wheel.

Another disappointment in a day of disappointments. He had started the engine and was ready to drive on when he noticed the dark shape of another jeep in the desert below.

Probably another UFO watcher.

As Ford watched, a figure stepped from the jeep. A tiny speck from this distance, he could see the stranger walk around to the front of his vehicle.

The first helicopter was much closer now, flying fast. It seemed as if it had noticed the lone man standing in the desert, for it made a beeline for him.

Ford's heart thrilled. Quickly he gathered up his camera once more, thinking he had stumbled on some clandestine government meeting.

The telephoto lens instantly enlarged the man to the point where the back of his head and shoulders were clearly visible. His hair was whitish-blond. The visible skin of his neck pale. His head was upturned as he faced the incoming helicopters.

For some reason Ford didn't understand, the man had raised his hands as if in supplication.

Probably some kind of code.

Excited, Ford began snapping pictures as the chopper raced toward the lone figure in the desert.

It was difficult to judge from his angle at the edge of the dead river, but it appeared to Arthur Ford as if the helicopter was nearly atop the distant jeep. Dust swirled up from the force of the rotor blades as the aircraft settled into a cautious hover above the man. The lone figure had yet to lower his arms.

Ford took another picture. Click, advance. Click, advance. He didn't know exactly what was going to happen, but if it was anything like—

There was a sudden blinding flash.

Shocked, Ford blinked sharply, tipping the camera away from his eye.

Some intense, unexpected burst of brightness in the desert below had shocked his eyes. Wild streaks of blue danced across his field of vision.

He blinked again, trying to force away the strange ghostly afterimage. Still it persisted.

It was only when he allowed his eyes to focus once more on the helicopter before him that he realized the flash that had blinded him was still occurring.

The constant image was easier to endure. The electrical arc from the hands of the man in the desert slammed into the belly of the big helicopter. The sparking blue charge enveloped the metal fuselage, racing down the long length of the tail and up to the stabilizing fin blades. Sparks flew hotly off the tail blades, crackling audibly.

Ford watched, stunned, as the surge of electricity raced up the main rotor assembly and out across the multispar stainless-steel blades.

As the dark figure shot more juice up into the

helpless helicopter, the snap of the current was overpowered by the hum of the rotors slowing down. They became plainly visible, cutting at the air more and more slowly until lift could no longer be sustained. At this point, the helicopter simply dropped out of the sky.

Crash-resistant features meant nothing under these battlefield conditions.

Deadweight now, the chopper thundered to its belly in a shower of bluish sparks. As soon as it hit the desert, the Hellfire missiles aboard the craft detonated, engulfing the helicopter in an enormous ball of brilliant flame.

A thick curl of black smoke rose like an angry cobra into the pastel-painted sky.

The other helicopter was visible now. It had flown in behind the first, hugging the ground.

As fast as the first chopper had moved in, this one came faster. It had none of the curious hesitancy of the first. Unlike the helicopter that lay shattered and burning on the desert floor, this one appeared ready for combat.

Standing back, away from the action, Ford was in shock. He could not believe what he was seeing.

A real live humanity-versus-alien battle was going on under his very nose. It was everything he had ever dreamed of. And if Arthur Ford had anything to say about it, he was going to be in the thick of things.

Flinging his camera into the jeep, he jumped behind the wheel. Leaving a huge plume of dust in his wake, Ford peeled off, bouncing crazily down toward the arena of intergalactic combat below.

ELIZU ROOTE WATCHED the second Apache tear across the desert toward him.

He had guessed correctly. Although he wasn't possessed with a great military mind, he still had an advantage. He knew Ironbutt Chesterfield was no great thinker, either. Obviously he knew the general all too well.

Chesterfield knew Roote's last location was near the Last Chance Saloon beyond Lincoln National Forest. He would concentrate all his forces in that direction, not even considering the possibility that Roote might have gone south before turning toward the eastern perimeter of the base.

Roote had driven through miles of empty desert with no interruption.

Until the Apaches showed up.

The first chopper lay twisted in the sand before him. Sparks from the wreckage had set off a few minor brush fires around the crash site. Those parts of the rotor blades that hadn't sheared off at the chopper's impact with the unforgiving ground spun lazy circles above the flaming aircraft.

The Apaches were being used for reconnaissance, blindly sweeping the lonely miles of desert in search of a single man. It was obvious that the chopper crews hadn't been told what that lone man was capable of. If they had, the first chopper would never have stopped the way it had. And the second wouldn't be racing to its doom.

Roote could tell they were going to open fire on him. The nose of the trailing helicopter was tilted down slightly, the 30mm Hughes chain gun beneath the cockpit directed at the spot before the stolen Army jeep where Elizu Roote stood waiting.

Roote wasn't interested in prolonging this contest. As the chopper soared toward him, the fiberoptic relays that connected his optic nerve to the targeting processor in his brain locked on the big gun beneath the aircraft. He raised one hand toward the helicopter, fingers cupped to maximize the strength of the stream.

Roote fired.

At a command from his brain, conductive fibers along his skeletal system sucked power from the backup capacitor sites buried in his torso. Electricity collected at his five metal finger pads, congealing into a single blue arc that surged through the air in the direction of the incoming helicopter.

The bolt never reached the Apache.

Roote knew all too well that electricity would naturally seek the shortest, fastest, most conductive route to the ground. Velocity compensators at his primary capacitor sites gave the extra boost his targeting systems needed to fire a controlled bolt at a given target. But he had drained those capacitors in his assault on the first Apache. Adrenaline had fooled his biological system into thinking that his mechanical system was at a higher operating level than it actually was.

As he watched in growing alarm, the heavy blue bolt of electricity turned a magnificent arc in the air, missing the Apache by dozens of yards. It blasted into the slowly revolving rotor assembly of the already downed helicopter.

Roote cut the power, staggering backward.

He felt the depletion all at once. His power was all but gone.

The helicopter continued to close.

Frantically, swaying wildly, Roote turned around.

He popped the hood on the jeep. As the aircraft rumbled inexorably toward him, Elizu Roote was certain that it would open fire any second. He visualized bullet holes erupting in his back, his body crumpling, bleeding, to the ground.

Fumbling, he grabbed hold of the top of the vehicle's battery. The wind at his back grew great. The roar of the chopper filled the desert around him.

He was almost dead. There would be no third chance.

Roote spun around. Sand from the downdraft ripped against his pale cheeks.

It was there. Fat and dark, hovering like some vision from the Apocalypse in the air before him.

They had not fired. They seemed content to watch him, unsure how to proceed.

Roote had no such hesitation.

He instantly channeled the power from the jeep battery directly up one arm and out the other. The blue arc exploded from his cupped fingertips, guided by his ocular systems to the slender angled gun barrel extending from the chopper's undercarriage.

The blue surge moved swiftly down the boron armor of the Apache. Random bolts were flung to the ground as the helicopter fought to stay aloft. There was a shriek of protest followed by a massive explosion as the ordnance aboard the aircraft detonated.

Roote barely had time to cut the power and scurry beneath the belly of his jeep before the big Apache crashed dramatically to the ground.

A few smaller explosions ripped through the air as the mortally wounded helicopter settled near the first in a plume of vicious dust.

Drained of nearly all power now, Roote could do nothing but cover his head with his arms. He crawled on his belly, away from the metal fragments thrown out from the chopper.

As he lay there, panting in fear and fatigue, he became aware of a new engine sound. It grew in intensity even as the roar of flames from the helicopter began to die.

A jeep. Almost as soon as he heard it, he saw it.

Tires slowed and stopped with a squeak. Roote saw them from the shade beneath his own jeep.

Feet appeared. They ran to a point before his own jeep, scuffing to a stop in the dust. They were aimed toward the nearest flaming helicopter.

"Wow."

The voice wasn't shocked. It was almost enthusiastic.

The boots changed direction. They ran over to the front of the jeep. Whoever it was dropped to his knees. An eager, sunburned face appeared in the square of light beneath the jeep's grille.

Roote's power was almost gone. He retreated from the newcomer, scurrying only a few inches back.

The stranger shook his head. He smiled.

"I am friend," Arthur Ford announced in loud, stilted English. He rapped his chest. "Me friend. Help you."

Flames crackled in the scrub around him. His capacitors were virtually empty. Elizu Roote hadn't much of a choice.

He extended a hand to Ford. The UFO enthusiast dragged one of the most dangerous men in the world from his hiding place beneath the jeep of the MPs he had murdered.

"Army bad. Government bad." Arthur nodded, as if indulging a dim foreigner. "I will take you to safe place." A thought suddenly occurred to him. "Do you want to phone home?" he offered cheerily.

"Shut up," Elizu Roote drawled weakly.

The words startled Ford. His alien had mastered Earthling vernacular already! Probably from watching television broadcasts while in orbit. This was obviously a creature of superior intelligence.

Thrilled that his alien spoke English and unmindful of the fact that the extraterrestrial's first suggestion had been rather on the rude side, Arthur Ford hustled the creature away from the flaming helicopter wreckage and to his waiting jeep.

10

Remo was sitting up in bed, a steaming bowl of yellowish liquid cupped in both hands.

Although he was still pale, thanks to the Master of Sinanju's ministrations, much of his strength had returned. Blowing away some of the steam, he raised the bowl carefully to his lips and sipped a tiny portion of the liquid.

His expression instantly soured.

"Bleah," Remo said, a disgusted look on his face. He pushed his tongue around, feeling the thick tang of the unpleasant flavor on the roof of his mouth.

At his bedside Chiun stood, almond-shaped eyes narrowed expectantly like an actor awaiting a career-making review. He was clearly not pleased with Remo's assessment.

"Bleah?" Chiun bristled, insulted. "I toil for hours to restore you to health, I scour this encampment of cheap amateur killers for the necessary ingredients for this admixture, and one of the first grunts of language that passes your blubbery white lips is 'bleah'?"

"So shoot me," Remo said. "It tastes horrible."

"Would you rather it taste like fudge-cake-ripple-marshmallow-flavored ice cream?" Chiun mocked.

"Yeah, actually," Remo replied. "Even mud would be an improvement."

Chiun crossed his arms imperiously. "Too bad. It tastes as it tastes. Drink."

Remo took another reluctant sip. His face puckered once more. "Bleah. It tastes like goat piss," he complained.

Chiun's eyes narrowed in suspicion. "Who has told you the secret ingredient?" he asked.

Remo shot a look at the old Korean. There was a hint of buried mirth in his teacher's eyes. Still, Remo wasn't certain if he himself was the joke. Steeling himself, he tossed back the bowl, drinking all of the liquid in one wretched gulp. He shivered afterward, handing the cup back to Chiun.

"Happy?" Remo asked, a deeply unpleasant expression on his pale features.

Chiun inspected the bowl for a single drop of liquid. Finding none, he nodded crisply, placing the bowl on the nightstand beside the bed. He settled, legs folded beneath him, into the lone seat next to Remo's hospital bed, the better to see his pupil.

Remo's gaze wandered to the half-open blinds on the nearest window. From this area of the infirmary, only a portion of the parade grounds was visible. Still, the view was such that many of the soldiers preparing for combat in front of Chesterfield's headquarters were plainly evident.

Remo's face took on a worried cast. "They're going after him," he commented softly.

"Who?" Chiun asked blandly.

"You know who," Remo said.

"Ah, yes." Chiun nodded. "The evil demon who shoots electricity from his fingers. Perhaps after they have slain the villain, they will concentrate their efforts on the wicked boogerman and Frankenpoop's monster."

Remo settled back in his pillow. "You're not really helping matters," he muttered, voice distant.

"No, of course not," Chiun replied tartly. "You were only unconscious and near death when I arrived. Your heart was bouncing like a drunken grasshopper around your chest, and any fool with a boomstick could have killed you with but a single shot, yet *I* am not helping. Forgive me, Remo. The next time you are about to die I will allow you to, thereby ingratiating myself to you for all eternity."

"Sarcasm doesn't help, either," Remo sighed, eyes closed.

"No," the Master of Sinanju admitted, bored, "but at least it gives me something to do while you sprawl like a calving bison in that Western bed." He fussed with the hems of his kimono.

After coming around an hour before, Remo had

told Chiun about Elizu Roote and his apparently remarkable abilities. The Master of Sinanju had been more than a little skeptical.

Secretly, Chiun hoped that Remo was lying to cover the embarrassment he felt for allowing his body to somehow become exposed to a near lethal dose of electricity. However, he knew that this was not like his pupil. Even if he were embarrassed, Remo wouldn't lie. Not to Chiun.

The only other alternative was one that Chiun dared not speak aloud.

Remo had gone mad.

If this were the case, the circumstances for the House of Sinanju would be catastrophic. Remo was Chiun's heir. As student of the Reigning Master, he was destined to one day assume the title himself. If he *had* gone insane, the future of the House was in grave jeopardy, for Chiun was far too old to train another pupil. Inwardly Chiun prayed to his ancestors that Remo would come through this trial, sanity intact.

"Is Smith still around?" Remo asked suddenly.

"Somewhere," Chiun replied vaguely. "I believe he has gone to speak with the oaf who commands this legion."

"Chesterfield," Remo murmured. "That bloated tin soldier set me up." He shook his head, as if reaching some internal decision. "I have to talk to Smith," he announced.

"No, you have to recuperate," Chiun replied.

"I feel pretty good," Remo said. "That bowl of hot whiz you gave me really hit the spot." He tapped his fist against his chest as he pulled weakly at his bedcovers.

Chiun was up and at the bedside instantly. Five slender fingers pressed against Remo's chest, pinning him to the bed. With his other hand, Chiun drew the sheets back into place.

"You need more time."

"Look, Little Father," Remo said, his tone reasonable, "that psycho is still on the loose. If *I* had a hard time with him, those soldiers don't have a prayer."

"You must rest."

Although he wished it were not so, Remo knew his teacher was right. The proof was beneath his very nose. Chiun's wrinkled hand barely brushed Remo's flesh, yet he couldn't budge an inch. He didn't even attempt to struggle. Surrendering, Remo collapsed back on the bed.

"At least get Smith in here," he said wearily.

"As you wish," said Chiun. "I will tell him that you worry Electricity Boy might ravage the province of Upstart Mexico with his powerful rays of death."

Remo closed his eyes tiredly. "I'd prefer it if you let me tell him. Somehow it loses something in the translation."

Chiun nodded curtly. Releasing his pupil, the old Korean turned from the bed. He left the hospital room fearing not only for Remo's health but for the future of Sinanju if his pupil had indeed succumbed to madness.

THE DESERT SUN CAST brilliant shades of evening red across the sky. Still, Harold Smith waited.

He sat patiently on the side steps of General Chesterfield's one-story headquarters, his battered leather briefcase balanced carefully atop his knees. The waning sunlight splashed across his gaunt features.

The activity in the main parade area was dying. Most of the soldiers and vehicles had dispersed to other spots on the sprawling base. One by one, Smith watched them go.

Earlier that day, the CURE director had used his briefcase laptop to tap into the computers at the Pentagon. He could find no reason for the flurry of activity at Fort Joy. That meant only one thing. Rogue operation.

In spite of the desert heat, the thought gave Smith a chill.

In many other nations, the possibility of the country's armed forces falling behind a crazed military dictator was a constant danger. Coups were so commonplace in undeveloped nations that they took place seasonally, like winter snow or autumn harvest. But this had never been the case in America.

In spite of the absurdity of the idea, Smith had

to consider the notion that General Delbert Chesterfield was planning to use his men in some sort of rebellion against Washington. After all, the cover story that all of this activity was to apprehend a single man was ridiculous.

But Chesterfield had only a few thousand soldiers under his command. Clearly not enough for any great campaign.

Fort Joy was too remote for the general to consider any kind of direct assault against the nation's capital. What else would he do, march against Santa Fe or Albuquerque?

El Paso was closer. So was Mexico. Did Chesterfield plan to invade either Texas or America's southern neighbor?

All of the scenarios the CURE director came up with led to more questions.

It would have been far easier to use Remo or Chiun to neutralize the general. But Remo was not yet well enough for action and Chiun refused to leave his pupil's bedside. The last time Smith had checked in, Remo was just coming around. Chiun had said that it could be hours before he completed his recovery. Smith knew that whatever was going to happen could take place long before then.

Smith had considered using his far-reaching computer access to bring troops in from around the nation to contain the soldiers of Fort Joy. However, he would only do this after he had exhausted all other strategies. After all, he didn't know how loyal the Fort Joy soldiers were to their commander. And Harold Smith did not wish to be the man responsible for setting American troops against one another for the first time since the Civil War.

All that was really necessary to resolve this was Chesterfield. Smith was confident that the general was key to unlocking whatever was behind this obvious madness.

According to an aide, the general had been out in his mobile command unit touring the eastern perimeter of the base for the past several hours. So, with nothing more to do, Smith was waiting for him to return.

It was nearly six o'clock when the general's command truck at last drove into view. The big vehicle slowed to a stop in front of the barracks-type building.

The truck rocked visibly on its shocks as the great bulk of General Delbert Xavier Chesterfield climbed down from the back. He slapped his riding crop against one thigh.

Smith rose from the simple wooden slat steps of the HQ building. He walked briskly over to meet the general.

"General Chesterfield," Smith called.

The military man had been marching determinedly to the main door of his headquarters. However, he balked at the sight of the thin, gray civilian coming toward him.

"Are you still here?" Chesterfield shouted. "I figured you'd be back in Washington cooking up some other problem for me to solve by now."

"Precisely what problem is it you think you are solving?" Smith asked.

"As if you don't know," Chesterfield snorted. He aimed his riding crop at Smith. "You started this whole mess, and now it's up to the good ole U.S. Army to pull your spook bacon out of the fire. I'll have you know I just got a report that two of our choppers were downed by a hostile force down along the southern perimeter."

"What hostile force?" Smith asked.

"Nice try, CIA man," Chesterfield said, shaking his head in mock sympathy. He started to sidestep Smith, but the CURE director slipped back before him, blocking his path.

"It is Roote, isn't it?" Smith insisted quietly.

Chesterfield hesitated. His mind was already racing, trying to figure out what Smith could know, attempting to determine what he should admit to. In the end, he settled on giving a noncommittal grunt.

"He has killed a number of people," Smith pressed. "It is for him that you are preparing your men for a major battle. What is so special about one man?"

Chesterfield relaxed. The spook didn't know a thing.

"I'm busy," the general barked loudly.

He tried to step toward his office again, but Smith placed a firm hand on the much larger man's chest. It would have been comical if Smith did not seem so determined.

"General, we *will* discuss the current situation," Smith insisted firmly.

"Current," Chesterfield mocked. "Pretty telling choice of words, considering what you and that buddy of yours have cooked up down here." He jutted his uppermost chin vaguely in the direction of the infirmary. As he did so, he snarled. "Here's another one of your damn spooks."

Smith glanced around, hoping to see Remo. Instead he spied the Master of Sinanju gliding swiftly across the wide parade grounds.

"What do *you* want?" Chesterfield demanded loudly as Chiun stepped up beside Smith. "Can't you see I'm up to my armpits in Army business?"

Chiun ignored him. "Remo is awake, Emperor," he said to Smith. "He wishes to speak with you."

Chesterfield's eyes went wide. "Awake? Grant said he was in a coma."

"He has awakened," Chiun said flatly.

"Is he well?" Smith asked.

The Master of Sinanju shook his head somberly. "His breathing is correct, as one would expect. I fear, however, that his heart is not yet working properly. Out of sync, it has altered his body rhythms."

Forgotten were the hours Smith had spent awaiting Chesterfield's return. He was more interested now in getting whatever firsthand information Remo might have concerning Roote and this mysterious Shock Troops. The CURE director had suspected that this was the reason for the heightened military activity around the base. His brief meeting with the general had confirmed those suspicions.

Smith began heading for the infirmary with Chiun, but a looming shape suddenly blocked their path.

"You're not allowed back in there," Chesterfield said in his usual bellow. His eyes belied his concern. "I can't let you CIA types conspire on your cover story. Before you know it, they'll be blaming *me* for what's going on down here."

Standing in the huge shadow of the hulking soldier, Chiun narrowed his eyes to razor slits.

"May I?" he asked Smith. His expression was steel.

"Do not kill him," Smith advised.

Chesterfield had to laugh at their audacity. As if for one minute, either of these two pipe-cleaner men could—

The general's world suddenly spun at a weird angle. The sky flew around to where the ground had been a second before. He had the brief sensation of being held aloft, followed by an incredible, liberating feeling of flight. This was instantly succeeded by the sharp crackle of wood and glass, as well as a great pressure at his back. Gravity took hold all at once, and the Army general thundered to a solid wood floor.

It took him a moment to orient himself.

General Chesterfield soon realized that he was lying on the floor in his office, surrounded by shattered clapboards and broken window panes. Through the man-shaped hole in the wall, he saw the two CIA types heading across the courtyard toward the infirmary.

Chesterfield sat up amid the debris. Splinters rained down from his close-cropped white hair.

"I guess one little face-to-face with the injured won't hurt," he said. His voice lacked its usual boom.

As the faces of a few concerned soldiers stuck hesitantly in around the gaping hole, the general lumbered uncertainly to his feet.

11

If science fiction had taught him one thing, it was that all aliens were not necessarily good. Arthur Ford considered this notion as he bounced across the desert in the company of his own personal Man Who Fell to Earth.

Rescuing the alien who called himself Elizu Roote had been very exciting at first. Especially after the dramatic display he had put on defending himself against the evil Army helicopters. It was like in *Starman,* except it wasn't Karen Allen in the driver's seat, but Arthur Ford, ufologist. But Ford's illusions about all space aliens were soon shattered when he began to sense how downright nasty his passenger was.

"Careful on the bumps, asshole," Elizu Roote muttered, one ghost-white cheek propped against the seat. "I already feel like I'm gonna upchuck."

Roote had looked sickly pale when Ford had dragged him out from underneath his stolen jeep. His batteries low, he had only gotten sicker as they drove into the setting sun.

Gripping the steering wheel tightly as they

crested a slight hill, Ford glanced over at Roote. The dust on his face had turned to mud as beads of perspiration broke out across his waxy forehead.

"It's our fault isn't it?" Ford said, concerned. "We've poisoned our water and air to the point where they've made you sick. We've built up an immunity to the toxins, but an innocent like you couldn't possibly have. Damn this shortsighted military-industrial society!" Ford balled an angry fist, punching down on the steering wheel. The horn beeped. Ford jumped.

Roote rolled his head toward Ford, fixing him with a baleful eye. If he could have worked up the strength to electrocute him, he would have. But the truth was, he was feeling completely drained from his earlier exertions.

There hadn't been enough gasoline in the Last Chance generator for him to recharge to capacity. The battle with the Apaches had depleted his remaining reserves. With his capacitors virtually at nil he felt a numbing fatigue.

He hadn't been told about this feverish, enervated sensation by the so-called experts at Fort Joy. Probably it wasn't anticipated. He was the first. This was just an unforeseen side effect.

The liquor hadn't helped. On top of everything else, Elizu Roote was hungover. As Arthur Ford's jeep sought out every uneven surface in the vast desert, it was an effort to keep down the frothing acidic liquid in his belly.

"I said watch the bumps," Roote snarled. A small spark hopped between his thumb and fore-finger.

"I'm *trying*," Ford apologized. "We just passed the first Fort Joy sign," he added hopefully.

It was a struggle, but Roote pushed himself up in his seat. In the side mirror he saw the receding image of a battered wooden sign sticking up out of rock and sand.

A thick droplet of mucus ran down from one nostril. Roote sniffled at it, pulling the thick slime, as well as a line of trailing black mud, back into his nose.

"Think ole Ironbutt'll welcome me home?" he asked. His demonic eyes were watery as he glanced, smiling, at Ford.

Arthur Ford didn't know what his alien passenger meant. He wondered if the cryptic phrase referred to the spaceship that had crash-landed up in Roswell decades ago. He also wondered why an alien from an obviously advanced civilization would choose to speak English with a Southern accent.

But as the speeding jeep bounced closer to the perimeter fence of Fort Joy, the ufologist dared not ask either question.

REMO WAS OUT OF BED and dressed when Smith and Chiun returned to his hospital room.

"Remo, I'm surprised you are up," Smith said.

"Can't keep a good man down," Remo replied with a tight smile. He was still pale, but seemed otherwise fine.

"How do you feel?" Smith asked.

"Never better," Remo said. "Chiun's bedpan cocktail was a real pick-me-up."

"Next time I must remember to brew a shut-you-up," the Master of Sinanju said, crossing to him. "Sit."

"Chiun, I'm okay. Really."

A glare from the elderly Korean stifled further protest. Throwing up his hands, Remo sat on the edge of the bed.

Scowling, Chiun pressed his slender fingers on the white cotton T-shirt Remo had found in the infirmary linen room. The examination was over in two seconds.

"Your heart still does not beat correctly," the Master of Sinanju pronounced.

"Yes, but it's filled with love." Remo held up a hand, stemming any protest. "Look, I've adjusted for it," he said. "And my system has almost corrected the problem. It's gotten at least ten times better in the last five minutes."

"Is this true, Master Chiun?" Smith asked.

Chiun nodded grudgingly. "He is healing quickly." Hands met inside his voluminous kimono sleeves.

"See?" Remo said to Smith.

"He is still pale," Smith pointed out.

"Hey, I'm no George Hamilton, but at least I'm not gunmetal gray," Remo countered, peeved.

Smith ignored the insult. "Has he recovered enough to return to active duty?" he asked the Master of Sinanju.

Chiun nodded. "If you insist, Emperor. With supervision," he added quickly.

"That is a relief," Smith said. He turned his attention to a more urgent matter. "What happened, Remo? Presumably Elizu Roote caused these injuries."

Remo leaned his fists on the unmade bed. "Chiun didn't tell you?" he asked, raising a skeptical eyebrow.

"No."

"I did not want the Emperor to think I endorsed your tall tale," Chiun interjected. Frowning, he sank to a lotus position in the center of the floor.

Remo took a deep breath. "Okay, first off, this is gonna sound crazy, Smitty," he cautioned.

"Go on," Smith pressed.

"I found the guy in a bar off the base. There were three bodies there already. They all looked like burned toast. When I tried to take out Roote, he zapped me."

Smith crinkled his nose at the word. "What do you mean?"

Remo raised his hands in an impression of Elizu Roote. "Zapped," he explained. "There was this kind of...jump of electricity. From all of his fingers. He had some kind of weird fingertips. Like metal. Anyway, the voltage must not have been as high as what he used on the dead guys, because I was able to throw most of it off. He did manage to overload my system. Next thing I remember was waking up with Chiun staring down at me."

"An angelic vision after your walk through the valley of the shadow of death," the old Asian said blandly.

"Chiun thinks I'm crazy," Remo said.

"I believe no such thing, Emperor Smith," Chiun interjected quickly, lest their employer think madness an excuse to seek a discount for their services. "Remo has been gravely injured. I believe his mind, as well as his body needs time to heal properly."

It was as if Smith didn't even hear Chiun. He took a seat next to Remo's bed.

"Out of his *fingers?*" he asked, intrigued.

Remo seemed mildly surprised that Smith hadn't already laughed him out of the room.

"Yeah," he said. "He aimed both hands at me like he was freaking Bela Lugosi, then fired."

"What about his fingers?" the CURE director pressed.

"What do you mean?"

"You said they were metal?"

"Oh, yeah," Remo nodded. "Sort of. But not all of them. Just the tips. The electricity came from there."

Smith considered Remo's words. After what seemed like an eternity, he nodded slowly.

"It makes some sense," he admitted somberly.

"It does?" Chiun asked, surprised.

"It does?" Remo echoed, just as amazed.

"Yes," Smith said, "it does." He turned to the Master of Sinanju. "Master Chiun, you must admit that it would take a powerful force to overcome Remo's training."

"Of course," Chiun sniffed. "He is Sinanju."

"Therefore, although you are understandably skeptical, you know that Remo must have encountered something unusual. Surprising, in fact."

"Possibly," Chiun conceded slowly.

"What could be more surprising than that which Remo has described to us? And are his injuries not consistent with a struggle with just such a man as Remo claims Roote to be?"

"Perhaps," Chiun said, unhappy to be swept along in Smith's speculative current.

For his part, Remo seemed bolstered by the leap of faith the CURE director had taken on his behalf. "I'm surprised you're the one in my corner, Smitty," he said.

"Your story is incredible," Smith admitted. "But there is much that is strange going on here. This entire base appears to be focusing its energy and resources on a single individual. That would make him special in the extreme. In a bizarre way, what you have said helps to explain a lot." He got to his feet. "I must meet with Chesterfield," he said determinedly.

Remo stood, as well. Chiun was quick to rise to his side.

"While you do that, I'm going to look for Roote," Remo announced.

"That is ill-advised," the Master of Sinanju insisted.

"You said Remo was well enough to complete his assignment," Smith challenged.

"Yeah, Little Father," Remo agreed. "I'm healthy as a horse. Don't worry. I'll be fine."

"Excellent," Smith said. "Now that you know Roote's abilities, you will not be taken by surprise. You two will have a better chance than anyone of stopping him. While you are gone, I will attempt to get to the bottom of this."

Without another word, Smith stepped from the room.

Once the CURE director was gone, Remo glanced at the Master of Sinanju. Chiun was staring intently at him, seeming to scrutinize his every facial feature.

"What's wrong?" Remo asked with a sigh.

The old man's voice was perfectly level. "I was attempting to determine who was the greater madman. You or Smith."

"Oh," Remo said dully. "Care to pick a winner?"

Chiun stroked his thread of a beard pensively. His intelligent hazel eyes were clouded in thought.

"The jury has not yet rendered a verdict," he intoned.

THE ROUGH ATV PATH they had taken through the desert spilled out onto a worn access road that ran parallel to the chain-link fence marking the southern perimeter of Fort Joy.

Signs warning intruders away had caused Arthur Ford concern for the past two miles. Although he had followed this route as a ufologist several times in the past without being bothered by the Army, he had never done so in the company of an extraterrestrial. He hoped the military hadn't put any special sensing equipment in place that would alert them to Roote's presence.

More and more, Ford was thinking that the creature he was with might not be a benign alien. He had hoped for the kind of life-affirming fun in his encounter with a creature from another planet as was the norm in movies and television. But even *Star Trek* had its share of villains. Maybe Roote was like a Romulan or Cardassian. Or even like the Klingons used to be, and sometimes still were.

These thoughts distracted him as they sped along the lonely desert road.

"The rear gate's comin' up soon," Roote drawled. "Bring me over to the fence."

They were driving at a slight angle on the uneven sand. The dusty earth spread up a short incline to a lone strip of sage-covered rock. The base fence had slipped behind this rise of land a moment before.

Dutifully Ford stopped the jeep. He hurried around to the other side, helping Roote out.

In spite of the desert heat, Roote's skin was clammy to the touch. All except his metal finger pads. These were warm as they clutched at the back of Ford's neck.

Embracing Roote around the waist, Ford helped him climb up the steep side of the scrub-covered bluff.

The first thing Ford saw when they crested the hill was not the fence, but the line of tanks and soldiers beyond.

"*Look out!*" Ford screamed, pushing Roote to the rocky ground.

He had thought to save his precious alien with his gallant act. But in truth, until Arthur Ford yelled, the soldiers hadn't even been looking their way. The men were farther along the fence, positioned closely to the desolate desert base entrance.

The nearest soldiers instantly turned toward the intruders. A shout carried down the line, bringing the attention of the rest.

Gunfire erupted instantly.

The ground around them was pelted with a flurry of bullets. Some pinged off the chain-link fence, the sparks of ricochets flying crazily through the desert twilight.

Arthur staggered and fell, accidentally dropping to safety behind a pile of black rock. A hail of bullets rattled against the hard rock, flinging flinty shards over the cowering UFO enthusiast's head. Bullets pelted sand, throwing puffs of powder into red-tinged sky.

The sound was deafening. Ford screamed. His voice was buried in the thunderous roar of automatic-weapons fire.

Covering his ears, flopping on his belly in the dust, he scrambled around on long legs, searching desperately for Roote.

His starman was *gone*.

Fear gripped Ford's chest.

Roote had been beamed up. And not a bogus beaming, like with that G-man earlier in the day. This time, it had really happened. Elizu Roote had gone back to his mothership, abandoning Ford to the mercy of the U.S. military. Men who consistently—if the movies he saw were accurate—showed no mercy.

Screaming turned to sobbing. Arthur Ford was weeping fat tears of terror into the bone-dry dust beneath his fearful face when he spotted a flicker of movement near the fence.

He blinked back his burning tears.

Feet kicking. Someone belly-crawling through the dust.

Hope swelled instantly within Ford.

It was the alien!

He was protected by the far edge of the out-cropping of rock. The men didn't appear to notice him. Not one bullet flew his way. The soldiers all seemed to be directing their fire at Ford.

As it was dawning on Ford that his actions might actually have saved Elizu Roote after all, his alien was reaching a weak, shaking hand for the fence.

He must not have seen the high-voltage signs posted along the electrified hurricane fence.

Ford started to scream a warning...too late! As he watched in helpless horror, Roote clamped down firmly on a cluster of chain links near the desert floor.

And then things got strange.

Over the waning gunfire, Arthur Ford distinctly heard the hum. *Felt* it. It filled the air all around him. It was the sound of a large factory whose many machines inexplicably powered down at the same time.

The hair on Ford's arms and neck tingled.

The soldiers stopped firing. They must have heard and felt it, too. Confused shouts issued from beyond the fence.

Even as the men were trying to figure out what was happening, Roote was rising swiftly from the scrub brush.

He held on firmly to the fence with one hand, jutting the fingers of his other through the chain link. The hum turned into a whining crescendo, and before another bullet sang from the other side of the fence, Roote fired.

The raw power surge was staggering.

It hit the nearest tank. The armor plating crackled as a million crisscrossing blue sparks raced along the vehicle's length. The blue glow was a brilliant contrast to the bloodred sky.

The electrical surge hopped from one tank to the next, to the next, enveloping the entire row in a matter of seconds. In between, it leapt to gun barrels, bouncing crazily down the line of men like some insane arcade game come to life.

Every metal surface grabbed hold of the charge, sizzling, blasting the electricity down into the ground.

Men were thrown back, arms fried. They screamed in agony as they fell. Still Roote fired.

Shells within tanks detonated, blasting out huge jagged chunks of hot shrapnel. In a matter of seconds, the entire defensive line was turned into a glowing, moaning killing field. More than three hundred men lay dead or critically wounded.

Victory mattered not to Elizu Roote. Energy channeled from the fence continued to pour through him out over the field long after any danger had passed. The electricity flowed from the hand that gripped the chain link over to the other even as his cybernetic microchips were siphoning precious power into his capacitors, restoring them to full operating levels.

Farther down the hill, behind Roote, Arthur Ford watched all of this with sick horror.

Roote was like a man possessed. He killed blindly. Horribly.

The thrill of meeting an alien vanished in a flash. In that moment, Ford's fear got the better of him.

He threw himself backward, tumbling end over end down to the access road at the base of the rocky incline. He landed, bloodied and bruised, on the hard-packed sand.

His jeep was forgotten. Flight was all that mattered.

Staggering, limping, Ford flung himself out into the desert. As he ran, the horrible crackle of electricity was carried to him by the warm breeze. And intermingled with the crackles was Elizu Roote's crazed laugh of triumph.

12

Ten minutes after Remo had scrounged a jeep from the Fort Joy motor pool, he and the Master of Sinanju were following the dusty path that skirted the artillery range.

Smith had caught Remo on his way out of the barracks area, telling him that Chesterfield had reported two Apache helicopters had been downed in the desert south of their position half an hour before. According to reports the CURE director had overheard, a major battle had also just taken place at the southern gate.

Remo's face was stern as they drove into the growing darkness. He wasn't right. He *knew* it.

In Sinanju, breathing was all. Remo had had this drilled into him forever, to the point where it was beyond second nature. But now there seemed to be something more.

Roote's attack had sent his system spiraling away from the perfection of mind and body that was the most ancient of all martial arts. It wasn't his breathing that was off; it was his heart. The muscle had taken a pounding and now seemed unable to correct itself. And a single imperfection in a Sinanju-trained body was like a ripple on a pond, it eventually reached all shores.

For anyone else on earth, a recovery like Remo's would be a miracle worth celebrating. But for Remo it was intensely frustrating. And in his line of work, anything short of perfection wouldn't cut it.

Since regaining consciousness in the Fort Joy infirmary, Remo had been thinking about the story of Master Cung. He was a Sinanju master who fell victim to a sickness of breathing. Rather than fight his illness, Cung surrendered to it. It took the death of his pupil and a Japanese invasion of the village of Sinanju for Cung to realize that the weakness was a thing to be overcome, not revel in. His lesson—proper breathing is all, but proper attitude is everything.

If the story was true, Cung had banished his physical problem in an instant. But for Remo, that didn't seem possible. And his inability to master so simple a thing in his own body frightened him.

As they drove along the slithering rutted road, Chiun glanced furtively several times at his pupil. Eventually, Remo could take it no more.

"I'm fine," he insisted, feeling the pressure of his teacher's gaze for the tenth time in as many minutes. Frustration mingled with annoyance.

"I was watching the sunset," Chiun replied nonchalantly.

"It doesn't set in my ear," Remo pointed out.

"No," Chiun admitted. "That would imply that light enters your skull at least part of the day. As far as I have ever been able to tell, that melon atop your shoulders is cast in perpetual gloom. There was a time I considered growing mushrooms in it."

"Har-de-har-har," Remo said. "Considering what we're up against, maybe you should ditch the chipper mood."

"Yes. The human lightning bug," Chiun sighed. Thoughts weighty, he stared out at the desert. "If only I had presence of mind to bring a canning jar from Castle Sinanju. We could have captured the dastard and placed him on the mantle in triumph."

"Listen to me, Little Father," Remo insisted harshly. "I'm serious. I want you to be careful."

The earnestness in his tone was what touched Chiun. Remo truly believed what he was saying. And in that belief was a genuine concern for the well-being of the Master of Sinanju. It was moving. It would have been more so, had it not been for Remo's obvious decline into madness.

Chiun turned to his pupil. "Would it make you feel better, Remo, if I said I believed you?" he asked, a sad smile on his parchment face.

"Only if you meant it," Remo said. "This guy is really dangerous, Chiun. I don't want you getting caught off guard like I did. Whether you believe me or not, just promise me you'll be careful.''

Chiun nodded thoughtfully. It wouldn't hurt to humor his mad pupil. ''I will take care,'' the Master of Sinanju said gently.

Remo didn't seem entirely satisfied. It was clear Chiun was just paying lip service to him. Having the Master of Sinanju to worry about on top of everything else would make his next meeting with Elizu Roote all the more difficult. But if push came to shove, Remo wouldn't allow the demented soldier to harm his teacher. Even if it meant protecting Chiun with his own life.

Each lost in private, disturbing thoughts, neither man spoke as they sped on into the encroaching night.

THE MEDICAL CORPSMEN screamed orders as they ran from one charred body to the next.

Enlistees hauled the dead into a special cordoned area near the fence, lest precious time be wasted rechecking those who were beyond help.

Soldiers still alive were carted with little care onto stretchers. There wasn't time to worry about their comfort. Just keeping them alive was top priority.

The worst were loaded onto waiting helicopters. The rest were packed on shelflike racks in the backs of waiting ambulances.

Army choppers crisscrossed the gray-to-black

sky, glaring searchlights illuminating wild patches of blowing scrub and frantic human activity.

Sirens blaring, Army trucks adorned with crosses of red tore back toward the main base.

The scene was one of utter chaos when Remo and Chiun arrived. They parked next to the row of twenty tanks.

The desert was already growing cool as they stepped down from their borrowed jeep. They avoided the hustling stretcher-bearers and approached the last tank in line.

Large sections of the tank turret had been blown away in the internal explosion. The main cannon had been ripped partially off and now lay against the nose of the crippled vehicle. Even so, most of what was below the deck structure remained intact. This was the area on which Remo focused his attention. He didn't need to search long.

"It was him," Remo announced instantly.

He pointed to a spot above the big tank treads to a blackened area a foot in diameter. The armor plating within this zone had partially melted to slag. It had dripped down the side of the tank, solidifying once more in slender droplets behind the tread.

"That's not consistent with an explosion," Remo said with certainty. "Something hit this thing from the outside."

Chiun frowned as he studied the odd marks in the metal. They matched nothing known to him.

Even so, the Master of Sinanju remained silent as Remo led him around the rear of the tank. They found a similar melted area on the opposite side.

"It came out here." Remo pointed.

They stepped over to the next armored vehicle.

"It must have hopped the space between and slammed right into here," he said excitedly, pointing at yet a third melted section of armor. The surrounding area was scorched, as well. "*Now* do you believe me?"

"It is odd," Chiun admitted.

"Damn right it's freaking odd," Remo said.

The two of them went around to the front of the tanks.

There were bodies everywhere. Hands were burned to shades of black and bloody purple. Blisters had erupted on the faces of some. Groans and sobs rose up in pathetic chorus from the remorseless desert sand.

Remo's features could have been carved from granite as he surveyed the scene of carnage. He looked down at one soldier propped up against a tank. The man's flesh was smeared black. One arm was thrown across his face as he rolled in slow agony in the dust.

With an effort, Remo tore his eyes away from the grisly sight.

They used the side of the first tank to judge the angle from which the initial blast of electricity had come. When they reached the hurricane fence,

Chiun was first to see the strange marks in the links.

"There," the Master of Sinanju said, pointing.

Remo looked to where the fence was buckled outward very slightly in the direction of the desert. There were five black marks in the metal, consistent with the pads Remo had seen on Roote's fingertips. They were about five feet off the ground. Another set of similar marks was visible much closer to the ground.

"It's electrified," Remo said.

They had both sensed the thrill of power from the fence. To Remo, the sensation was an unpleasant reminder of his encounter with Roote. His nearness to the fence seemed to make his heart fibrillate. It was as if his body expected bolts of electricity to come leaping for him once more. He banished the uncomfortable feeling.

"He must be able to channel it somehow," he said.

The frown Chiun had been wearing throughout their investigation grew deeper. The old Korean looked back toward the field of carnage.

Flashing red ambulance lights and streaks of helicopter searchlights illuminated the macabre tableau. Someone had finally come to attend to the soldier they had seen on their way to the fence. A stretcher was brought forward.

"I will concede that it is possible," Chiun said finally. He almost sounded as if he meant it.

Remo didn't allow his relief to be too great. After all, they still had much work ahead of them.

"There are footprints outside the fence," Remo said. With a nod he indicated the scuffmarks in the sand where Roote had obviously stood. "We'd better see where they lead before anyone else gets killed."

Turning, they hurried back to retrieve their jeep. Driving past the battlefield, they headed through the gate and out onto the desert path.

They found the abandoned jeep a moment later.

"Dollars to doughnuts it's his," Remo said.

He looked up the rocky incline beside the parked jeep. Although darkness had fallen, Remo's eyes were able to pull in enough ambient light to see almost as well as if it were full daylight. He spotted the crushed sage and tumbled stones instantly.

Chiun saw it, too. "Someone has fallen down this hill recently," the Master of Sinanju said from his seat next to Remo.

Remo glanced across the path.

"There," he said, pointing. "He ran into the desert."

Without waiting for Chiun to echo his obvious conclusion, he put the jeep in gear. The two of them drove off into the deepening desert night, little realizing that the man they were trailing was not the man they were truly after.

UP THE INCLINE, within the perimeter fence of Fort Joy, an Army medic was checking on the soldier

Remo and Chiun had noticed before heading toward the fence. Two corpsmen stood anxiously nearby, leaning against a stretcher.

Although the wounded man's face was smeared with grime, he didn't appear to be injured like the rest. His arms weren't burned in the least. His eyes were screwed into closed knots of pain. When the medic tried to see his hands, the man squeezed them more tightly shut and groaned loudly.

The medic wheeled on the waiting corpsmen. "Load him up with the others," he ordered.

"Chopper?"

The medic shook his head. "Superficial wounds at best. Ambulance." He slapped the nearest corpsman on the shoulder for support, dashing off to the next injured soldier.

The groaning soldier was loaded onto the stretcher and carried into the back of a waiting ambulance. No one noticed that his hands were now partially open. Nor did anyone see the contours of the faintly visible metal pads on his fingertips.

Siren whining, the ambulance headed onto the base.

13

This time, there was no attempt to avoid him. Harold Smith was ushered by an efficient young aide directly into General Delbert Xavier Chesterfield's office.

Old Ironbutt was seated behind his big desk.

Although the glass shards and wood splinters had been swept away, the flimsy clapboard wall had yet to be repaired. A thick sheet of unrolled plastic had been stapled to the Chesterfield-shaped hole in the wall.

The plastic rattled wildly in the downdraft thrown off by perpetually landing helicopters. Sand pelted the flimsy material, giving the odd impression of a violent hail storm that had swept up unexpectedly in the middle of the previously tranquil desert evening.

Through the plastic, Smith noted the weirdly gauzy lights from the arriving helicopters and ambulances as he took his seat before General Chesterfield's desk.

The general's big face was a shade of red not seen in nature. It looked as though his shirt collar was at least three sizes too small. Porcine eyes regarded the CURE director with disdain as Smith settled primly into his chair, resting his briefcase on the floor at his feet.

Chesterfield leaned back in his own seat. He cradled his fingers to his ample belly. "What is it now?" His booming voice competed with the commotion in the courtyard.

"It is time you told the truth," Smith said. "Obviously there is something very wrong here."

"I'll say," the general replied. "This is shocking. You CIA boys should be ashamed. I've written a report on the matter." He dropped a big mitt to a closed manila file on his desk. "You are mentioned prominently, *Mr. Jones,*" he added with smarmy confidence, little realizing that the name Smith had given at the gate earlier that day was merely a cover.

"I am with the FBI," Smith said blandly.

Chesterfield jumped forward, dropping his hands loudly atop his desk. "Bullshit. I had you pegged for a spook the minute you drove through my gate. And it figures. Your little experiment escaped and you came scurrying up out of your spook hole to see what happened to it."

"Roote," Smith said, his face pinched.

The general leaned back once more. "All in the report," he said, his smile returning.

"I would be interested to read it," Smith said.

"Oh, I bet you would," the general said. A hand

slapped down on the report again. Sliding it ever so slowly toward his ample paunch, the military man dumped the file into an open drawer. He slammed the desk drawer closed.

"I presume there is something in there about your Shock Troops project?" Smith asked.

The general's confident expression faded. "You don't know anything," he bluffed.

"I know that there are wounded men being brought back here after some bizarre attack at your southern perimeter. Soldiers I have seen are suffering from severe electrical burns. I know that you are reporting virtually nothing of the events of the past few days to your superiors, short of overt hints that the CIA is responsible for some great project gone awry." Smith's grew angrier. "I also know that one Elizu Roote has been altered in some way that allows him to emit controlled bursts of electrical energy. And I know that you are responsible for all of this, General."

Chesterfield's eyes grew wide at the accusations. "How dare you!" the general screamed. He rose, stabbing a fat finger at Smith. "This is all *your* fault! You come in here, kill dozens of my men and then try to blame it on me! I will not take it, sir! I will live to see your spook hide nailed to the wall for everything that's happened here!"

The fit was calculated. Chesterfield had planned to explode this way. It was why he'd allowed Smith a meeting in the first place. The general wanted everyone within earshot to hear him blame this CIA spy. It would be better for Chesterfield at the inevitable inquest afterward. But he was somewhat discomfited by the fact that Smith seemed to actually know some of what was going on at Fort Joy.

Smith was not fazed in the least. He sat calmly in his chair, unmoved by the general's tirade. By the end of his diatribe, Chesterfield's face looked ready to explode. Puffing, the military man collapsed back into his seat.

Smith didn't miss a beat.

"It might interest you to know that I have some access to CIA files," Smith said, not even caring about the security risk that could go along with such an admission.

"No surprise there," Chesterfield panted.

"It might further interest you to learn that there is absolutely, unequivocally no—repeat, no—trail either paper or electronic leading from Langley to Fort Joy. I have accounted for every significant aspect of the Central Intelligence Agency budget and there are no outlays for a project of the nature likely being carried out here."

Chesterfield thought quickly.

"You covered your trail," the general offered. "You fellas do that all the time. Everybody knows that. The public doesn't trust you." Chesterfield smiled. "Face facts, spy boy, as my dear departed pappy used to say, that dog of yours just won't hunt."

Smith shook his head. "You do not understand. There is not the additional funding for Shock Troops or any other such project at the CIA. It does not exist. Period. However, I have found in my research that a clerical error in Washington significantly increased your base maintenance stipend last year. It was part of the last-minute emergency defense expenditures prior to the last mid-term elections. You failed to report the increase to your superiors. Furthermore, the money—as far as I have been able to discern—has been spent."

As Smith spoke, the crimson face of Chesterfield's tirade had returned. His mouth opened and closed as he attempted to speak. For the first time in his adult life, no boom came out. Little more than a pathetic squeak rose from the great throat of General Delbert Xavier Chesterfield.

"Lies," he managed to say eventually. When the word came, it sounded as if he'd been sucking on a helium-filled balloon.

"I am sorry, General," Smith said efficiently. "I have followed the money trail directly to you. Roote is part of your Shock Troops project. Presumably the first and only."

Chesterfield shook his head slowly. His dark eyes were glazed. "I deny everything," he said.

"It does not matter," Smith said. "All that matters is the truth, which will be made clear."

The general was still in a fog. "If you know about Shock Troops, you somehow got into closed base files." A light dawned. "Yeah," he said, eyes coming back into focus. "If you got into my locked files, you could have done anything. Even planted a phony money trail."

Smith had had enough. "This is ridiculous," the CURE director snapped. "Assume I created a false trail. Assume I did everything. Tell me what we are up against."

Chesterfield nearly knocked his chair over in the excited struggle to get to his feet. "You take the blame?" he asked cagily.

"I do not care," Smith said, perturbed.

"For all of it? Shock Troops? Roote? Everything?"

"Whatever," Smith replied. "What I need now is all information available on Elizu Roote."

The general smiled broadly. He picked his riding crop up from his desktop, slapping it up under his armpit.

"Sir, I think we can come to what my ex-wife's lawyer used to call a mutually satisfyin' accommodation," General Chesterfield boomed.

MAJOR GRANT HAD EXHAUSTED nearly all of the painkillers in the Fort Joy infirmary. Still, more patients arrived.

He had lost ten already. Three had died on their

way from the battle scene. The others were too far gone to help.

Of the soldiers still alive, Major Grant had already sent many on to burn units in better-equipped hospitals off base. Army doctors waited in the courtyard, picking through the wounded as they arrived, deciding at a glance who would be kept and who would be immediately transferred.

Triage for those brought into the infirmary building was being conducted by Grant and another harried doctor. From what Major Grant had seen so far, they were *all* in pretty rough shape.

Grant stepped over a minefield of legs as he searched for patients he had not yet examined. As had been the norm for the past half hour, he found one instantly.

Down the corridor from where the major was working, two corpsmen were carrying an injured soldier into the infirmary. There was no longer any room in the main hallway, so they leaned him alone in the alcove of the supply hallway.

Grant was angered by the carelessness of the corpsmen. If he hadn't seen the two men running from the spot with a stretcher, he never would have known the soldier was there.

Ducking down the corridor, Grant found the private lying in the shadows. The soldier's eyes were open. He appeared more alert than the rest. In fact, at Major Grant's appearance, he actually pushed himself upright.

"What's your problem, soldier?" Grant demanded, crouching down before the man.

"I—" The soldier giggled. "I think I love you."

Laughing out loud, Elizu Roote slapped his palms against either side of Grant's head.

The surge was short and powerful. The major's brain was literally fried by the wave of electricity that fired across every synaptic pathway at once. Hair smoking, the Army doctor toppled over onto Roote's legs.

"Mama always wanted me to marry a doctor." Roote snickered. He pushed the twitching corpse away.

Roote knelt beside the body. He used the tail of the major's white coat to wipe off the worst of the oil and grime that he had smeared on his face before joining the men he had attacked at the fence.

Once he was through, Roote stood calmly. Strolling at a leisurely pace, he wandered across the main infirmary hallway and out the swinging doors.

REMO'S VISION WAS NOT as keen as it had been before his encounter with Roote. He realized it once they had traveled a few hundred yards away from the activity at the Fort Joy gate.

Although the area immediately around the jeep was clearly visible, he was having a difficult time with objects in the distance. It was part of the same problem that afflicted his entire system.

While they drove through the desert, Remo was forced to rely on the Master of Sinanju for directions.

Chiun was having some difficulty, as well, but not for the same reason as Remo. In spite of his exceptional night vision, the aged Korean was having difficulty following the fresh trail across the desert because it was so uneven.

The path was erratic. Even so, it would have been easy for Chiun to see if it had been exclusively through sand. Apparently their quarry had raced across stone surfaces and through fields of thick sage. It was obvious to Remo that the Army private they sought had been in a blind panic as he fled the site of the massacre.

Concentrating so as not to have to ask his mentor for every twist and turn in the route, Remo steered the jeep in a zigzagging pattern, following the trail to a point, losing it, doubling back, picking it up once more, following to the next twist. It was an arduous process that led them miles away from the Army camp.

Far behind, the tiny lights of Fort Joy helicopters swooped back and forth across the night sky.

Chiun sat at the edge of his seat, peering intently at the ground as they drove along. The amber headlights seemed to bounce and settle in wild spurts as the jeep hopped rocks and minor bluffs.

"There," the Master of Sinanju announced. A bony finger was aimed at a tangle of brush beyond a long, flat rock.

Remo turned the jeep without question. As they drove off in this new direction, he quickly spied the single footprint in the sand beneath the bush that had signaled Chiun they should turn. He blinked hard, annoyed that he hadn't seen the print himself.

"He couldn't have gone much farther," Remo commented. Sage scratched like the talons of groping demons along the side of the jeep. "There wasn't that much time."

"He is close," Chiun admitted, nodding.

A wave of fresh concern took hold of Remo as they broke through the far side of the field.

"There," Chiun said once more.

Remo followed his outstretched hand. He instantly spied the footprints heading away from the cluster of desert brush. They led up a slight incline.

Remo followed like a dog on a scent.

A rough path had been left by all-terrain vehicles crossing the side of the long hillock. Remo followed the trail to the crest of the hill.

The winding path of a dry riverbed opened up below the jeep. Above the barren river, Remo no longer needed Chiun to guide his vision. He saw the body immediately.

Lying facedown at the very center of the deep furrow was a lone, battered man.

Stopping at the bank of the long-dead river, Remo cut the jeep's engine. Leaving the headlights on to illuminate the scene below, he climbed down to the dust.

Chiun got out the other side.

"You think he's dead?" Remo whispered.

"Open your ears," Chiun replied tightly.

It was an effort, but Remo forced himself to listen more intently. Straining at the effort, he eventually picked up the sound of the man's heart.

The heartbeat was frantic. Although it was pounding madly, at the moment it sounded more confident to Remo than his own. The thought was not comforting.

"You think he's playing possum?" Remo asked, his voice still pitched low.

"I am not going to stand out in the desert with you all night playing the world-famous Remo Williams 'You Think?' game," Chiun said, peeved.

And tugging up the skirts of his kimono, the Master of Sinanju promptly began hiking down the dry embankment. Remo hustled to catch up with him.

"Be careful, Little Father," Remo whispered.

Chiun nodded tersely.

Side by side, the two of them stepped cautiously over to the prone form.

As they approached the body, Remo noted that he didn't feel the same telltale thrill of electricity in the air that he'd noticed during his first encoun-

ter with Roote. It was possible Roote had exhausted all of his supply on the attack back at Fort
Joy.

There was not a hint of movement from the body
as they slid up to it, each on one side.

Remo was relieved to see the Master of Sinanju
was being more cautious than he'd expected. Some
of what the old Korean had seen and heard this
night had made an impact.

One of the prone man's hands was jutting at an
awkward angle from beneath his body. Chiun bent
at the waist to examine it. After only a glance, the
Master of Sinanju rose to his full height, a disgusted look on his face.

One sandal stabbed forward, catching the man
under the chest. Before Remo could object, Chiun
flipped the body over.

Lying on his back at the bottom of the ancient
river, Arthur Ford blinked madly. He looked up at
Remo and Chiun, his eyes blobs of white in his
dirt-smeared face.

"Ben?" he asked.

"It's not him," Remo announced to Chiun. For
the first time he realized that the man had been too
tall to be Elizu Roote. He seemed deeply disappointed.

The Master of Sinanju nodded. "His hands were
not as you described."

"Then Roote must still be near the base," Remo
said, his face growing concerned.

Chiun nodded. "We must hurry." He turned to go.

"Ben Kenobi, is that you?" Ford persisted. He was staring hopefully at Chiun.

"What do we do with this guy?" Remo asked, ignoring the question from the dirt-covered man on the ground.

Pausing at the edge of the river, Chiun looked disdainfully down at Arthur. "The buzzards will enjoy whatever the wolves do not finish." Hiking his skirts up around his ankles, the Master of Sinanju marched up the incline.

"Help me, Obi-wan Kenobi," Ford pleaded. "You're my only hope." He reached out a hand to Chiun's departing back.

"I guess we should take him back," Remo called.

Although it was offered somewhat as a question, Chiun had already crested the hill. The old man disappeared behind the glare of the jeep's headlights.

Remo glanced reluctantly at Ford.

"Assuming he *wants* to go back," he said to himself.

Ford sat up, suddenly animated. He blinked exhaustion and delirium from his bloodshot eyes. "To the *future?*" he asked excitedly.

"It's going to be a long ride home," Remo sighed.

Bending down, he hefted Arthur Ford up onto his shoulders.

As he climbed back up to their jeep, the ufologist was humming loudly. It was the theme to *Star Wars*.

14

PROJECT SHOCK TROOPS
FORT JOY, NEW MEXICO
CLASSIFIED
TOP SECRET

Smith read the main screen of the computer in the drafty warehouse laboratory of the Fort Joy special-projects unit. A thick file containing much of the same information stored in the system lay open on the desk beside him.

Behind him, the huge tank in which Elizu Roote had been imprisoned lay empty. The water had been drained the day before. The rubberized isolation cell that had contained the Army serial killer was gone, destroyed on orders from General Chesterfield himself.

The bodies of the men he had electrocuted during his escape were also gone. A faint smell of chlorine hung in the air-conditioned coolness.

Chesterfield hovered over Smith as the CURE director navigated further into the system. The general was chewing nervously on one thumbnail, his arms crossed over his big chest, one forearm resting on his belly.

"Some of those files might have Fort Joy security codes on them," Chesterfield said. "Hell, they might even have my name and authorization on them. Depends on how thorough you were when you tapped into our system."

Smith did not look his way. He continued to work at the computer as he spoke.

"I will accept your fallacious premise if you agree to stop trying to sell me on the concept," he said thinly.

Chesterfield raised his hands in apology. He fell mute, clasping both hands behind his back as Smith accessed the necessary information.

The laboratory computer network was a closed system, which was why Smith hadn't been able to access any of the Shock Troops information earlier. None of the computers in the big laboratory building were hooked into any outgoing telephone lines. Smith soon saw why.

It was horrific. Page after electronic page detailed the procedure used to transform Elizu Roote into a creature of frightful power.

Given the green light by General Chesterfield, the scientists hired with funds mistakenly sent to Fort Joy had set out to marry biomechanical systems with Roote's natural biological system. In effect, they had created a bionic human being.

The Shock Troops team owed a great deal to

Nicholas Rashevsky, Smith noted as he scanned a sick eye across the material. Rashevsky's mathematical analysis of the various functions of the central nervous system had been a virtual primer for the insertion of flexible metal cords along the length of Roote's spinal cord. In their notes, the only problem the science team foresaw was possible paralysis of the test subject. The level of dispassion expressed in the notes was horrifying.

The brain and eye surgeries were a veritable breeze for Roote after the stress of bionic alteration coupled with the months of recuperation time.

The nonconductivity of fiber-optic cable made this material crucial to the next stage of Roote's alteration. It would not do to have their subject electrocute himself along the internal pathways of his own targeting system. Fortunately for the Fort Joy scientists, this particular type of cable was commonly used for tactical military applications. When they requested it, the cable was readily supplied by the base commander.

Much of the research into the encoding process of the visual system had already been done by other research groups around the world. Optical recognition systems had advanced to the point where it was a fairly simple procedure to install the necessary fiber-optic cable along the Army private's ocular nerve.

The scientists wove one end of the cable into the mechanical systems of Roote's lower body.

The other was threaded through the optic line directly into the brain.

Specially designed microchips connected to the cerebellum and were linked to parts of the subcortical basal ganglia, thus creating an artificial system that would be able to decipher and coordinate the new information taken in by Roote's ocular targeting implants. In effect, the man-made system explained to Roote's brain what was taking place at any given moment along his complex artificial assemblage.

From the spinal cord, surgically implanted insulated wires were installed along Roote's entire skeletal structure. Primary atomic capacitors capable of storing vast quantities of electrical energy were buried in his shoulders and hips. A pair of secondary capacitors was wired into the system at his thighs and functioned as emergency backups.

As Smith read the overview of what had been done to the pathetic soldier, one word continued to creep into his horror-struck mind: why? Why, why, why?

He hadn't realized that he had spoken the word aloud until he was interrupted in his work.

"What did you say?"

The voice of Chesterfield bellowed behind him, jarring Smith from his thoughts.

The CURE director turned in his seat. He shook his head in dumb amazement. "Why would you do something so appalling?" he said softly.

There was no accusation in his voice. Just a genuine, human curiosity. The kind that surfaced in seasoned homicide detectives when studying a particularly gruesome crime scene.

Chesterfield appeared somewhat apprehensive. He shrugged his massive shoulders. "Of course, I'm not admittin' to anything. This is all purely off the record."

Smith nodded his acceptance. By not agreeing aloud, the CURE director would technically not be reneging on a promise when the time came to remove General Chesterfield. It was not in Harold Smith's nature to lie.

"You see these, Jones?" Chesterfield asked, dropping a finger to the bar on his left shoulder. He tapped the two gold stars. "Got the second of these ten years ago. Haven't seen one lousy promotion since."

Smith was aghast. "You did this for advancement?" he asked.

"Not just any advancement, sir," Chesterfield said, insulted, as he stood at attention. "*Army* advancement. I've been languishing at the bottom of the upper ranks for too damn long. Sometimes in this man's Army it becomes necessary to make your own opportunities. What you're lookin' at right there is a made opportunity. Or was."

Smith looked back at the computer screen, which displayed a schematic of Elizu Roote's mechanical system. The skeletal frame was shown in red, and the artificial implants were highlighted in white.

Contacts at the back of the soldier's neck and at his elbows shunted the power down to the conductive pads buried in his fingertips. The pads were fashioned from solid gold, the best conductor of electricity.

The CURE director turned back to Chesterfield.

"You are mad," Smith said simply.

The general shook his head firmly. "Just extremely pissed off. The Shock Troops project was supposed to get me my seat on the Joint Chiefs of Staff. At this point, we'll be lucky to sell Roote to Ma Bell for scrap."

Smith was amazed at the general's unconcerned attitude. There was nothing he could say that would be appropriate to such a confession of monumental egotism. He turned back to the desk, dropping a hand atop the paper printouts.

"Shock Troops Project, Subject Roote: Classified."

Bracing himself for the contents of this particular file, Smith opened the manila folder.

Of course Smith already knew that shock troops were men chosen for offensive work because of their extremely high morale, as well as for their training and discipline. But as he read the psychological appraisals contained in the file, he found that Private Elizu Roote had nothing in common with the definition.

As a soldier he was a virtual washout. He was sullen and withdrawn. Prone to fights, he had been a discipline problem several times in his Army career.

Smith read through six pages of single-spaced text before finding evidence of Roote's homicidal tendencies. At the point when the CURE director thought that nothing else could shock him about this operation, he found himself more astonished than ever.

"He murdered two people," Smith said flatly.

"Two confirmed, yes," Chesterfield readily agreed. "A local first, then a nurse. Of course, the nurse was after the procedure so she don't rightly count. That's when we drugged him and stuck him in the box."

"There were more," Smith said. The file speculated that Roote was the likeliest suspect in several unsolved murders.

"Probably. He fits the serial-killer profile. Young, white, in his twenties. Soldier about to be dishonorably discharged. The works."

"And you proceeded to alter him in spite of your knowledge of his mental condition?"

"Are you kiddin' me, son?" Chesterfield mocked. "That's what made him perfect. He was shit out of luck on this murder thing. We had him dead to rights. It was either the gas chamber or volunteer."

"How could he refuse."

The general missed the irony completely. "Absolutely," he enthused. "And it worked, too. The plan always was that he'd be the prototype. We'd be able to build more once we were sure all the bugs were worked out. An army of invincible soldiers marching for the good ole U.S. of A." Even as he finished boasting of his great scheme, Chesterfield's shoulders began to droop. "Then he goes off and escapes and screws up the whole works. I might never get my stars now."

"Forgive me if I take no pity on your dashed career hopes," Harold W. Smith said sarcastically.

Chesterfield didn't appreciate his tone. His brow furrowed as he watched Smith take his laptop computer from his battered leather briefcase.

"Listen, buddy, are you gonna be all right here?" the general asked, annoyed. "I've got some stuff I've got to take care of. Don't forget, we've still got a maniac on the loose who most likely wants to fry my ass."

"I will need some time here," Smith said.

"Take it," the general said, backing toward the door. "Take all the time you need."

He watched for a moment as Smith set up his computer on the table next to the lab monitor. With nimble fingers, the CURE director hooked into the back of the lab computer, accessing the hard drive. He began downloading files.

As the Shock Troops data was being transmitted to CURE's Folcroft mainframes via the portable laptop, Smith hunched back down before the monitor. He began to study Elizu Roote's schematics, hoping to find a weakness. Anything that might give them an advantage.

AT THE DOOR, the general could not help but smile.

The whole Shock Troops idea had been an unquestionable disaster. Until now. Chesterfield now had a scapegoat in Mr. Harold Jones. Jones could shoulder the blame even as the general took whatever credit might arise. And there could very well be some.

Chesterfield had been on the phone again with one of his superiors in Washington. There was genuine interest in what had been going on at Fort Joy. In spite of his complaints of being stuck at two stars, the future might not be as bleak as it had earlier appeared.

As the general left the lab for the last time, self-preservation was the order of business for the career soldier. It was cover-your-ass time in a major way. Let Jones and his two operatives clean up this mess. When the shit finally hit the fan at Fort Joy, General Delbert Xavier Chesterfield had no intention of being anywhere near the messy splat.

15

"It's my fault," Arthur Ford wailed.

The jeep was prowling swiftly across the desert toward Fort Joy.

The stars were diamonds, scattered across the heavens. Out here they were bright enough to illuminate the vast tracts of empty land in a thin wash of ethereal white.

"Are you going to ask him?" Remo said to Chiun.

"No," the Master of Sinanju droned. "And if you know what is good for you, neither will you."

Neither one of them had to ask. Ford volunteered the answer on his own.

"I failed to understand him. I'm lucky enough to meet an actual alien and *I* have to run away. Now he's at the mercy of the military." As if cradling a baby, Ford clutched to his chest the water bottle he'd found in the back of the jeep. "Oh, how terrible it must be for him. To have to face the hostile military of an alien world on his own."

"I think the military has to worry more about

him than he does about it," Remo commented aridly.

"No, no," Ford moaned. "You don't understand. No one understands." He stared out into the lonely desert night.

"You think you've been tooling around the desert all day with Robby the Robot and you're telling me *I* don't understand?" Remo said.

"Remo, why are you still talking to it?" Chiun complained, his parchment face a scowl. "You are only encouraging it."

"Why didn't I sign a mutual nonaggression peace treaty with him?" Ford lamented to the desert night.

"See?" Chiun demanded, swatting Remo on the arm.

"I don't think he needs much encouragement, Little Father." Remo frowned, rubbing his stinging bicep. He was about to say something more when Chiun touched him on the forearm.

When he glanced over at the Master of Sinanju, the old Korean was nodding surreptitiously to the back seat.

All was silent. For the first time since Arthur Ford had come back to what passed for his senses, the UFO enthusiast had stopped talking.

Chiun placed a long finger to papery lips. "Shh," he said in a cautious whisper only Remo could hear. "With any luck he has swallowed his tongue and is choking to death."

The silence lasted all of three seconds.

"Maybe if we'd agreed on terms, the military would have been persuaded to go along," Ford announced abruptly. "After all, the United Federation of Planets has a military dimension, but it has benign intentions. Maybe this could have been the start of a new world order."

Twisting in the passenger's seat, the Master of Sinanju stared, irritated, at Ford. He frowned as he examined the features of their passenger. Bouncing morosely in his seat, Ford didn't seem to notice the scrutiny.

"Is he insane?" Chiun asked Remo.

"He wasn't in the desert long enough to be dehydrated," Remo offered, steering up an incline in the dusty path. The hurricane fence surrounding Fort Joy was a dark strip in the distance. "And it wasn't daytime, so he couldn't have suffered sunstroke. My guess is he's the real deal."

"Hey, aren't you the guy who was with that G-man at the Roswell airport?" Ford blinked, noticing Chiun for the first time.

"G-man?" Remo questioned.

"Smith," Chiun replied, facing forward once more.

"Oh."

Ford had already forgotten his own question. He sank back into the pool of despair he had created in the rear of the jeep.

"How is history going to remember me?" Ford

complained. "I missed an opportunity for a cultural exchange with an extraterrestrial. Think of what he could have taught us."

"How to kill for fun and profit?" Remo suggested blandly.

"That was only a defensive mechanism," Ford insisted quickly. "The Army shot first."

"Only because they know what he can do," Remo said.

"And are *afraid* of him. Typical. A visitor comes all the way from another planet and we greet him with guns."

"He's no more an alien than I am," Remo said, irritated.

Ford's eyes suddenly narrowed. He stared intently at the back of Remo's head, as if searching for antennae. "Are you?"

"Of course not," Remo snarled.

Ford accepted the denial even as he scooted to the far corner of the back seat. Just in case.

"Think of the science we missed out on because of me," Ford complained from his new perch. "Maybe if I'd stuck by him when he needed me, he might have given me the secret of an inverse proton propulsion system or some other method of interstellar travel. Otherwise it could take years for humans to travel from Earth just to the nearest star."

In the front seat, Remo and Chiun glanced quickly at one another.

"I'll pay for the ticket," Remo volunteered hastily.

"One way," Chiun added swiftly.

SMITH BECAME AWARE of the sound as he was completing his work on the Shock Troops files.

The pulsing explosion was like that of a transformer blowing up. The noise swelled in a loud thump, then receded. Thumped, then receded. It was as if an awkward giant were taking huge steps across the grounds outside the laboratory.

Smith assumed the sound was just more of the crazed activity that had followed Roote's assault against the perimeter fence.

There were fewer helicopters rumbling over the roof now. The dead and wounded had been returned to the main camp area. The sound he was hearing was probably just the Army involving itself in some exercises preparatory to another attack.

Disregarding the noise, he detached his laptop from the back of the lab terminal.

Every scrap of information contained in the computer had been transferred back to Folcroft. As soon as the transfer was complete, Smith destroyed the hard drive. He proceeded to do the same to all the other computers within the lab. He would deal with those in the outer offices later.

Using a special wand from his briefcase, Smith

magnetized every floppy disk he could find, destroying the contents of those, as well.

As he worked, Smith could not help but think of what General Chesterfield had done here.

The casualty list that had caught Smith's eye while at CURE headquarters was woefully inadequate. He had found a far more detailed inventory of Elizu Roote's victims on the base computer system. It was a grisly roster with a few notable exceptions.

During and after his escape from isolation, Roote had killed virtually all of the scientists involved in the procedure that had made him what he was. Their deaths, coupled with the destruction of all records, guaranteed there would be no resumption of these horrible experiments.

All that was left was the general himself.

Returning to the workstation where he had completed the bulk of his work, the CURE director gathered up a few last items. He replaced his laptop in his briefcase, sliding in beside it the thick dossier left him by General Chesterfield. With both thumbs, he was careful to make certain that the two briefcase latches were secured tightly.

Smith stood, scanning the area to see if there was anything he had forgotten.

Thump!

The noise was closer than before. It filtered through to Smith's consciousness, though he paid it little real attention.

Yes. His work was finished in the lab. All he had left was whatever information remained in the outer offices.

Thump! Very close. Followed by a muffled shout.

To Smith, it still sounded like a transformer exploding. He thought of this as he began strolling to the lab door.

Thump! A scream.

It hit Smith all at once. His face registered the shock of sudden realization.

A *transformer*.

Thump! More cries of panic.

Knuckles white on his briefcase handle, Smith ran from the coolness of the lab out into the hallway. He found a window in one of the tidy offices. As he peered outside, there came a brilliant flash, as from lightning during a fierce thunderstorm.

But, Harold Smith knew, this storm was anything but natural.

The flash was accompanied by the same massive thump he had heard before, this time no longer muffled by the laboratory walls. The window panes rattled at the sound waves from the electrical blast.

Smith blinked the dancing spots from his eyes as he sought out the source.

He found it with chilling ease.

The dark shape of a man strolled out from behind the white-painted clapboard base chapel. The instant he did so, an uneven stream of energy pulsed seemingly from out of the thin air before him.

On the far side of the courtyard, a jutting rifle barrel caught the charge. The soldier holding the weapon shrieked in pain and was flung backward by the powerful jolt of electricity.

There were shouts from outside. More troops raced forward, darting for cover behind buildings and parked vehicles. Methodically, without any sign of hurry, Elizu Roote took out each of the men in turn.

Smith watched the scene with growing horror.

It seemed as if every soldier who drew a bead on Roote with a weapon became an automatic target for a bolt of electricity. Smith knew that this was a feature of the defensive hardware wired into Roote's central nervous system.

The soldiers were having no effect whatsoever on General Chesterfield's Shock Troops prototype. It didn't take long for them to realize they were fighting a lost cause.

The cry for retreat was called. The wounded were gathered up and carted away amid sporadic bursts of feeble weapons fire.

The Fort Joy courtyard had been relinquished to Elizu Roote. With a contemptuous arrogance, the private sauntered out from behind the chapel. Thumbs tucked into his waistband, he wandered off in the direction of Chesterfield's headquarters.

Smith watched as the rogue private went.

There was no sign of Remo or Chiun in the courtyard. Either they had tried to stop him and failed, or Roote had slipped past them.

Smith could not chance waiting. If his two operatives were dead and he failed to act now, Roote might escape. He couldn't allow that to happen.

Tucking his briefcase into the well under a desk, Harold Smith slipped from the office. As he ducked into the shadows of the laboratory hallway, he wondered how he could hope to succeed when both Masters of Sinanju, as well as the United States Army, had failed.

THE TANKS WERE LIKE creatures from some bygone age— dinosaurs left to erode to bone and dust in the desert heat.

There were no men in sight as Remo, Chiun and ufologist Arthur Ford tore back through the desert gates of Fort Joy.

Remo slammed on the brakes, sliding to a stop inside the rear gate. Slipping from behind the wheel, he hit the sand at a run, racing over to the spot where Elizu Roote had gripped the electrified fence.

He found the footprints that had misled them earlier. A single print half-hidden beneath a cluster of sage indicated Roote's true direction.

The new path led onto the rocky ledge that spread for several yards on the other side of the fence. At the spot where the rock stopped, the tracks began anew. Remo traced them all the way over to the gate and directly to the line of silent, crippled tanks.

Remo ran back to the jeep, hopping in behind the wheel.

"He got through," he announced, grimly.

"He's here?" Ford asked excitedly. Leaning forward, he grabbed on to the tops of both front seats. "Are we going to liberate him from the evil clutches of the military?"

"Only long enough to liberate his psycho head from his shoulders," Remo said somberly, throwing the jeep in gear.

They took off with such speed, Ford was thrown back into the rear seat. The jeep steered a certain course for the heart of the base.

ELIZU ROOTE HAD a great tradition of killing without compassion. He'd started young.

His mama—for Elizu Roote there was no daddy—hadn't much liked it when he took out his youthful frustrations on the various neighborhood pets. The neighbors liked it even less. But it was only after he'd taken a pair of vise grips to the toy poodle belonging to the preacher's daughter that the authorities first took notice.

A deputy with a thing for the hysterical young girl and a shovel in his hand uncovered the animal graveyard in the back of the Rootes' tenement in Charleston, West Virginia.

Mama Roote had been all too eager to let the state take charge of her troubled son. When she hadn't been dominating him, she'd treated him as an inconvenience. For her, the mound of rotting animal corpses spelled freedom.

At thirteen Elizu started the cycle of counselling and foster homes that would continue until his eighteenth birthday. Of course, the killing never stopped. But he was more careful than he'd been as a kid.

He would adopt dogs from animal shelters in nearby communities and take them for a final trip deep into the woods. Their pitiful yelping cries helped to slake his thirst for blood during those long, awkward teenage years.

To celebrate his high-school graduation, Elizu joined the Army and killed his first prostitute all in the same day. After that, the next few years were a blur.

There were more women, of course. He'd never stopped the killing. He had no other hobbies, no other interests to fill the void of his life.

Roote knew he fit the famous FBI profile of a serial killer. Other men might not like to be shoehorned into a narrow category like that. But Elizu Roote didn't have any friends, either from the Army or from his youth. He shied away from group activity, he was not exactly a joiner. For him, to be a serial killer was to be part of something. A member of a select group of like-minded individuals.

In a life that was gutted of everything meaningful, Elizu Roote needed to define his existence. He was a serial killer. For if he wasn't that, he was nothing.

At least that was what he always thought. But now, thanks to the United States Army, he was much more.

As ELIZU ROOTE STROLLED with impunity through yet another empty Fort Joy street, a soldier appeared from the shadows beside an officer's house.

Before Roote even realized there was a threat, he'd targeted the soldier and his hand flew up.

The thump of a solitary burst of electricity exploded across the night air.

His gun barrel snatched the surge of energy like a lightning rod and the soldier dropped.

Roote walked past the twitching body. He recognized the dead man. But although the face he looked upon was familiar, no emotion accompanied the recognition.

Just a body. Another corpse to throw on the growing pile. Elizu Roote was a god stepping on ants.

He had had the same reaction upon seeing the faces of the other men he had killed this night.

Not one of his fellow Fort Joy soldiers had even noticed when he'd disappeared months before.

While the surgeons and scientists were conducting their sick alterations on him, no one thought to look for him. Not one of them came to help while he was being held captive in his rubberized tomb.

He had been nothing to them. They were nothing to him.

The chorus of voices in Roote's head sang with glee as he fired three rapid shots at a trio of skulking soldiers. Only the last of them managed to squeeze off a few rounds before the intricate tracking system connected to Roote's finger pads blew him away.

Bullets ripped through the air around him. But none kissed the flesh of the godlike Elizu Roote. He walked through the hail of lead unharmed, stepping beyond the latest smoking bodies. Moving toward his ultimate target—the headquarters of General Delbert Chesterfield.

SMITH'S RAPID ANALYSIS of Roote's internal systems had proved correct so far. Shadowing Roote across the grounds of Fort Joy, Smith had no doubt that he had survived thus far only because he hadn't attempted to shoot the private. Therein lay the CURE director's dilemma.

He had ventured out after Roote in order to stop the deranged killing machine. However, the moment he attempted to do so using conventional means, Roote's systems would target him as a threat and destroy him.

Helpless to act, Smith could only watch as more soldiers died at the hands of this frightening horrid manufactured aberration.

Smith leaned into a barracks wall, feeling the rough texture of the wood beneath his hands. The uneven lines of the clapboard building pressed against his back. Cautiously he peered out across the courtyard.

Roote was only a few dozen yards away. The soldier was meeting less and less resistance the closer he got to Chesterfield's headquarters.

Angled floodlights positioned in pairs along the exteriors of all buildings facing the courtyard spread an even coat of brilliant white on the dusty grounds.

Though Roote appeared to be careful to stay to one side of the yard so as to avoid a full-out assault at the center of the parade grounds, it was more an instinctive reaction than a conscious one. He didn't seem outwardly concerned.

And rightly so. As far as Smith could tell, the private had nothing to fear from the troops he met.

Focusing on the deranged soldier as he continued on his remorseless trek toward the base headquarters, Smith hadn't been paying attention to his immediate surroundings. He was startled to hear a foot suddenly scuff the dirt beside him.

Whipping away from Roote, Smith spun toward the noise. He came face to face with a group of four young soldiers. They were sliding up to the

CURE director. Their boyish features registered clear apprehension.

"Out sightseeing, sir?" one of them asked, his voice a husky whisper.

"What the devil is going on here?" Smith demanded with quiet anger. He waved a hand in Roote's direction. "These men appear undisciplined. The only possible defense against Roote is a full-blown assault from every direction at once. All I have seen are sporadic attacks."

The soldier's eyes were dead. "That's what happens when command structure breaks down," he said bitterly.

Fury sparked the gray flint of Smith's eyes beyond his rimless glasses. "I am not interested in your problems, soldier," he snapped, his voice a sharp whisper. "That man is a threat that must be neutralized. I believe he is going after General Chesterfield."

"He ain't going to find him there," a soldier at the rear mocked, youthful voice fraught with tension.

"Why? Where is he?"

"Old Ironbutt left."

"Left?" Smith frowned. "What do you mean?"

"He's gone. Took off. Chopper airlifted his fat ass out of here twenty minutes ago."

Shocked, Smith glanced back at the headquarters. Roote was nearly there. But if what these men were saying was true, he would not find his quarry inside.

A decision was instantly made.

The CURE director turned back to the soldiers, addressing the man who seemed to have taken over as their leader.

"Gather every last man you can find," Smith ordered. "Arm victims from his previous assaults if they can walk. Medical personnel, civilian staff. *Everyone*." He pointed across the grounds to Roote. "That man cannot be allowed to leave this base. Only a full assault from all sides can bring him down. Even he will not be able to withstand such a barrage."

The soldiers seemed heartened to have someone assume command so authoritatively. Their nervousness fled, replaced by a sudden eagerness for action.

"Yes, *sir*," the first private said, nodding sharply.

Smith checked his watch. "It is 9:39. At 9:50 you will commence your assault. Expect him to head for the main gate by then. Bear that in mind as you plan your offensive."

The CURE director began to slip back down the rear of the building, away from Roote. The men stopped him.

"What about you?" a soldier asked.

"I have a plan that could render your assault unnecessary," Smith informed him. "If it succeeds, you will know it, for you will not encounter Roote.''

"And if it fails?''

Smith didn't miss a beat. "If it fails, I will be dead,'' he said with grim detachment.

Without another word, he slipped off into the night.

THE ELECTRIFIED FENCE had been constructed around a vast area of New Mexico desert. There was much vacant ground to cover on their race from the rear gate.

Remo and Chiun had already seen the flashing pulses of light while they were still miles away from the central part of the base. In spite of the constant background glow of the normal base lights, the shocks of blue were plainly visible.

It was like a ground-based fireworks display.

"If we're lucky, that's coming from the Fort Joy disco,'' Remo commented tightly as they flew up the hard-packed road.

In the rear, Arthur Ford watched the strobing pulses with silent awe.

The wind as they drove tore mightily at the wisps of hair at Chiun's chin and above his ears. The Master of Sinanju was deep in thought.

More and more, Chiun had begun to accept Remo's seemingly unbelievable story. As he did so, his concern for Remo had grown proportionally. He glanced at his pupil now.

Remo's jaw was clenched. His expression was dour as the jeep flew along the desolate path.

Chiun focused his hearing on Remo's heart.

It was still remarkably good, all things considered. His body was working overtime to right itself.

Inwardly Chiun was impressed. The abilities of his son in spirit rivaled those of the greatest Masters of Sinanju. Even surpassed some. The time of Remo's ascension to Reigning Master was overdue.

But no matter how quickly Remo healed now, it would matter little if he fared as poorly in his second encounter with this mysterious creature as he had in his first. For in his current weakened state, Remo would not survive.

Remo's frown deepened as he sensed his teacher's eyes upon him.

"Stop staring at me all the time," he griped abruptly. "I told you, I'm fine."

"I am not worried about you," Chiun said mildly, looking forward once more. "I am trying to decide how to explain your failure against this alleged creature in the Sinanju scrolls. Perhaps the electricity was attracted to your nose or ears," he suggested. "They would be obvious targets."

"He hit me in the chest, Chiun," Remo said, irked.

Chiun nodded. "Therein lies my dilemma."

"I bleed for you."

"Of course, it would be easier for me if you did not fail again."

"I'll do my best," Remo promised.

"That *would* make my task as chronicler of your misadventures simpler. I would hate to have to bend the truth in the Masters' scrolls."

If he weren't so concerned with what they were about to face, Remo would have laughed out loud. As far as the sacred scrolls of Sinanju were concerned, Chiun was notorious for twisting the truth into whatever pretzel-shaped contortions suited his carp of the day. Instead of commenting on this fact, Remo concentrated on the road ahead.

He had only a few miles to correct his erratic heartbeat, and at the rate he was going he'd never be at his peak by the time they reached their target.

Beside Remo, the Master of Sinanju sensed the concern of his pupil.

Deeply troubled, both men stared silently ahead at the hypnotic pulsing flashes that rose from out the heart of the desert night.

ROOTE CREPT SILENTLY alongside the command center.

He was alone. The sporadic attacks he had fended off since leaving the infirmary had stopped. The men had either fled or were regrouping for another assault.

It wouldn't matter. By the time they came back at him, Chesterfield would be dead. Afterward,

Roote would stroll right out the main gate. Anyone who tried to stop him would be killed, too. Thanks to Ironbutt Chesterfield, Elizu Roote was certain to come out on top.

As he approached the general's office, Roote could see a vague dark shape moving on the other side of the thick, translucent plastic that covered the hole in the wall.

Roote didn't move too quickly. He was careful not to make a sound. He wanted nothing more than to surprise General Chesterfield with his sudden appearance.

The plastic had been torn roughly along one edge. As he braced his back against the wall, Roote took the jagged section between his metal finger pads.

There were staples running all along the top and sides of the sheet. With a single, mighty tug, he wrenched the plastic free of the wall. As fast as the sound came, he had already slipped in through the opening.

Without hesitation, Roote fired bolts from all ten fingers at the startled figure across the office.

The surge of electricity caught the man in the chest. Eyes flew open in shock as he was lifted off the floor. An instant later, his back slammed against the far wall.

The officer collapsed to the floor. Dead.

The satisfaction Roote had expected on entering

the room never materialized. The soldier wasn't Chesterfield.

Roote vaguely recognized the dead lieutenant.

So it wasn't the officer he'd been looking for. So what? Chesterfield was here. Somewhere. And Elizu Roote would find him if he had to kill every last soldier on Fort Joy in the process.

He was about to duck back through the hole in the wall when the general's desk telephone jangled to life.

A perverse curiosity took hold of Roote. Striding across the room, he dropped into Chesterfield's chair. His gold fingertips clicked on the receiver as he lifted the phone to his ear.

"General Chesterfield's office," he drawled pleasantly. A smile crossed his face as he glanced at the smoking corpse lying on the floor.

"Please inform the general that his jeep is ready at the motor pool," a tart voice commanded.

Roote sat up. "What for?" he questioned.

"General Chesterfield intends to leave the base," the pinched voice said. "It is my understanding that he wishes to conduct a counteroffensive from a remote location. Please let him know—" The voice paused. "Never mind. He has just arrived at the motor pool."

The line went dead.

Roote quickly climbed to his feet, replacing the receiver. Thanks to the caller, he now knew where he would find Chesterfield. And where he would kill him.

Leaving the body of the lieutenant to mind the office, Roote slipped back out through the flap of plastic.

REMO'S JEEP SKIDDED to a stop at the nearest soldier. There were many more massing at the periphery of the first base outbuildings.

"What's going on?" Remo demanded.

"We're getting our lunch handed to us, that's what," the young man complained. "Dead and wounded everywhere. Big offensive starting in a couple of minutes."

Remo glanced quickly at Chiun. The Master of Sinanju's mouth was stretched into a concerned frown.

As he looked back at the soldier, Remo's expression mirrored that of his teacher.

"Where's Roote?" he asked.

The soldier snickered at the name. He was obviously an acquaintance of the private. "He was spotted near HQ a couple of minutes ago."

Remo spun to Arthur Ford. "Get out," he ordered.

"No way," Ford replied firmly. "It's my fault he's in the evil clutches of the military. For humanity's sake, I've got to do what I can to help him." He clutched determinedly at the seat.

"Kill him or ditch him, Little Father?"

"He is tall," Chiun pointed out with thin impatience.

"Gotcha," Remo nodded.

Hoping Arthur's height would attract the first bolt of lightning, he spun back around, jamming hard on the accelerator. The jeep bounced forward, toward Elizu Roote's last known location.

HIS POWER WAS DRAINED.

The circuitry within him was so familiar to Roote and so integrated with his biological systems, it was as if he'd been dealing with depleted capacitors since he was a child. The sensation was similar in nature to hunger or exhaustion.

His violent trek through the base had forced him to tap into his reserve power. His backup capacitors had been partially sapped, as well.

Although his store of energy was low, Elizu Roote knew that he had a sufficient supply to take care of General Chesterfield. He would recharge afterward.

As he slipped through the open bay door of the Fort Joy motor pool, he tapped his digits together in a twisted parody of finger snapping. Tiny blue sparks accompanied a sound like clacking castanets.

The interior of the building was dark. When he flipped the light switch inside the door, he found that the power had been cut.

They'd expected him. They thought to keep him

from recharging by severing the line to the motor pool.

"It ain't gonna work, Ironbutt," Roote taunted from the doorway. "I still got enough juice to fry your fat ass."

As he took another step into the building, Roote noticed a set of jumper cables attached to a solid metal pole just beyond the open door. For some reason, someone had pounded the metal rod into the earthen floor.

He disregarded the post, moving beyond the open bay door and into the shadows of the motor pool.

Roote had just stepped past the door when he sensed someone move out from behind it. In his peripheral vision, he caught sight of a man rushing toward him, something clasped in his hands.

His targeting scanners didn't match the object with any of the potential threats that had been stored on the small microchip buried in his brain. Automated system or no, the decision to kill was instantaneous.

In the instant the man appeared, Roote started spinning toward him, fingers extending to deal flashing death.

But to his shocked astonishment, he never got the chance.

Something painful latched on to a spot at the back of his neck. Clawing pincers. Soft flesh yielded to jagged metal.

The tearing sensation was short-lived. It was

completely overwhelmed by a body-racking jolt of pure pain. And to his shock and horror, he felt the bottom drop out of his capacitors. Roote's entire store of electricity was siphoned off in half a heartbeat.

In agony, he stood rigid during the split-second power surge, helpless to act.

And as quickly as it had begun, it was over. His capacitors were completely drained. As was Elizu Roote. With no electricity to animate him, the private collapsed like a rag doll to the floor.

Sapped of life.

THE SAME BLAST that racked Elizu Roote's body flung Harold W. Smith backward to the dirt floor.

Although he knew it would endanger his own life, it had been necessary for Smith to be in close to attach the free end of the jumper cables.

The schematics of Roote's mechanical system had suggested to Smith that the metal contact buried beneath the flesh at the rear of the soldier's neck might be a kind of Achilles' heel to his cybernetic systems.

At that moment, the CURE director didn't know that his supposition had been correct. He lay flat on his back near the open door of the motor pool. As still as death.

A few yards from Smith, Roote kicked feebly at the dirt floor as a few residual sparks hopped from his bleeding neck to the steel rod Smith had pounded into the floor.

16

Remo spied the first bodies lying in heaps of tangled limbs near the infirmary.

"Looks like our little glowworm's been glimmer-glimmering," he said coldly as they drove past the grisly scene.

"These are not burned like the others," the Master of Sinanju commented, hazel eyes narrowed.

"He had more power to work with back at the fence," Remo suggested. "When he's using his own store, maybe he has to hold back a little."

"It's terrible," Arthur Ford gasped. He was leaning between the two seats, looking out the windshield as they drove past the many smoldering bodies.

"Glad you're finally coming around," Remo said, assuming the gruesome scene had at last dispelled the UFO-chaser's notions of Elizu Roote as benevolent alien.

"What they forced him to do," Ford lamented, shaking his head sadly. He was practically in tears. "It must have been terrible for him."

"What planet are you from?" Remo demanded, astonished that Ford was still unmoved.

"Earth," Ford replied seriously, as if there truly was another option. He sniffled in solidarity with Elizu Roote as they passed another cluster of electrocuted corpses.

The bodies were scattered along a direct path to the base headquarters, like a macabre trail of breadcrumbs.

Remo slowed to a stop near the building where they had gotten their jeep.

Remo and Chiun climbed out. When Arthur Ford attempted to follow, Remo pushed him back in his seat.

"As annoying as you are, I'd still recommend you don't wander away," Remo said reluctantly.

Ford considered for a moment, glancing at one of Roote's nearest victims. Finally he fell back into his seat. "Just promise me you'll let him return to his ship if he agrees to go," he said, crossing his arms morosely.

"I'll put him in orbit myself," Remo promised.

Ford didn't like the way he said it.

Remo and Chiun left him in the jeep. Side by side, they moved swiftly across the courtyard.

The two men hugged the shadows, becoming one with the patches of darkness. Their moves were identical and instinctive as they hurried forward. As they rounded one of the many flat one-story buildings on the base, the rear of the HQ building suddenly loomed before them.

"Think he's after Chesterfield?" Remo asked as they passed another body.

"That bellowing pork belly commands these legions," Chiun said reasonably. "The bodies lead to his burrow."

Remo nodded agreement. "Be careful, Little Father," he warned.

"And you, as well, my son," Chiun replied softly.

The weight of shared apprehension heavy on their shoulders, neither man spoke again as they slipped around the side of Chesterfield's headquarters.

ARTHUR FORD SAT nervously for several long seconds after Remo and Chiun had gone.

He had done it again. Here he had been given yet another chance to help out the poor misjudged alien, and he had allowed fear to get the better of him.

Sitting in the back of a jeep. A fearful lump. A pathetic waste of humanity. No more.

There was one thing Ford was certain of. A warp field wouldn't form around a stationary object.

Screwing up his courage, the ufologist climbed out of the Army vehicle. His heart gripped tightly at his chest as he surveyed the area around the Fort Joy motor pool.

There didn't seem to be any bodies in the immediate vicinity. Maybe Roote hadn't gotten this far.

Remo and Chiun had headed north. Arthur Ford decided to strike out in the opposite direction in search of his alien.

He hadn't walked more than three yards when he spied a body sprawled in the open door of the motor pool.

Ford recognized the man instantly. It was the same government agent he had spotted at the Roswell airport.

The G-man lay sprawled on his back, unmoving.

Setting each foot carefully—one slowly before the other—Ford crept deliberately up to the motor pool door.

Leaning against the wood frame, he peered down at the government agent.

The man was alive. Barely. Ford could see the faint movement of his chest beneath his gray vest. That put him one up on the other victims they had passed.

As he moved closer, Ford also saw that the G-man was not singed like the others. It was as if someone had used a stun gun on him. Aside from the fact that he was obviously unconscious, there didn't appear to be anything dramatically wrong with him.

Taking a wide berth, Ford inadvertently stepped into the deep shadows beyond the door.

His ankle hit something solid.

Ford jumped back. Heart thudding madly, he stared into the darkness, trying to see what he had bumped.

As his eyes adjusted to the blackness, he was surprised to see the contours of a foot take shape. Beyond it lay another sprawled body. Another soldier.

The face was so pale it was almost visible in spite of the pervasive darkness. It almost looked like...

Ford recoiled.

It *was!*

He glanced out at the courtyard beyond the open motor pool door. Remo and Chiun would be back any minute. He didn't have much time to make up his mind.

The decision came surprisingly easily. He had shirked his responsibility as a galactic citizen back at the Fort Joy security fence. He would not allow it to happen again.

Stooping, Ford gripped Elizu Roote by both ankles. Walking backward, he began dragging the unconscious alien to the waiting jeep.

THE ONLY OCCUPANT of General Delbert Chesterfield's office was a five-minute-old corpse.

"Fresh kill," Remo said, glancing away from the body of the lieutenant.

Chiun was across the room. A tapered fingernail

pressed against the interior of the thick plastic that covered the hole he had made in the wall. The plastic sheet moved away from one side at the gentle touch.

"This was his egress," Chiun announced.

As Remo crossed over to him, Chiun raised both hands high in the air. Slashing long fingernails across the heavy plastic, the Master of Sinanju opened up a more respectable doorway. He and Remo ducked through the larger opening and out into the courtyard.

Ten minutes of searching turned up nothing. As they were doubling back past Chesterfield's HQ, Remo and Chiun were approached by a group of suspicious soldiers. Remo waved his FBI identification under their noses.

"Have you seen him?" he demanded urgently.

There was no question to whom he was referring.

"Nope," an anxious soldier replied. "We've been waiting at the front door." He jerked his head toward the main gate.

"You think he might have doubled back?" Remo asked Chiun. Before the Master of Sinanju could respond, the soldier cut in.

"Maybe the old guy took him out," he suggested hopefully.

"What old guy?" Remo asked.

"Civilian," the soldier explained. "He kinda took charge when Chesterfield bugged out."

Remo had a sinking feeling. "This old guy," he said worriedly. "Three-piece gray suit? Looks like he gargles with grapefruit juice?"

The soldier nodded emphatically. "That's him," he agreed. "He told us he was going after Roote alone. Said if he failed, Roote'd be coming our way. Since he never showed up, maybe your buddy figured out a way to stop him."

Remo's concerned expression was mirrored by Chiun's.

"We must find Smith," the Master of Sinanju intoned gravely.

As the Fort Joy soldiers fanned out in their search for Roote, Remo and Chiun doubled their efforts to locate the missing CURE director. Their tour brought them back around to the motor pool. The Master of Sinanju frowned as they neared the building.

"Our conveyance is not here," Chiun commented.

"That UFO whack-job must have taken it," Remo mused. "Probably went for a spin around Alpha Centauri."

They spied the body the moment they passed the open motor pool door. Racing inside, the two men squatted next to the supine form of Harold W. Smith.

"He's alive," Remo breathed, relieved.

Chiun was already examining Smith's frail chest.

He found at once that the CURE director had not been hit in the same manner as Remo or the others. That was fortunate, since Smith already had a congenital heart defect, as well as a pacemaker. He would never have survived a typical Roote attack.

Chiun began massaging Smith's chest. At the same time, he reached around to a spot at the base of the CURE director's spine. A single finger probed the area.

It was like flipping a switch. At Chiun's expert healing touch, Smith's eyelids fluttered gently open.

Remo had been examining the set of jumper cables attached to the pole in the floor. For some inexplicable reason, a torn chunk of ragged human flesh was caught in the claw of the free end. When Smith's eyes opened, Remo dropped the cables and slipped back beside the Master of Sinanju.

The CURE director's eyes rolled around in their sockets for a moment—seemingly with a life of their own. All at once, they cleared, settling on Chiun first, then Remo.

"How do you feel, Smitty?" Remo asked with a comforting smile.

Smith didn't respond to the soothing words. He was trying to see past Remo and Chiun. "Where is Roote?" he asked weakly.

"We've been looking, but we came up empty," Remo said.

"Save your strength, Emperor," Chiun cautioned. "Find speedy recovery in the knowledge that Sinanju will locate this demon and eradicate him if we must track him to the very ends of the earth."

Smith shook his head. "You do not understand. He is here. I believe I found a way to short him out."

Smith tried unsuccessfully to push himself to his elbows. With Chiun's aid, he settled back into the dirt.

Remo was shaking his head. "He's not here, Smitty," he insisted. "We've looked everywhere." A thought suddenly occurred to him. "Uh-oh," he said, hollow of voice.

"What?"

Remo seemed hesitant to speak. "We found some nutcase in the desert. He kept babbling on about how Roote is really just a misunderstood alien." He shook his head, hoping that he was wrong. "If I'm right..."

He left Smith's side.

Almost at once he found the marks in the earth where something heavy had been dragged. They led from where the jeep had been parked back in to the spot where Roote had fallen. For the first time, Remo noticed the scorched area around the base of the pole. He realized all at once what Smith had done.

Stepping back across the floor, he crouched down beside the CURE director.

"He's gone, Smitty," Remo said apologetically. "Ford must have taken off with him in our jeep."

Smith closed his eyes. As he did so, Chiun shot a dirty look at Remo. It was his "don't let the idiot know when you've done something stupid" look.

Remo shrugged helplessly. "He'd find out soon enough."

Chiun's eyes went wide. He was readying another nonverbal remonstration—this one much harsher than the last—when Smith's eyes opened once more.

"Do you have any idea where he would go with Roote?"

"Mars isn't an option, so I'd say back the way we came. Jeep tracks look like they turn that way."

Smith nodded. "The base defenses were concentrated in the other direction. Roote's pattern was that of a man unconcerned with confrontation. Given his own choice, that is the path he would have taken."

"A wise assessment," Chiun agreed.

"That does us no good now," Smith replied tartly.

He tried once more to push himself to his elbows. This time, he succeeded. He took a deep breath, glancing up at Remo and Chiun. There was work to do.

"Please bring me to my computer," Harold Smith said tiredly.

17

Luck was with Arthur Ford. Now if his good fortune would just hold out for a few hours more...

Though he expected to be stopped at any minute, he didn't encounter even one of the soldiers stationed at Fort Joy as he tore back across the desolate stretch of land between the main base and the southeast gate.

The row of charred tanks stood like somber sentries from another world as he flew back out the rear gate and onto the packed desert path. Swerving out behind the lip of black rock, he raced down the short hill, coming nose to nose with his own abandoned jeep at the bottom.

Struggling with the deadweight, he transferred Elizu Roote from the Army jeep to his own.

The private never made a sound. He was as limp as a pile of laundry when Ford dumped him into the rear footwell. For added protection, Ford tossed a dusty blanket over the body before running back around to the driver's side.

In another two minutes they were racing back

out into the vast barren wastes of New Mexico desert.

Even though he expected helicopters to rake the sand with searchlights at any moment, none materialized. They were not in pursuit. Apparently, the Army was still licking its wounds from its encounters with Roote.

Good. It served the military right for being on the wrong side of every significant extraterrestrial event of the past half century.

Ford knew just where he'd take Roote. It was someplace safe, where people would understand him. Someplace where he would never be found. Not if he lived to be a million years, which, Ford knew in some aliens, was possible.

The red taillights bobbed along the path for a few moments as the vehicle struggled to put greater distance between itself and the United States Army. But almost in a twinkling, the desert blackness swallowed the jeep. The engine sound faded just as quickly across the miles of empty desert.

18

Night burned off into the first muzzy streaks of pre-dawn gray above the endless flat desert.

The inevitable arrival of the rising sun revealed a level of destruction on Fort Joy greater than nighttime shadows had suggested. It was like the aftermath of a drunken New Year's party gone horribly awry.

Vehicles had been crippled during Roote's rampage across the base. Black scorch marks marred whitewashed walls where residual electrical energy had blown through the private's many victims. The wash of daylight exposed bodies previously undiscovered.

It was a horrific scene. Still, the chaos Roote had left was slowly coming to order.

Smith had arranged an interim command structure at the base. The breakdown in order among the troops the previous night had been more a result of General Chesterfield's lack of control than anything else. With the general out of the picture, things were coming back around.

Many of the dead had already been bagged and

stored. The injured had been nearly entirely relocated. Only those with the most superficial injuries remained at the base infirmary.

Damaged vehicles were being towed to where they could be repaired. Crews were already working to salvage the tanks at the southeast gate, as well as the Apache helicopters in the desert beyond it. The cleanup was going smoothly.

For a time during the night, Remo and Chiun had searched around the base for Roote and Arthur Ford. As expected, they had come up empty. By 3:00 a.m. the two of them had rejoined Smith at the Shock Troops lab where the CURE director had set up a clandestine temporary command center.

Remo's disappointment was great as he stalked around the big empty tank where Elizu Roote had been imprisoned. It was his hundredth circuit since their return.

Smith had largely recovered from his encounter with Roote. His system had been greatly shaken by the electrical discharge, but fortunately for him, most of the power had been channeled into the motor pool floor. Chiun had reasoned that Smith's heart condition was the real cause of his reaction to the relatively mild shock he had received.

To see Smith now, one would never have known he had come in contact with someone as dangerous as Elizu Roote only a few hours before. The head of CURE sat at one of the lab workstations, lost in cyberspace. For much of the night he had been typing rapidly on his laptop.

The Master of Sinanju sat in a lotus position on the floor near the CURE director.

Chiun's eyes were closed. As he sat—as still as a statue—an occasional loud honking snore would emanate from the nose of the greatest assassin on the face of the planet. The Master of Sinanju was oblivious to the noise.

This had been the division of labor for hours— Smith worked, Chiun slept and Remo paced.

As Remo completed another circuit, the CURE director lifted his hands from the laptop keyboard. He clenched his fingers a few times, working out the kinks that had developed in his hours of ceaseless typing.

Smith had said hardly a word to Remo since they'd brought him here. He had been working too feverishly to even speak. When the opportunity presented itself, Remo inserted himself into the sudden, silent vacuum left in the wake of the steady clatter of computer keys.

"Any luck?" he asked, strolling up behind Smith.

The CURE director blinked away weariness. "I have found nearly all there is to know about Arthur Ford, but I have yet to locate the man," he complained.

"Maybe he hasn't made it home yet," Remo suggested.

"That is likely. He lives with a friend in Bangor. The two are apparently space fantasy fanatics."

"How do you know that?"

"I had a warrant issued to the local FBI to search their apartment. The place was loaded with piles of science fiction bric-a-brac. Neither man was there."

"Maybe the friend knows about Ford and Roote," Remo suggested.

"Perhaps," Smith sighed. "He is at something called a *Star Trek* Convention in Los Angeles. It seems that the devotees of an old canceled television program assemble regularly around the country. To what end, I do not know."

"I've heard of them before," Remo said dryly.

"Really?" Smith asked, genuinely surprised. "I found the notion ludicrous. In any event, the L.A. police have been sent to collect Ford's friend. I doubt that his input will illuminate much, but we have little else to go on."

"What about Chesterfield?" Remo asked. "If you can't give me Roote, at least let me punch that bloated crapbag's ticket."

Smith shook his head. "General Chesterfield has fled east. He arrived at Washington National Airport earlier this morning. Beyond that, I have yet to attempt to locate him."

"Why the hell not?"

"Because Chesterfield is a side issue. He can be

dealt with in time. We must not allow ourselves to lose focus of the main objective here.''

Remo dropped into a swivel chair near Smith. ''Roote,'' he said bitterly.

''That is correct.'' Smith tapped a frustrated hand on the table next to his laptop. ''General Chesterfield has created in Elizu Roote a potentially unstoppable killing machine. If he reserves his energy, he can go for weeks at a time without recharging. His bionic and biological systems are flawlessly integrated. The science that combined to create him is as brilliant as it is terrifying.''

''Tell me something I don't know, Smitty.''

Smith's face grew grim. ''Roote's psychological make-up,'' he suggested.

''What about it?''

''He *likes* to kill.'' Before Remo could interrupt, Smith raised a hand. ''It goes beyond the obvious, Remo,'' he said. ''Roote fits the psychological profile of a serial killer to a tee. The psychosis he is displaying now has not manifested itself as a result of his physical alterations. He was most likely insane long before the general got his hands on him.''

''So Chesterfield and his pals took a stir-fried, finger-painting loony and turned him into a freaking walking power plant,'' Remo said flatly.

''It is arguable who was the greater lunatic, but essentially, yes. That is the case.''

"Who here's ready to reinstitute the draft?" Remo said, shaking his head in disgust.

Smith's sleep-deprived eyes were glazed. "A being with a combination of Roote's dangerous psychological temperament and man-made abilities was a disaster waiting to happen at the outset."

"And now he's in the hands of some dip shit Buzz Aldrin wannabe," Remo muttered.

"Yes," Smith said, his voice trailing off. He stared beyond Remo for a few long seconds. At last, he turned back to his computer.

As Smith began typing, Remo was rising to his feet. He resumed his endless cycle around the huge tank.

On the floor, the Master of Sinanju continued to snore, unconcerned.

19

Earth was doomed. Everyone who didn't already know it would find out soon enough.

It was an ecological thing. It was a political thing. It was a whole damn human race thing.

The entire world was going to hell.

People in the know realized that imminent global disaster had as much to do with the destruction of the rain forest and the polluting of the oceans as it did with the planet's leaders. And ultimately the leaders in the United States were the ones that mattered most of all. A sad fact, but true.

For some reason unknown to Beta RAM, the world looked to America for leadership. Even those who claimed they didn't care about the opinions of the U.S. were obviously intensely jealous of the richest nation in the world. The United States set the terms for the global game. And when it fumbled the ball, the world suffered. But Beta RAM knew that this was only part of the story.

The U.S. government was in bed with special interest groups. And no matter who was in charge in Washington, the special interests dictated the rules on a host of different topics. The results were predictable: pollution, germ warfare, nuclear proliferation, the destruction of old-growth forests.

Further, Beta knew that behind the so-called special-interest groups was a cabal of seeming humans who controlled everything, for one evil purpose: to destroy the world. Beta RAM knew that the members of the Association of Evil were men only in appearance. In truth, they were Squiltas—alien beings from the swamps of the second moon of the third planet circling Ursa Minor. Fearful of the fact that man was on the threshold of intergalactic travel, they had taken on the appearance of men in order to bring about the destruction of mankind.

Beta had tried to warn four consecutive puppet leaders of America of this grave danger to humanity. He found to his great horror that the influence of the Association was strong. He had been mocked, harassed and—after bringing a concealed weapon to a George Bush rally back in 1992—even imprisoned.

The only figure in recent years to express an interest in his story had been Ross Perot, but Beta RAM had hesitated to ally himself with the Texas billionaire. After all, he didn't want to appear crazy.

Beta RAM—who had been born Bobby Jack Balbo—would have almost given up all hope, con-

demning the world to the whims of the Squiltas, if
not for one thing. Salvion.

Salvion was of the planet Tragg, whose inhabitants were the natural enemies of the Squiltas. In
his native Traggian tongue Salvion meant "faith."

Salvion was a being of light who had come to
Beta RAM many times over the course of his life.
Appearing in glowing robes, he spoke of a future
for a select few humans, separate from that or-
dained by the Squiltas. On several occasions, Salvion had even brought Beta aboard his celestial
ark, taking him for rides around the cosmos.

The trips they took together were always breath-
takingly beautiful and, oddly, seemed to coincide
with Beta's most intense peyote and phenobarbital
sessions.

As a result of his meetings with Salvion, Beta
had withdrawn from society into the wilds of New
Mexico. There, at Camp Earth he gathered around
him a group of followers who awaited the inevitable end of time, when the Squiltas would succeed
in their designs to destroy the planet. Only then
would Salvion land with his celestial ark to shep-
herd the men and women of Beta RAM's camp to
the safety of a distant star system. Where they
would establish the paradise of New Earth.

Until that time, all Beta RAM could do was
wait. And, as the mood struck him, drink.

The mood had hit him pretty hard lately.

As the desert sun rose higher into the clear blue

sky this day, the brilliant stabs of sunlight burst through the corrugated tin sides of Beta's tumble-down hut. The light from the yellow star Sol, around which he had travelled more than once, spilled across his sleeping eyes.

Reluctantly Beta opened one bleary eye on the new day. He saw a foot.

Beta blinked the eye, as if trying to clear a fuzzy sleep image from his waking thoughts.

It was no good. The foot was still there. And it was dirty. Dark crescent moons of mud had col-lected beneath the too-long toenails.

Still with only one eye open, Beta dragged his gaze all the way up the rest of the filthy, naked body. He had to scuff his cheek against his tattered surplus Army blanket in order to get as far as the face.

When he saw who she was, he shivered in spite of the steamy heat inside the tin hut.

His companion was one of the Indian girls who had glommed onto the hope offered at Camp Earth. Her face was as flat as a crepe and as big around as a basketball. Above her three chins, rotten teeth were exposed with each sucking, snoring breath.

As he rolled over onto his itchy back, Beta opened his other eye. He stared at the white streaks of light slicing through the holes in the roof of the hut roof. He sighed.

"I gotta tell Salvion. When we load up the ark for New Earth—no pigs."

Clearing the morning phlegm from his throat, Beta RAM scanned the dirt floor for his pants.

FIVE MINUTES LATER, Beta RAM was dressed and touring the temporary shelters that comprised Camp Earth, which was erected on a flat plateau in the Caballo Mountains west of the White Sands Missile Range.

The squalid camp was the sort of pathetic shantytown that normally sprang up across the border in Mexico, eighty miles south.

Old car hoods, sections of discarded tin, even the hull of a broken boat were leaned together into makeshift hovels. Ratty tarpaulins and sheets decorated with cartoon characters whose popularity had faded a decade before formed the outer skin of teepees. The skeletal framework beneath consisted of broom handles and steel rods lashed together with scrap wire.

Like Beta RAM, the men and women of Camp Earth had begun crawling out from beneath their piles of rubble to greet the new day. Before the pathetic homes, a few of the disciples of Salvion had already started breakfast.

Rocks were formed in circles to contain crude fires of brush and twigs. Cans of everything from stew to baked beans were being warmed on metal racks. A few more enterprising individuals burned strips of fatty bacon in filthy pans.

Beta walked past all of this activity.

In one of his earliest visitations, Salvion had informed Beta RAM that the item that fell to Earth during the famous Roswell incident had been an escape pod from his own ship. Also on the pod was a group of Squiltas that Salvion had been conducting to a penal colony on Pluto. The evil aliens had transmitted the coordinates of the planet to their home world before being recaptured. Salvion had rounded all of them up—or so he thought.

One had escaped, and this lone Squilta had coordinated the rise to power of the Association of Evil on Earth.

The White Sands Missile Range eventually became a landing strip, as well as a departure point, for the Squiltas on Earth. The arrival of the end time would be made obvious by the increased activity in the desert around the secret base.

Beta thought that the climactic moment he'd been awaiting had finally come the night before, when the lights in the sky swept the desert all around White Sands and Fort Joy. A lot of the people at Camp Earth had begun to pack up their belongings in preparation for boarding the ark. Only when their lookouts stationed in the desert below confirmed that the lights belonged to ordinary terrestrial helicopters did depression finally set in at Camp Earth. With the disappointment came the drinking.

Walking away from the nausea-inducing breakfast smells, Beta RAM was trying to purge himself of that awful hungover feeling by pulling in deep breaths of clean mountain air.

His head felt like a balloon that had been filled to twice its capacity.

Blinking, tasting the film that had collected on his tongue, Beta paused at the edge of the plateau.

The sight was breathtaking. It was a sheer drop down to the Rio Grande far below. In the distance the river snaked off around the side of another hill of rough rock.

Faced with the combination of the awesome majesty of nature and the gallon of cheap whisky and beer in his otherwise empty belly, Beta RAM, Prophet of Salvion, Guardian of Camp Earth, Preparer of the Great Migration, could do only one thing. He vomited as if there were no tomorrow.

It took more than ten seconds for the puke to hit the river. By then, Beta was already vomiting again. He puked and puked and puked some more until he thought his stomach would come up through his mouth. It was ten long minutes of painful, ceaseless retching.

When his stomach was at last empty, Beta RAM wiped the bile from his chin. With a thick snort, he pulled back some mucus from his nose.

"Time for breakfast." He coughed, spitting a glob of phlegm into the sparkling river.

He turned and headed back for camp.

Before Beta had even reached the first tin house, he knew something was wrong. The pilgrims of

New Earth had abandoned their fires and breakfast plates. They were moving en masse to the mouth of the narrow road that led down to the flat desert on the other side of the rocky hill.

Beta heard the shouted voice as he approached the rear of the crowd.

"Intruder alert! Intruder alert!"

The voice echoed up from the road, filtered through a tinny megaphone. The speeding jeep crested the hill a moment later, skidding to a stop near the line of vehicles belonging to the Camp Earth inhabitants.

The men in the jeep were fellow Salvion disciples. They were part of the crews that toured the desert around the flat hill. As Camp Earth's first line of defense, they would warn the residents of any Squiltas invasion.

Beta RAM pushed his way through the excited crowd, catching up with the breathless arrivals as they jumped from their vehicle.

"What's going on?" Beta demanded.

"Someone's coming!" the driver said excitedly. "We spotted him moving up the road a few minutes ago."

Beta glanced at his disciples. "Squiltas?" he asked nervously. The people behind him withdrew in fright.

The driver shook his head. "Human. At least he appears to be."

"I think it might be Arthur Ford," the other man

said, panting. "I couldn't see too good with the binoculars."

Beta RAM relaxed somewhat. He knew Arthur Ford. The ufologist was not a disciple of Salvion, but at least he was a believer. But since he would not be part of the chosen few invited to board the ark, Beta had no idea what Ford would want at Camp Earth.

A few minutes later, Ford's jeep raced up the path and squealed to a rapid stop, kicking up a cloud of sand and stones. Ford hopped out before the jeep had rocked to a stop.

"What can the people of New Earth do for you, friend Arthur?" Beta said by way of greeting.

Ford was covered with desert grime. His eyes were bloodshot and rimmed with black from lack of sleep.

"We've got trouble," Ford announced seriously. "On a *galactic* scale."

Without further warning, he reached in through the open door of his jeep. With a yank, he pulled off the blanket he had thrown over Elizu Roote.

The pale, sweating form of the Army private hunched uncomfortably in the rear footwell of the jeep. The heat had caused red hives to erupt on his doughy white skin. Although hours had passed since his encounter with Smith at the Fort Joy motor pool, he remained unconscious.

Beta RAM leaned over to examine the almost phosphorescent-white body. Ford had crammed

Roote in the back of the Jeep so tightly, Beta couldn't see him very well.

"Who is he?" Beta asked, turning to the ufologist.

"An alien," Ford insisted.

Beta raised an eyebrow. "A Squilta?" he asked.

"I thought they were supposed to be amorphous," Ford said, confused.

Some in the crowd snorted derisively at Ford's obvious ignorance.

"They're capable of taking on human characteristics," Beta said impatiently. "Bill Gates? Need I say more?"

Ford shook his head. "I don't think he's Squilta. At least he hasn't manifested any signs to me."

"*I'll* be the judge of that," Beta announced.

He ordered his followers to carry Roote into the light. They did as they were instructed, stretching the Army private out in the dirt before the jeep.

Beta stooped to examine the pale, wasted form more carefully. He found the finger pads immediately.

"What are these?" he said, awestruck.

"Defensive system," Ford explained. "Used only when threatened by the United States military."

A thought occurred to Beta. "All that junk going on in the desert last night, was that him?"

Ford nodded. At this, Beta RAM whistled his approval.

Continuing his exam, Beta found the spot of ragged flesh at the rear of Roote's neck. What little blood was present had dried.

Beta tapped a finger against the partially exposed subcutaneous plate. It clicked.

"No doubt about it," he said, standing. "This boy's not human."

The people of Camp Earth accepted their leader's conclusion with surprising ease. After all, for some of them, this was not their first alien.

"He doesn't look too healthy," commented one of the men who had been first to see Ford approaching.

"Probably the contact with Earth's polluted atmosphere," Beta said, looking down on Roote's stricken body. "Damn Squiltas." Scratching his belly, he glanced up at Ford. "What can we do to help?"

Ford smiled, excited and relieved to finally be among people who truly understood what Roote was.

He took a deep breath. "We need to gather up all the car batteries we can get," Ford exhaled urgently.

20

Dr. Harold W. Smith had always thought that when he reached a certain age there would be nothing left that would surprise him. On this day, he learned that he could not have been more wrong.

The director of CURE fought the urge to let his mouth drop open in shock as he scanned reams of material on the World Wide Web devoted entirely to alien conspiracy theories.

Smith knew there always had and would be lunatics out there. But he was amazed to find an entire subculture devoted to the ludicrous notion that the United States government was deliberately covering up the fact of regular alien visits to the planet Earth.

Forget that Earth was a relatively obscure planet in a relatively isolated part of the Milky Way. Never mind that the odds of anyone ever stumbling upon Earth in the vast expanse of the cosmos were beyond astronomical. Overlook the obvious notion that it would be easier to hold a nuclear explosion in a hatbox than to contain a secret on the level being posited by the UFO devotees. None of these considerations warranted concern for those whose eyes were turned hopelessly starward.

To the rational, analytical, staunchly terrestrial mind of Harold W. Smith, the whole discussion was utterly incredible. He wondered if it would seem less unbelievable if he had not been so tired. He doubted it.

Smith had been working for hours without sleep.

Police in Los Angeles had rounded up Arthur Ford's roommate. The man had known nothing beyond the fact that his friend was somewhere in New Mexico.

So far, the usual checks had been fruitless. There were no credit-card transactions, no airline tickets, not even a simple traffic violation. It was as if Arthur Ford had vanished off the face of the planet.

The irony of that thought occurred to Smith the moment it passed through his weary brain.

No, Ford was still on Earth. Somewhere.

But where?

It was possible that he and Roote had run out of gas and were dying in the desert right now. Perhaps they had even crossed the border into Mexico. It was a big, big world. And in order to track his quarry, Harold Smith needed something, anything to go on. So far, he had nothing.

"Blast." Smith muttered the rare curse under his breath as he dropped back in his seat.

"Nothing yet?"

Remo's voice startled him. Chiun had awakened

from his untroubled night's sleep hours ago. He and Remo had gone for a walk around Fort Joy. Smith had been so involved in his work that he hadn't heard them return.

The CURE director sighed. "I would have an easier time locating a single grain of sand in the desert," he complained. Removing his glasses, he rubbed his weary eyes.

"I have great faith in your oracles, Emperor," the Master of Sinanju offered. Hands clasped behind his back, he was looking at them through the wall of the huge tank. The Plexiglas distorted his wizened form.

"Thank you, Master Chiun," Smith said. "But I do not think you appreciate the difficulty of this search. There is a network of individuals out there who I am now certain would be more than willing to aid Elizu Roote. They would be as convinced as the young man we met at the airport that they were dealing with an alien being."

"You haven't even found Ford yet?" Remo asked. He was leaning against the side of the tank.

Smith shook his head. "He has vanished."

"Any friends in the area?" Remo asked. "Maybe there's some other nut nearby who might help him out."

Smith turned to a pad beside his laptop. In a dull monotone, he began reading from the hasty notes he had collected from the Internet.

"Alien Guards, Alien Sentries, Alien Watchers,

Binary Ring Party, Brotherhood of the Stars, Brothers of Aliens, Brothers of Man, Camp Alpha, Camp Beta, Camp Earth, Camp Gamma, Camp Omega—not to be confused with Omega Camp, Omega Brotherhood or a dozen other sites around the area.''

Disgusted, he tossed the notepad back to the table.

"We could check them all out," Remo offered.

"It would take years," Smith said, shaking his head. "There are hundreds of groups camped out from the Rio Grande to Roswell. Some have permanent settlements, some come back at a specific time each year. Others are nomadic, moving from one place to another rapidly. Their paranoia does not allow them to stay in one place very long. If Ford has gone to any of these, it would be nearly impossible to find him."

"If this creature is as you both claim, it will surface again," Chiun said with certainty.

"And the only way we'll know is when someone shows up on the nightly news smoking like a bucket of extra crispy," Remo said.

Chiun shrugged. "It will be a trail to follow."

"No way we're waiting," Remo insisted. "I'm not letting that nutbar toast anyone else."

"Remo, we have no choice," Smith said, forcing a reasonable tone in his tired voice.

A small electronic beep suddenly emanated from his computer. Smith turned back around, checking the thin band on which only a few lines of text could appear at one time.

The four Folcroft mainframes had continued to troll the Net since Smith's return to the Shock Troops lab. A satellite connection transmitted any relevant data to the CURE director's briefcase laptop.

As he read the information his computers had gathered, Smith felt the weariness melt away.

"I have something," he said, his lemony voice tense.

Stepping rapidly across the room, Remo and Chiun gathered around the computer.

"What is it?" Remo asked.

"Arthur Ford has used his Discover card."

"Where?" Remo pressed anxiously. "And don't say Neptune."

Smith was typing rapidly at the small keyboard, accessing the pertinent information.

"The Wal-Mart in Truth or Consequences."

Remo scrunched up his face. "Wasn't that an old game show?" he asked.

"The city was renamed after the success of the program," Smith explained as he worked.

"There's a brain trust I'd steer clear of," Remo said dryly. "What was their fall-back option, 'Let's Make a Deal Falls'? Probably Assholeville'd be more appropriate, huh, Little Father?"

"Silence, chatterbox," Chiun insisted. He was watching intently as Smith typed at his computer.

"I have located several other individuals whose credit-card uses roughly match the purchase time of Arthur Ford. I have traced them all back to a single location. They are all residents of a place called Camp Earth."

Remo seemed surprised. "That's pretty slick, Smitty," he said, impressed. "How'd you do that?"

"Ford bought an unusually large quantity of a single item, as did the others. There was a clear correlation between all of the purchases." He didn't seem pleased by his discovery. "They have effectively cleaned out the entire area of this one item."

"What is it?" Remo asked.

Smith looked up at him. When he spoke, his voice was tight. "Automobile batteries."

ARTHUR FORD DIDN'T HAVE a clue what he was doing.

The ufologist had borrowed a set of jumper cables from one of the Camp Earth inhabitants. Carefully he clamped a clawed end to one of the many batteries sitting on the dirt floor of the corrugated tin shack.

"How much juice does he take?" Beta RAM asked. He was crouching in the doorway, hands braced on his knees.

The leader of the Salvion movement glanced

around at the huge number of car batteries arranged around the supine form of Elizu Roote.

"I'm not sure," Arthur admitted. "I saw him drained once before, but never this bad."

Crawling on his knees, he gently lifted Roote's head with one hand. Squeezing open another of the jumper cable claws, he found the metal patch on the Army private's spine. Carefully he clamped the hook onto the nub.

Beta RAM and Arthur Ford actually heard the hum from the battery. It was a rapid powering-down noise.

Once Ford removed the clamp from the battery, Beta used a tester to confirm their suspicions.

Both were right. The battery had been drained of all its juice.

There was no reaction from Roote. He continued to lie there, eyes closed, breathing shallow. Not so much as a solitary muscle spasm disturbed his slender frame.

"His power must be really low," Ford commented.

Leaving the far end of the cables hooked to Roote's neck, he moved over to the next battery, latching on to another terminal with one of the free claws.

The results were the same as before. A loud hum, followed by a total lack of any reaction from Elizu Roote.

"This is going to take forever," Beta RAM complained.

Arthur wasn't paying attention. Sliding on his knees through the dirt, he had already moved over to the next battery. He hooked into Roote's system once more.

"We're going to need more batteries," Ford commented as he worked.

"You've got a couple hundred already," Beta RAM said. "We'd have to go all the way to Las Cruces for more."

"We *need* more," Ford insisted. "He's sucking down juice like there's no tomorrow."

Beta RAM sighed. "If he's working for the Squiltas, there might not *be* a tomorrow," he muttered. Shaking his head, he added, "I'll see what I can do."

The leader of Camp Earth ducked back out the door of the small shack, leaving Arthur Ford to his work of reviving a man more dangerous than any of the creatures of Beta RAM's fertile imagination.

BY THE TIME Remo and Chiun arrived at the Truth or Consequences House Warehouse store, it was a little after three in the afternoon.

"Why are we here?" the Master of Sinanju asked as they walked through the huge air-conditioned building. Shoppers filled the aisles.

"Camp Earth is one of the few alien-chasing wacko groups without its own Web site," Remo explained. "Smith doesn't know exactly where it is."

"And he believes someone here knows?" Chiun asked. He appeared to be extremely doubtful that any of the people they were passing could know anything. The men all looked as if they had just stepped in from the bowling alley next door, and the women seemed to be practicing for the Olympic gum-snapping-and-halter-top-wearing competition.

"Maybe," Remo said. "Someone from there bought a ton of batteries here and at other stores in town. It's possible the locals know where they were bringing them."

"Knowledge is no doubt scarcer than hen's teeth in this toilet-seat emporium," the Master of Sinanju sniffed. Tucking his hands inside the sleeves of his silver kimono, he trailed Remo reluctantly up the aisle.

They found the manager of the automotive department at the rear of the building. The man expressed sympathy for their situation, but explained with a sad smile that he had no more automobile batteries in stock.

"Gee, I'm really sorry," he said, "but a couple guys came in this morning and cleaned me out."

"I heard," Remo said. "We were hoping you knew who they were. Maybe where we could find them."

The man shook his head in apology. "Sorry,"

he said. "Didn't really know them. If you really need a battery that bad, I've got another batch coming in on Tuesday."

Remo shook his head. "Thanks. We'll check somewhere else."

As they turned to go, the manager called to them.

"Good luck," he said with an apologetic shrug. "The whole town's cleaned out. In fact, I just heard from our sister store down in Las Cruces. Someone already put all their supply on reserve. Maybe if you hurry you can sneak in and get one before they pick them up."

Remo spun back around. "How long ago did you talk to them?" he demanded.

The man's face clouded. "Five minutes," he said. "Customer made a cell call to make sure the store held on to all the batteries. Told the manager down there to check with me when he asked if they were on the level." He shook his head. "Why's there such a big run on batteries?"

The manager found that the last words he had spoken were to himself.

The two men he had been speaking to were suddenly nowhere near him. When he craned his neck over the crowd of shoppers, he was just able to spy them as they raced around the corner of the long aisle at the distant front of the store. A moment later he could barely distinguish the bright silver flash of the old Asian's kimono in the parking lot as the pair raced past the long windows beyond the line of cash registers.

"Have fun driving to Las Cruces without a battery," the manager muttered, annoyed at their rudeness.

Glancing down, he returned to work.

21

The old rusted Dodge truck that Beta RAM drove down into Las Cruces was so battered it almost looked as if someone had stuck four bald tires on one of the Camp Earth shanties and pushed it down the hill.

The sun was sinking lower in his rearview mirror as the Prophet of Salvion steered the rattling pile of metal down the sticky black streets.

Beta was not a happy Camp Earth camper.

For several years now his followers in the Salvion movement had been willing to do anything and everything he asked of them. Even though they were all dancing on the precipice of Armageddon, in a strange way it had truly been a golden age for Beta RAM. In just a few short hours, Arthur Ford had changed all that.

The people were no longer talking about Salvion and the Squiltas threat, they were discussing creatures called the Power Players of Andromeda.

It took some arm-twisting to find out that they were talking about the race from which the companion of Ford's had apparently come.

Ford had described the creature's amazing abilities to the people of Camp Earth. How he could channel and launch electricity with his fingers. How he killed only when he was threatened. How he was being stalked by government agents.

Slowly those at Camp Earth were beginning to believe their ultimate salvation, as well as the hope of all mankind, lay in the hands of this E.T.-come-lately.

Beta RAM knew what would come next. His followers would denounce Salvion. They would disregard the Squiltas threat. They would toss out Beta himself as part of the old orthodoxy,

The prophet of Salvion would be without his beloved followers. Perhaps when the celestial ark finally did come, he would be forced to bring along pigs after all, assuming the more attractive females in the movement went with Arthur Ford.

It was all utterly ghastly. On a cosmic scale.

These things weighed heavily on the mind of Beta as he drove his rickety red truck into the big parking lot of the House Warehouse store in Las Cruces.

After parking the truck near the front of the lot, he walked toward the store.

Car batteries were pretty heavy, he thought as he approached the large building. He had helped move a few of the many that had been brought back to Camp Earth earlier that day and had had a difficult time lugging them.

Hmm...

Maybe he could drop a battery on Roote's head and blame it on the Squiltas. If Arthur Ford objected, Beta could give him the battery treatment, too.

As the electronic entrance door slid open before him, Beta reminded himself that the government secreted cameras in the motion sensors in order to keep videotaped records of every American citizen. Beta RAM covered his face with both hands and ducked his head away from the black sensor box as he stepped into the air-conditioned store.

THEY HAD BURNED UP the highway between Truth or Consequences and Las Cruces, twice avoiding the flashing lights of state police cruisers by sheer reckless driving.

Within the city limits, Remo did his best to stay within the posted speed limits.

As they drove down one traffic-filled street, the Master of Sinanju glanced at his pupil.

"Your driving on the highway was more reckless than usual," he commented.

As Remo steered the rented car he had borrowed from Smith through the thick traffic, he shot a look at Chiun.

"I wouldn't talk if I were you," Remo said. "I've been strapped in when you were behind the wheel. It's like being in a turbo-charged bumper car."

"Allow me to refresh your memory, O Forgetful Caster of Aspersions. I am thinking of a certain truck you tipped over on me in Germany," the Master of Sinanju said dryly.

"Water under the bridge," Remo said. "And besides, I apologized for that about a billion times."

"And forgiving soul that I am, I considered accepting some of them," Chiun replied. "Even though you nearly killed me, we were transporting my gold—thus your carelessness in haste was almost excusable. However, there is no treasure in this vehicle other than me. Therefore there is no need to risk my precious life."

"Have you been paying attention the last couple of days?" Remo asked. "That guy tried to fry my cullions. I want to settle his hash. It's as simple as that."

"If by simple you mean simple-minded, I agree," Chiun said.

"Are these insults strictly for pleasure, or is there a point behind all this?"

Chiun nodded somberly. "You are behaving rashly. You are rushing into a conflict without any concern for the possible outcome."

Remo was genuinely surprised. "You think I can't beat this asswipe?" he asked.

"If he were an ordinary foe, I would say yes, my son. Without hesitation. But neither you nor Smith believe this man to be ordinary."

"He isn't," Remo insisted.

"This have I conceded," Chiun agreed. "So why do you hasten to meet him again? Give yourself time to heal. Knowledge is our ally when confronted with the unknown. While you grow strong, Smith will learn more of this creature. When the time comes we will face it together, you and I."

"Nope. Roote is a killer, Little Father. He was a maniac before they stitched all that hardware into him. Thanks to Chesterfield, he's a hell of a lot more dangerous. He has to be stopped now. Case closed."

Remo hunkered down behind the steering wheel, his face pulled into hard lines.

"You are still not one hundred percent," Chiun pointed out after a moment's silence.

"I'm fit as a fiddle," Remo said dismissively.

"You are strong, Remo, but you are not invincible."

"I'm not woman, either," Remo interjected, his tone deeply sarcastic.

"What is that supposed to mean? Of course you are not," Chiun spit. "And since you insist on being pigheaded, when we find this villain, *I* will deal with him."

"What?" Remo asked. "No way. Roote is mine."

"You are not well enough to face him again."

"I told you, I'm fine."

They were at a red light. He slowed to a stop behind a line of cars.

"In another day you may be fine. In another week perhaps you will have healed completely. But at present your body is still not right."

"Absolutely not, Chiun. When we find Roote, *I'm* the one who gets to punch his ticket."

Chiun's voice took on a cold edge. "Are you forgetting who is Reigning Master of Sinanju?"

Remo closed his eyes. A honking horn behind him told him that the light had turned green. Opening his eyes, he started forward once more.

"No," Remo muttered morosely.

"Who is?"

Remo snapped one hand against the steering wheel. "*You*, okay? Geez, Chiun. Fine. If you want Roote, you've got him. He's yours. Take him with my blessing. Sheesh!"

In the passenger's seat of the rental car, Chiun's wrinkled face split into a broad smile.

"I now see why so many people join the militia in this nation, even though they are not required to do so," the Master of Sinanju said.

"Why?" Remo asked sullenly.

There was a twinkle in the old man's eye.

"It is fun to pull rank."

TEN MINUTES LATER, they were in the parking lot of the House Warehouse superstore.

Remo steered the rented car up and down the

lanes, looking for a parking space. He found one near a battered red truck that looked as if it were being held together by rust and a thick film of desert dust.

As he got out of the car, Remo noticed an emblem on the side of the truck door. The grime was so thick that the logo was difficult to read.

He dragged one hand across the door. The cleared logo depicted a bluish planet Earth. Above it hovered something that looked like a dinner plate with running lights. Below the planet a semicircle of letters spelled out Camp Earth.

"I think we've hit pay dirt," Remo called to Chiun. He dusted the grime off his hands as the old Korean came around to the truck.

Frowning, the Master of Sinanju inspected the Camp Earth logo. "And I think Americans have far too much idle time," he pronounced contemptuously.

Remo leaned against the side of his car. "We can discuss the stagnation of American culture while we wait for them to beam out," he said with a tight smile.

BETA RAM HOPED that Salvion's ark would land before his credit-card bill came due.

The head of Camp Earth emerged from the big exit doors of House Warehouse dragging a metal dolly filled with boxes of batteries. A store clerk followed, pushing another cart that was equally full.

Sweating in the late-afternoon heat, they hauled both wobbly carts over to the rear of Beta RAM's truck.

After Beta had dropped the tailgate, the clerk helped him load the batteries into the back.

"Are you a survivalist or something?" the young clerk puffed as they worked.

"If the Association of Evil has its way, none of us will survive," Beta replied. He was standing in the rear of the truck, pushing the batteries up against the cab.

While he was working, Beta noticed two men sitting in a car next to his. Neither of them were looking his way, nor did they appear to be looking anywhere else in particular. He felt a sudden knot tighten in the pit of his stomach.

"Association of Evil. What, is that like the Mob or something?" the clerk asked as he wiped the sheen of sweat from his forehead with the tails of his untucked shirt.

Ordinarily Beta didn't shy away from a potential convert to the wisdom of Salvion. However, the people in the next car had made him very nervous. One of them was Asian, possibly Japanese. And everyone knew the Squiltas had replicated android duplicates of that entire country's population during the 1980s.

"Something like that," Beta said quickly.

He scurried down from the rear of the truck, mumbling thanks to the young clerk. As the kid began dragging the carts back to the store, Beta closed the tailgate.

He shot another glance at the car in the next space. The two men still hadn't looked his way.

The sweat under his arms turned cold.

Fumbling in his jeans for his keys, Beta headed around the bed for the cab.

"HE HAS SEEN US," Chiun announced.

Even though they hadn't glanced in Beta RAM's direction, they had both sensed his gaze upon them.

"He looked at us," Remo replied. "It doesn't mean anything. We weren't even looking at him."

Beside them, Beta climbed in behind the truck's wheel, slamming the cab door shut.

"Start the engine," Chiun commanded.

"I don't want to make him suspicious," Remo said. "I'll give him a little head start first."

All at once Beta's truck lurched out of its space. For something that looked to have been pieced together in a junkyard, the truck moved with surprising speed.

Weaving in and out of parking-lot traffic, the truck flew toward the exit. In seconds, it had bounced back out onto the main street.

"Is that enough of a head start for you?" the Master of Sinanju asked aridly.

Remo wasn't listening. He had already twisted the key in the ignition. Throwing the car in gear, he slammed his foot on the gas, flying out of their space after the fleeing truck.

Drivers were forced to squeal their brakes as the big sedan flew across the lot. Horns honked angry protests as Remo twisted in and out of traffic.

Flying off the speed bump at the exit, the rented car landed in the street, a hail of sparks spitting from the vehicle's undercarriage.

Beta RAM was already far down the road. Swerving to avoid striking cars and pedestrians, Remo raced after the fleeing prophet of Salvion.

22

Arthur Ford had drained fifty batteries already, and Elizu Roote's condition hadn't changed one volt.

The Army private was breathing shallowly. He didn't seem in any immediate danger, but he remained pale and his skin was still clammy to the touch.

The cables connected to his neck continued to transfer power from the batteries to his body.

At first Ford used the tester on every battery just to make certain they had been drained. Eventually he had only checked sporadically, then gave up testing them altogether. The batteries were fine, it was Roote who no longer worked properly.

The time it took to suck the batteries dry had become progressively longer. Although the first few had been drained in an instant, the past thirty or so had taken increasingly longer amounts of time to deplete.

Still, Roote slept.

Forte was beginning to think that it might be necessary to turn his alien over to the military after all. Maybe they had deliberately done something to his physiology to make him dependent on them. It was also possible that if the ship that had crashed at Roswell was Roote's, something might be aboard that could yet save his life.

Even as he considered his options, Ford continued to drag batteries into place. He hooked them up almost out of habit now. When each was done, he'd drag it dutifully away, pulling another one through the dirt to his alien patient.

Arthur Ford had completely lost count of what battery he was on when Elizu Roote finally opened his eyes.

Ford didn't know how long he had lain there like that. He only noticed the washed-out pink eyes of the private when he glanced over, bored.

Roote didn't blink. He stared up blankly at the tin roof of the shack.

His breathing was more determined now. Like someone who had just returned from a long trek through rough terrain.

Crawling on his knees, Ford moved swiftly over to Roote's side.

"Are you feeling better?" Ford asked hopefully.

The eyes twitched, moving spastically. A single blink followed. All at once, the eyes rolled in their sockets, turning slowly over to Arthur Ford. Trailing in their wake, Roote's head lolled in the same direction.

"I saved your life," Ford whispered proudly. "They were trying to kill you. But I revived you."

Roote didn't hear.

As Ford watched, the private's eyes rolled back dramatically, irises eclipsed by fluttering lids.

Consciousness fled once more.

To Arthur Ford, it didn't matter. He had just gotten all the encouragement he needed. Gone were any thoughts of turning Roote over to the Army. The treatment Ford had prescribed was obviously the proper one.

Scurrying back through the dirt, Ford collected the next battery. Working feverishly, he redoubled his efforts to revive his precious alien.

23

Harold Smith was sitting anxiously before his computer when he heard the familiar muted chirping sound emanate from his tattered leather briefcase.

His cellular phone automatically rerouted phone calls from both CURE's dedicated White House line and the special line used by Remo and Chiun. Smith hoped that it was not the president who was calling as he dug out the phone and unclipped the collapsible mouthpiece.

"Smitty, we need help, fast," Remo's familiar voice announced.

"What is the situation?"

"The situation is that car you rented is a piece of flaming horse dung. We were tailing one of the Camp Earth nuts and it overheated. We lost him somewhere off of I-25."

Smith was already typing at his laptop. "Are you able to acquire alternate transportation?"

"I already boosted a car, if that's what you mean," Remo replied. "But the guy we were chasing is long gone."

"That is unfortunate. But at least you have narrowed our search parameters. Where did you last see him?''

Remo told Smith they were a few miles away from an abandoned diner near the Caballo Mountains.

''Stay near this number,'' Smith said. ''I will get back to you.''

Terminating the call, Smith placed the phone on the desk near his laptop. Using the CURE computers, he began issuing orders to the Fort Joy command.

ROOTE WAS AWAKE AGAIN. The private's eyes appeared to be more focused now as he took in his squalid surroundings. After scanning the entire one-room structure, his gaze finally settled on the eager face of Arthur Ford.

''You're looking a lot better,'' Ford enthused.

Roote closed his eyes wearily.

The Army private had seen the many batteries lying in the dirt of the shack. Apparently too weak to speak, he beckoned Ford to bring one of the batteries over to him.

Ford was eager to oblige. He shoved the heavy object through the dirt to Elizu Roote's makeshift sickbed.

Once the battery was in place, Roote opened his tired eyes. Struggling at the effort, he lifted one hand from the sand at his side and dropped it atop the battery.

The hum was loud and abrupt. As it had been the first time Ford patched into Roote's system.

There was a brief blue sparking around the private's metal fingertips. As soon as it started, it was over. The battery was dead.

The change was instantaneous. A glow suffused Roote's pale cheeks. He closed his eyes once more, a smile playing at the corners of his thin lips.

Panting, Elizu Roote said but one soft, nearly inaudible word: "More."

FROM THE PARKING LOT of a lonely desert gas station, Remo and Chiun watched the helicopters soar out of the thin red twilight clouds in the east.

It seemed that everything from Fort Joy still capable of flight had been thrown at the Caballo Mountains. Almost thirty aircraft of several different types flew in formation. The collective sound was deafening.

"Smitty isn't taking any chances," Remo commented as the choppers raced overhead.

The aircraft soared off toward the mountains, black in contrast to the brilliant setting sun.

"Learn from your Emperor's lesson," Chiun said. He was looking up at the passing aircraft, face impassive.

Remo sighed. "I promised to give you first crack at Roote," he said.

"Do not forget," Chiun replied.

"If I did, would you let me live it down?" Remo asked.

"No," the Master of Sinanju replied simply.

"So there we go," Remo surrendered.

"Assuming you were alive afterward," Chiun added somberly.

His hazel eyes were unreadable slits as he watched the helicopters rattle off into the nearby hills.

HE WAS ADDICTED. There was no doubt in his mind.

Roote hadn't been certain of it until now. But he felt the change come over him with each successive battery.

He had tried a few different drugs in the past, but never really liked them. Alcohol had been his mind-altering substance of choice. And the buzz he was getting right now was not unlike the feeling he got when drunk.

The squalid room seemed to rise up from the shadows around him. It was as if with each successive battery someone were gradually turning a dimmer switch higher.

But there was no switch. He was the only source of true power in the tiny metal shed.

An addict. A freak.

A monster.

They had made him like this. When his power

was drained, he had collapsed. A marionette without strings.

A fail-safe? Probably not. They had never expected him to be careless enough to allow himself to be grounded.

Lying in the dirt, Roote dropped a hand onto yet another battery. The jolt was immediate. Even pleasurable. It was taking time, but his capacitors were slowly filling up once more. His implanted systems were coming back on line.

The dizziness and nausea he had been experiencing since regaining consciousness were gradually receding. And as the sickness fled in the growing light around him, the voices scurried up out of the darkness of his mind.

There was panting somewhere near the door of the shed.

Roote rolled his head to one side, seeking the source of the sound.

Arthur Ford was breathless from his exertions. He was scurrying around the interior of the shed, hauling the remaining batteries over to where Roote lay.

Roote had enough power stored already. He could satisfy the killing urge within him.

But Ford was a male. There wouldn't be much pleasure there. When the chorus of voices began their song of death, Roote found that women were always preferable to men. The difference was that between simple fun and pure rapture.

Besides, he needed Ford. For now.

"Give me another," Roote commanded.

With his returning strength, his voice had gotten stronger.

"There aren't many more," Ford puffed.

When the inhabitants of Camp Earth had brought their initial supply of car batteries to the shed, those that wouldn't fit inside were left out front. Over the course of the past hour, the ufologist had brought all of the remaining batteries inside.

The private had an unquenchable thirst for electricity. Ford could see that they weren't going to have enough to bring him back to full power. He had dragged the last of the drained batteries outside and deposited the final fully charged batteries just inside the door.

Roote pushed himself up to a sitting position. Ford had removed the jumper cables from his neck as soon as the private had been able to use his gold finger pads.

"Help me up," Roote insisted.

Ford hesitated. "Are you sure you're okay?"

Roote didn't respond. Verbally.

He aimed a single index finger in Ford's direction. Eyes locking on target, he sent a small bolt of energy toward the door beyond Ford. The brilliant streak of lightning struck the metal frame and instantly coursed all around the interior of the metal shed.

Ford cowered beneath the blue glowing tin. He felt like a turkey on Thanksgiving day, trapped inside a massive oven.

The electricity abruptly sought its way to the floor, pounding harmlessly into the dirt at their feet.

Ford didn't need to be asked a second time.

The UFO aficionado immediately hurried over to Roote. Grabbing him around the back and up under the armpits, he hauled the Army private to his feet.

"Over there," Roote said, nodding to the door.

Ford helped him across the room. He thought they were leaving, but Roote had him pause just inside the doorway.

The private lowered his hands, palms flat, over the remaining fresh batteries. There were only about ten left.

Ford felt the hair rise on his forearms as a powerful burst of bluish electricity leapt from the tops of all the fresh batteries at once, surging up into Roote's finger pads.

Ford watched in wonder as the batteries rose slowly off the ground. Roote was like a magician doing some remarkable levitation trick. But the sleight of hand was real.

The perfectly pressed rectangles of dirt where the batteries had sat became visible as the heavy objects hovered for a moment several inches off the ground.

There was another loud hum—that of all the batteries losing power at once. Abruptly the electrical flow cut off. As one, the batteries thudded back to the earthen floor.

Leaning against the door frame, Roote took a deep, cleansing breath. He seemed stronger now. More in control.

Hooded eyes settled on Arthur Ford.

"That's better," Roote drawled with a smile. "You got more of them things?"

"Those were the last ones," Ford admitted nervously.

Roote closed his eyes for a moment. His head was clearing. Even so, he still needed more power.

"They got generators around here?" he asked.

"Not that I've seen," Ford said.

The private opened his eyes. They settled on Ford's jeep, which the ufologist had parked just outside the open door of the hut.

"Over there," Roote ordered, pointing with his chin.

Ford knew enough not to refuse.

Grabbing Roote by one arm, he helped the hobbling killer out into the dying sunlight. He leaned Roote against the fender of the jeep.

"Open her up," Roote commanded.

Roote's intention was clear. And it was just as clear to Ford that he was helpless to stop him. Reluctantly he lifted the hood of the jeep high into the warm evening air.

Like some sort of perverse faith healer, Roote laid hands on the battery while it was still hooked into the engine. He drained it in a sparking instant.

Although he said nothing, Ford looked dispirited as he dropped the hood back into place.

"You-all had best call Triple-A," Roote slurred through his Cheshire cat grin. "Any more cars?"

Ford nodded. "The Camp Earthers keep them on the other side of the huts. Near the road."

The killer pushed away from the jeep. He accepted Ford's assistance, though he was almost strong enough to stand on his own.

"Let's go power walkin'," Elizu Roote enthused.

As dusk settled around them, the two men struck off across Camp Earth.

BETA RAM RACED through the growing twilight up the winding path to Camp Earth.

Even though he had lost his tail several miles before, his heart still thudded in his chest. The sedan had chased him all the way from Las Cruces to the Caballo foothills. The entire time his pursuers were behind him, Beta had the distinct impression that they could have overtaken him at any moment. The driver of the other car—whoever he was—matched Beta's every move flawlessly. It was as if the two vehicles were wired to the same steering wheel and gas pedal.

He was dead. It could have been anyone: Squiltas, Army, any of a number of shadow government agencies. They were going to get him. No doubt about it.

But then the miracle happened. Thick billowing clouds of gray-white smoke began to pour from his pursuers' hood. It was as though Salvion had personally intervened to save Beta.

They had broken off. Fallen back.

As they pulled over to the side of the road, Beta had stomped down even harder on the gas pedal of his rickety truck. His only thought was to put as much distance as possible between himself and the two strange men.

It was stupid, he told himself in retrospect, to have taken the direction he had. They wanted him to lead them to Camp Earth. He had practically done that.

Beta remonstrated himself as he drove rapidly up the steady, boulder-lined incline, a plume of heavy dust rising in his wake. Stacks of batteries bounced against his tailgate, threatening to break free.

Even as he chastised himself, he was shifting the blame. It was Arthur Ford's fault. Him and that alien of his.

After all, when pursued by the government, where else would Beta have gone? Camp Earth represented safety to him. It was his haven from the doomed world. Of course he would go there when in danger.

Beta had gone into town hundreds of times without any problem. The Squiltas and their Association of Evil were afraid of Salvion. And since they knew the Being of Light protected Beta RAM, they left Beta and his followers alone. Because of the divine protection afforded Beta by Salvion, the Camp Earth leader had for years avoided a pitched laser battle every time he went to the local Safeway for toilet paper. The only difference this day was Roote.

For some reason, they were after Arthur Ford's alien friend. They'd followed Beta in order to reach their prize. As he raced along the twisting mountain road, Beta RAM was beginning to regret not turning Roote over to the authorities.

A sudden bounce. A twist in the road.

Beta turned the steering wheel sharply, taking the curve in a great skid of dust and sand.

Flooring the gas once more, he lurched ahead.

As the truck closed in on his encampment, he caught a flash of light in his rearview mirror.

For a sick moment he thought that the government men were back. But when he looked at the sliver of mirror that was held in its casing by strips of ratty gray duct tape, he realized that it was much, much worse.

There was light all right. *Lights.* But they weren't on the ground. They were in the blackening sky behind him.

Running lights. From an alien spacecraft!

Blaming Ford and Roote, Beta RAM slammed both feet firmly on the gas pedal. The truck was already moving at a dangerously high speed on the mountain trail.

Its speed failed to increase one jot. While its panicked driver screamed in terror, the battered truck raced closer to the camp. Ahead of the hostile starship.

Behind Beta RAM, the Fort Joy Army helicopter roared forward in hot pursuit.

HAROLD SMITH PICKED UP the phone on the first ring.

"Report," his lemony voice commanded.

"We've got a truck matching the description you gave us, sir," came the crisp reply.

The colonel who reported to him didn't know that the man he was speaking to was in a lab on base.

"Where?"

"Near Caballo Lake Percha, northwest of Grama. He's moving fast. Chopper's hanging back for now. Should we concentrate our search in that area?"

Smith considered. "No," he said finally. "Recall the others. Have only the one helicopter follow the vehicle back to its camp. When the location is confirmed, call me."

"Yes, sir."

They both cut the connection at the same time.

After Smith had placed the cell phone next to his computer, he tapped the plastic case with one idle finger.

He knew from a strong instinct honed by years of experience that this was the truck Remo had been following.

Smith even knew the owner's name. He had gotten the credit-card records from the Las Cruces House Warehouse store. The vehicle belonged to one Beta RAM.

The name appeared on the bar screen of his laptop computer. Smith's face pinched in displeasure as he read the obviously invented appellation.

Another lunatic to throw on the ever growing heap. Beta RAM could join the ranks of Chesterfield, Roote and Arthur Ford. Smith had met too many insane men in the past two days. It would be up to Remo to thin their numbers.

A steady gray hand clutched the cell phone. The CURE director waited for the call that would send Remo after Roote. He only hoped Remo was up to the challenge.

24

The inhabitants of Camp Earth had been told by their leader to stay away from the alien in their midst. Reluctantly they had obeyed the command. For the better part of the day, they'd been hunched before their huts, occasionally craning their necks toward the distant shack where the creature was being nursed back to health.

Beta RAM's edict was promptly forgotten the moment the alien appeared in their shabby make-shift village.

Elizu Roote was like a conquering hero as he was helped past the ramshackle homes of the Camp Earthers.

His stride seemed to improve with every step. At first he was like a stroke victim who was going through the arduous process of relearning to walk. By the time he and Arthur Ford reached the motley collection of Camp Earth cars, he was walking largely on his own.

At an order from the alien, the hoods of all the cars were sprung open.

The nine vehicles were arranged in a tidy line.

Roote walked down to the middle car. Stretching out his hands broadly to either side, he instinctively tripped his internal circuitry.

The flash was blinding as streaks of bluish lightning arced crazily from beneath the grimy hoods of all nine vehicles.

Hoods shuddered, some dropping shut, as the bionically enhanced killer sucked every vestige of stored power from the cars.

It was over in seconds.

A few faint puffs of smoke rose from the now dead engines, lifting gently into the warm evening air.

There was a pervasive silence for a few long seconds. Then, all at once, a single engine seemed to hum to life.

The sound took all of them by surprise. Even Elizu Roote seemed puzzled.

But the noise did not come from the line of Camp Earth cars.

"Intruder alert! Intruder alert!"

The panicked voice rose from down the road.

One of the sentries came running toward the crowd of Camp Earthers from his lookout post, his special night-vision binoculars clasped firmly in his hand.

"On the road," the man announced, breathless. "*Beta.*"

"It's about time," Ford complained. He was already wondering how he was going to sneak one of Beta's freshly-purchased batteries into his own jeep.

"He's not *alone*," the man cried frantically.

He was too out of breath to explain. And a moment later, his breathless silence didn't matter.

As the crowd watched, Beta RAM's truck suddenly broke into sight around the rocky outcropping that ran in a jagged semicircle around the upper edge of the main Camp Earth road.

Beta drew up to them a moment later, screaming even before he got out of the cab.

"I've got company!" he yelled.

As Beta threw his hand out behind him, the breathless camp sentry was also pointing to the black sky.

Dozens of eyes looked up into the post-twilight.

They saw the lights immediately. As the crowd gasped in horror, Beta wheeled on the Camp Earth visitors.

"This is all your fault," Beta accused Ford. He shoved the ufologist roughly, knocking him into the side of his rusted truck. "You brought him here. Now the Squiltas are coming after me."

Ford glanced at the lights. "Squiltas?" he scoffed. "Are you nuts? It's probably his mother ship." He nodded to Roote. "They're coming to take him back now that *I've* saved his life."

As punctuation, he shoved Beta RAM back.

"Denier of Salvion!" Beta snarled, pushing Ford.

"Salvion's an asshole!" Ford screamed. He pushed Beta with both hands.

Beta gasped. "*Blasphemer!* You'll never get on the ark. No matter how much you beg when the Squiltas finally destroy this benighted rock."

"Your *mother* is a Squilta!" Ford shouted.

That was enough. To have his mother thrown in with the sworn intergalactic enemies of mankind was too much for Beta RAM. Screaming in anger, Beta tackled Ford. The two of them fell to the dusty ground in a grunting heap.

As the pair of UFO enthusiasts rolled back and forth through the dirt grunting Klingon curses, Elizu Roote was staring up at the approaching aircraft.

The chopper came in from the direction of Fort Joy. From the sound it made, he figured it was most likely an older Huey.

They had found him.

Roote would need more juice if he hoped to get out of this alive. Fast. Time to inspire the troops.

Roote picked someone at random. It was the flat-faced Indian girl whom Beta RAM had soiled and later thought to exclude from the trip to New Earth.

As the two men continued to wrestle on the ground, Elizu Roote sent a two-handed bolt of electricity pounding into the girl's chest.

The shock lifted her high off the ground, flinging her backward. She landed on her ample derriere in the dirt next to the two wrestling men.

On the ground, Ford and Beta froze, arms locked around one another's throats. They were covered with dirt.

"Open those boxes. Now!" Roote commanded the crowd.

The Camp Earthers didn't need to be told twice.

Leaping over the twitching body, they descended on the truck in a mad huddle of arms and legs, wrenching at tightly glued cardboard flaps. The batteries were quickly dumped out and passed on to eager, grabbing hands at the open tailgate. They were arranged in hasty lines on the path.

As he had done with the cars, Roote positioned himself before the rows of batteries. He lowered his hands.

The crackle of energy in the warm air was palpable.

As Roote drained the power from the batteries, the lone helicopter flew in closer. Dust thrown up by the rotors pelted roughly against the faces of the Camp Earth residents.

Blades slicing madly at the sky, the chopper swept over their heads, banking south before swooping back toward the dark eastern sky.

It didn't get far.

One hand remained over the batteries while the other rose toward the departing craft. A single violent burst of electricity exploded from Roote's fingertips, skipping the distance between him and the helicopter in a heartbeat.

The blast caught the chopper in the tail.

Engine spluttering, the helicopter plummeted amid a hail of sparks behind the rising plateau. A moment later an explosion rocked the night. A single plume of fire rose up from beyond the rocky ledge. It was followed by a prolonged rumbling as the aircraft pounded in an awesomely slow crawl down the steep embankment. Next came an eerie, stunned silence.

Slowly Elizu Roote turned to the shocked Camp Earthers.

"Well, if they didn't know I was here before, I reckon they do now," he said.

The demonic smile he flashed drained all warmth from the evening air.

FORTUNATELY THE HELICOPTER had spied the Camp Earth cooking fires minutes before Elizu Roote blasted it from the sky. The chopper had quickly radioed the location to Fort Joy, where the message was relayed to Harold W. Smith. Smith in turn contacted Remo.

Ten minutes later Remo was racing along the highway in his stolen Camaro.

The Master of Sinanju sat in the passenger's seat, his hazel eyes fixed on the dark contours of the mountain range that skirted the desolate road.

"I see nothing," Chiun announced. "Were not Smith's legionnaires supposed to rendezvous with us?"

"That was the original plan," Remo said tightly. "But Smitty says they lost radio contact with the chopper at Fort Joy after it checked in."

"Given the incompetence of the gaspot who commanded that garrison, they are probably halfway to Mexico by now."

"I think they've hauled it together now that Chesterfield's pulled a disappearing act," Remo said. He was scanning the sky for any sign of the helicopter that would take them to Camp Earth. "All these mountains look alike to me. In case we don't meet up with them, are you sure you can follow Smith's directions?"

The Master of Sinanju fixed him a baleful glare. "If Mad Harold was sane when issuing his instructions, I will find the site. With or without the assistance of his unreliable soldiery."

An explosion of stars had taken firm hold of the night sky by the time they arrived in the general area Smith had described. Remo had been driving at speeds in excess of 120 miles per hour until now. As they ripped through this new area of desert, he slowed to eighty.

They had just flown around the base of a hill that looked like a giant's foot dropped in the middle of the road when the Master of Sinanju's head suddenly snapped to the right.

"Halt!" the old Korean commanded.

Remo left twin strips of smoking black rubber fifty yards long in his haste to follow the order.

"What is it?" Remo asked once they had come to a stop.

Chiun raised a silencing hand. "Backward," the Master of Sinanju insisted.

Dutifully Remo put the car in reverse. He backed all the way down the long black skid marks until he was at the point where Chiun had first called out. When they stopped once again, the Master of Sinanju aimed a perilously long finger to the soft shoulder of the road.

Leaning over to see out the passenger's window, Remo spotted the fresh tire tracks in the sand.

"So what?" Remo asked.

"They belong to the vehicle that eluded us," Chiun announced with certainty. He immediately thought better of his choice of words. "Eluded you," he amended.

Remo didn't seem convinced.

"Are you sure?" he asked. "We're wasting valuable time if you're just going to take us around in circles on some wild-goose chase."

"Need I remind you that you chased a goose into the desert yesterday, only to find a jackass."

Remo's face clouded. "I didn't hear you objecting too strenuously at the time."

"That is because I wished for you to get this crazed-gander pursuit out of your system once and for all. Now we go after our true quarry."

Smiling faintly, Remo shook his head. "Bullshit artist," he muttered under his breath. He thought he had spoken softly enough that Chiun hadn't heard.

"Coming from you, O Bullheaded One, I will take that as a compliment," Chiun announced loudly. Settling back in his seat he waved a bony hand dramatically toward the mountain path. "Drive, bovine!"

Steering off the main road, Remo tore up the shadowy mountain trail.

25

Pry bars were carried hurriedly from a dilapidated storage area near Beta RAM's hut. The heavy iron rods were dropped unceremoniously to the sand, followed by many of the residents of Camp Earth.

Crawling, squatting, sliding across the dirt, they worked feverishly to brush aside the sand and clay from the large wooden lid. The pry bars were hastily shoved into the space between lid and lip, and the nails securing the cover to the thick wooden walls popped free one by one. With a final, furious wrench, the lid was ripped free and tossed aside.

Most of the residents of Camp Earth had seen a movie years before where survivalists like themselves had hidden weapons in a hole in the ground. When the Camp Earthers had first moved into the wilds of New Mexico, they'd decided to copy their cinematic counterparts. No one realized that in the film the weapons cache had been carved in dirt.

It took months of dynamite and pickaxes for the Camp Earthers to clear the hole they stood in now. It hadn't occurred to any of them to dig where the sand was deep—two hundred yards away on the plateau whereon squatted the hut in which Arthur Ford had revived his precious alien.

Dust-covered tarps were pulled away. Automatic weapons were passed up out of the burrow. They were quickly distributed among the eager, grabbing crowd.

"Remember," Beta RAM called to his followers as he watched the men working in the hole. "This is not yet a confirmed alien invasion. We could be dealing with creatures in humanoid shape or humans in league with aliens. There is also a very remote outside chance that they are all humans."

One man snorted contemptuously. "Figure the odds."

A few more in the crowd laughed out loud at this third, outlandish possibility.

Beta RAM raised a silencing hand. "Just be prepared for all the typical alien deception." He began ticking off the possibilities on his fingers. "We're talking mind control, alien possession, false holographic images, transmutation, shape alteration. The works."

The residents of Camp Earth waited impatiently as he listed all of the most obvious alien ruses.

When Beta RAM was through issuing his warnings, he began dispatching men and women whom he deemed part of the first watch to the periphery of the camp. About half of the Camp Earth residents remained behind near the huts.

As the men were dispersing, Beta leaned down

into the pit. He pulled a pair of M-16s out by their khaki straps.

Carrying a gun in each hand, Beta wandered back through the bustling activity in the camp up to the lonely plateau shack.

Ford sat on one of the drained batteries before the hut's open door. He had decided that his chances for surviving the next few hours hinged on his proximity to Roote. The closer the better.

Ford looked up nervously as Beta approached. He didn't relax when he saw the automatic weapons in the Camp Earth leader's hands.

Beta stopped before him, looking down disdainfully at Arthur Ford.

"He's inside if you want to talk to him," Ford grumbled.

"He can handle himself," Beta replied, voice flat. "Here." Beta held out an M-16. "You're going to need it."

Ford accepted the rifle. He started to lean it against the side of the hut but suddenly thought better of the idea. He placed it across his lap.

"You really fixed us up good," Beta complained. "My people were happy to wait for Salvion's ark. Now you've dragged us into the middle of some alien war."

"I don't think so." Ford glanced at the open door. He pitched his voice low. "I think this is a government thing. When I got lost in the desert yesterday, the two guys who found me were looking for *him*."

"What two guys?"

It wasn't Beta RAM who asked the question.

Two sets of sick eyes turned to the door of the hut.

Elizu Roote had apparently adjusted to his new power levels. Standing in the open doorway, he appeared to Ford to be as good as new. The thought failed to comfort the ufologist.

"Just a couple of guys," Ford said, standing. "I saw one of them at the airport in Roswell the day before yesterday. A really old Chinaman. He was with another guy who I'm sure was from the government. Three-piece gray suit and everything. He had bureaucrat written all over him."

Beta didn't seem interested in the second man. "The Chinese guy," he said to Ford. "Was he wearin' some kind of crazy dress?"

"I think they call them kimonos," Ford said, nodding.

Beta glanced excitedly at Roote. "He was one of the ones that followed me from Las Cruces. I lost them a little while before I picked up the spacecraft tail."

"That was a helicopter," Ford said, rolling his eyes.

"They used their energy protection grid to throw off a false image," Beta explained dismissively, as if Ford were a complete idiot. "Forget about the ship for now. The old one was with a young guy. He was kind of scary looking. Had the deadest eyes I've ever seen."

Ford nodded to Roote. "He was the other one in the desert. They were both looking for you at Fort Joy. Luckily I saved you before they could get to you."

"Alien Detection and Eradication Unit?" Beta said, nodding to Ford.

"Probably," Ford agreed. "ADEU still civilian?"

"As far as I know," Beta replied.

Ford shrugged. "The military is in this, too. Could be the Army's Special Extraterrestrial Tactical Division."

"SETD?" Beta said, whistling. "Those guys are heavy-duty. I hear they reverse engineered a ton of junk from the Roswell craft. They've got alien technology that's light-years ahead of anything terrestrial."

"If they're coming after you, you'd better watch your step," Ford cautioned Roote. Beta nodded his agreement.

Elizu Roote wasn't even listening to the fools chatter.

"I met the young one already," he drawled softly. "Zapped him at the Last Chance a couple days ago."

Ford and Beta both seemed surprised. "Did he have any special gadgets? Any alien hardware?"

"Just a guy in a T-shirt. Thought I killed him."

"Maybe he has a personal energy field," suggested Beta. "I hear SETD has those."

"He didn't have nuthin'." Roote shrugged. "Just a guy in a T-shirt. Nuthin' special."

"He's the first person who's come up against you and lived that I know of," Arthur Ford said worriedly. "The fact he's still alive makes him special."

Elizu Roote didn't seem concerned.

"Won't be special for long," he said. His matter-of-fact tone chilled the spines of both alien enthusiasts. As the two men shuddered in fear, Elizu Roote wandered undisturbed back inside his tin shed.

REMO REGRETTED his choice of vehicle the instant he turned his stolen car onto the winding mountain path.

The Camaro took the dips and ruts like a bronco that had spent the day slurping from a spiked trough. When the nose wasn't dropping precipitously forward with every tiny hollow, the lightweight rear end was sliding back and forth as if they were driving on a skating rink. For the entire trip into the hills, the low undercarriage scraped a furrow along the dirt path.

The drag coming from beneath the car was so bad, Remo could imagine some enterprising Indians planting corn in the dirt they'd plowed up.

In the bucket seat beside him, the Master of Sinanju had placed one delicate finger against the ceiling to keep from being thrown around the interior of the car.

"This carriage is appalling," Chiun complained over the grinding and bumping of the Camaro.

"Yeah, but it looks cool," Remo pointed out.

"Laud its frigid appearance to your undertaker," the Master of Sinanju retorted. "One would have to be a lunatic to purchase one of these contrivances."

"Don't look at me. I didn't buy, I stole."

As a precaution, once they were only a few hundred yards up the path, Remo had turned off the car's headlights. The engine sound remained loud, but at least if Roote was above them somewhere, he wouldn't have as easy a target to follow.

In spite of the darkness, Remo and Chiun both saw the road clearly, although Remo was still having trouble with distances. The path pitched crazily ahead of them with every uncertain bounce of the Camaro's shocks.

Driving far too fast for safety along a particularly treacherous strip of road, Remo steered around a huge knot of tumbled boulders. The burning wreckage of an Army helicopter suddenly appeared before them, flying toward the nose of the car at incredible speed.

As soon as he'd spotted the crashed aircraft, Remo's heightened senses took over. Almost before his mind knew what was happening, he was slamming on the brakes.

The car completed a 360-degree turn as it skidded to a sudden stop on the desolate mountain road. While it was spinning, Remo heard a loud snap from beneath the car.

The Camaro finally slid to a stop, nudging the flaming Huey.

Chiun and Remo were both out of the car in an instant. Remo dropped down to his knees, looking for the source of the noise he had heard while they were twirling.

"I am not getting in that vehicle with you again," Chiun announced, breathless.

"Doesn't matter," Remo said, getting up. He dusted off his hands. "Transmission just dropped out."

Remo walked over to the Huey. He didn't expect to find any survivors, but he wanted to be certain. The Master of Sinanju trailed behind him.

"You are like one of those elderly people I see on television. Your driving skills have deteriorated with age, yet you refuse to relinquish your license."

"I got us here all right, didn't I?"

There were only two soldiers within the burning wreckage. Both were dead.

"We do not even know where here is," Chiun announced.

"Yes, we do," Remo said. Turning away from the bodies, he looked up the hill. The charred, mangled path the helicopter had taken as it crashed down the hillside was clearly visible. "Here is where we punch Roote's ticket once and for all."

His face a cruel mask of rigid determination, Remo headed for the rocky slope. And the killer that waited above.

26

Arthur Ford was beginning to second-guess his decision to bring his alien to Camp Earth.

The men and women were willing to help; that was clear. They marched back and forth at the edge of the camp, their silhouettes visible in the flickering light of a dozen separate fires. But they were still hopelessly mired in the pap Beta RAM had been feeding them.

It might have been better for Ford if he had taken Roote out into the desert on his own. They would have found a way to survive somehow.

Too late to go back now.

As he walked along through the shadowy night, Ford adjusted the M-16 slung across his shoulder. The strap was biting into his skin.

Technically he was not part of either watch. However, on further consideration he had decided that he couldn't sit and wait for the invasion to come. He had to be out there. With the troops. *Away* from Elizu Roote.

Not that Ford had suddenly become a doer. He was just having second thoughts about his theory that his safety hinged on his proximity to Roote. It had occurred to Ford that if government forces were going to descend on the camp to find Roote, perhaps next to the alien was not the best place to be after all.

And so Ford was away. Far, far away.

He strolled along the farthest point from Roote's tiny shack.

Touring the perimeter, Ford came upon a pair of men near the line of crippled Camp Earth cars. They were arguing in hushed voices.

"You saw what he did," said the younger of the two. "He's a Being of Light, just like Beta said."

"I don't know," said the other man. He was in his late forties and wore a shirt emblazoned with a single grimy marijuana leaf. "I guess it could be."

"Could be, my ass," the young one scoffed.

Startled by a sudden footstep nearby, the two of them spun to face Ford. When the young man turned to him, Ford saw that his T-shirt was decorated with the rough sketch of an alien head common to abductees—lightbulb head, large almond-shaped eyes, narrow neck.

The men relaxed when they saw Arthur Ford.

"You scared me, man," the young one exhaled.

"Anything yet?" Ford pressed.

"Nope. It's as quiet as a black hole out here," the older one announced.

Ford nodded his approval. "Stay alert," he commanded.

Turning, he headed back for the collection of huts.

As he walked away from the two guards, Ford was disturbed to find that he was suddenly getting the eerie sensation that someone was watching him.

He glanced over his shoulder at the two men. Neither was looking in his direction. They were both staring out into the inky blackness. Spooky.

Shivering, Arthur Ford picked up his pace, hurrying for the safety of the campfires.

"THAT'S THAT DIP from the desert," Remo whispered. He nodded to the retreating form of Arthur Ford.

"I have eyes," the Master of Sinanju replied.

They had scaled the sheer face of the mountainside, skirting Camp Earth entirely. The two of them were lying on a bluff overlooking the encampment.

From their vantage point, they had a commanding view of the entire camp. Beyond the cliff at the edge of Camp Earth, the sparkling, midnight-black waters of the Rio Grande shimmered off into the distance in either direction.

"So I guess this is where he brought Roote, but I don't see the psycho anywhere." He squinted down at the camp.

"How can you tell?" Chiun asked. "One dung beetle is indistinguishable from another."

"Come on, Chiun," Remo said. "Smith showed

you his file picture. Tell me if I'm missing something."

"You are missing a brain. And I do not see him, either," Chiun admitted, frowning deeply.

"So he must be in one of the buildings," Remo reasoned. "I'll start at the far end. You start down there. We'll meet in the middle."

He began to rise, but the Master of Sinanju placed a restraining hand on his forearm.

"Have you forgotten our bargain?"

Remo slumped back down. "I'm fine," he insisted.

"You mask it well, my son, I will admit," Chiun said softly. "But I have ears. Your heart yet beats incorrectly. Even now, when your eyes fail, you ask me to see for you. In spite of your protestations, you are not completely well."

Though it bothered him to admit it, Remo knew it was true. He had healed greatly since his encounter with Roote, but he wasn't yet one hundred percent.

Sighing, he settled back to the ground.

"Remember what I told you," Remo insisted morosely. "The guy packs a wallop. Watch yourself."

"Your concern is heartening, but not necessary," Chiun said, standing. "I will unplug the bulb from your lightning bug and return forthwith."

Gathering up the hems of his skirts, the Master of Sinanju marched down the hillside.

Remo followed him with his eyes. As his teacher's back faded into the shadows beneath him, Remo said a silent prayer to Chiun's ancestors. For both of them.

WALTER MALPA HAD BEEN claiming for many years that he was the victim of multiple alien abductions. He had claimed this even after his parents had thrown him out of their home. He claimed it after his family and friends had disowned him. He continued to claim it even after he'd lost his job.

But even though he claimed it loudly to everyone he met, there had always been a small, shameful part of Walter that actually doubted his own story. A tiny part of him that thought everyone might be right. He might actually be crazy.

That was, until today.

He had seen with his own eyes what Elizu Roote had done. The rest of the Camp Earthers could argue until the cows came home whether the aircraft had been a helicopter or a spaceship, but either way it didn't matter. Roote had blasted it out of the sky.

Elizu Roote was the real deal. A genuine, bona fide, absolute, definite space alien.

The only thing that troubled Walter was the fact that Roote didn't match the typical alien depictions.

Traditionally aliens had long fingers, large heads and big, elongated eyes. At least that was the way they were always being sketched. That was the way Walter claimed to remember them after each of his many kidnappings.

Walter felt that if Roote had only fit the proper alien description, everything would finally make sense. He could go back to his family and prove once and for all that he was not a head case. And that little niggling spot of self-doubt would be banished from his mind forever.

Walter sat on the hood of one of the Camp Earth cars thinking of proper aliens. As he cradled his M-16 in his lap, he stared blankly into the shadows down the road.

A real shame. A crying, crying shame.

As he sat lamenting his misfortune, Walter became aware of a gentle wash of movement at the very edge of his vision.

It was as if someone were slowly turning a control knob on reality, bringing forward from the darkness a shape that had always been there.

When the strange congealing of shadows was complete, Walter Malpa was startled to find himself confronting a genuine space alien.

The creature was dressed in a glittering silver robe. A hairless head was balanced atop the most delicate neck Walter had ever seen. Even the eyes were the right shape—teardrops turned on their sides, tugged up to tiny ears.

Walter slid off the car.

So enraptured was Walter with the wizened figure that strode toward him from the darkness, he didn't even realize he had abandoned his gun. The

M-16 lay on the hood of the car on which he had been sitting.

Mouth hanging open in shock, he tapped the shoulder of the man with him. The other guard had been looking in the opposite direction.

''What?'' the man said, turning.

Seeing the approaching creature, he stopped dead.

The second man looked at the alien image on Walter's T-shirt. He glanced back at the strange apparition. His jaw dropped open, as well.

Neither sentry said a word as the silvery phantom slid up the path and stopped directly before the two men.

The creature was so tiny, it had to lift its head in order to look them in the eye. When it spoke, its voice was a lyrical singsong.

''Take me to your leader,'' the Master of Sinanju commanded firmly.

ARTHUR FORD SPIED Chiun while the old man was still conversing with the two guards. He was stunned that the men didn't fire at him. His shock gave way to horror when he realized that one of the men wasn't even carrying a gun. For some reason, he had discarded it.

The other man still held his weapon, but it was down at his side, hanging by its strap. The second guard obviously had no intention of using it.

Mind control. That was the only possibility. Beta

RAM was right. Remo and Chiun *were* extrater-restrials.

The invasion of Camp Earth had begun, and their troops were falling under the spell of the invading army.

Roote would have to be warned. Though an alien himself, he was the last hope for humanity. And for Arthur Ford.

Running, tripping, Ford raced away from the cluster of huts to the lonely shed of Elizu Roote.

ABOVE CAMP EARTH, Remo spied Arthur Ford running in the direction opposite Chiun.

There was only a lonely tin hut beyond the main camp. Ford seemed to be heading toward it—and the Rio Grande.

Remo did some quick calculations. Ford had saved Roote once already. He appeared now to be a man with a purpose.

It didn't take long for Remo to come to a conclusion. There wasn't much doubt in Remo's mind where Arthur Ford was running now. And to whom.

Chiun didn't see Ford. From his position on the road, the dilapidated shacks of the main village blocked the Master of Sinanju's view.

Although Remo still felt out of sorts, he didn't think that he was in the dire condition Chiun claimed. As long as he kept his wits about him, he'd be okay. Besides, he'd just keep an eye on

Roote until Chiun arrived *and* watch the old Korean's back if he underestimated his opponent.

In spite of Chiun's warnings, Remo got carefully to his feet. He began to pick his way stealthily across the rocky ledge toward the lone shack.

27

"Behold, lesser mortals, the Master of Sinanju!"

Chiun held his arms out wide. His kimono sleeves flapped like the wings of a giant silver moth.

"Is that like a Time Lord?" someone asked.

Chiun's hazel eyes narrowed. "Is that something that is terribly powerful?"

Many of the Camp Earthers shrugged. "Sure. Yeah. Absolutely." The words were accompanied by confident nods.

"Then I am that, as well," he announced.

"See? What did I tell you?" Walter Malpa enthused. He pulled the hem of his untucked T-shirt in order to better display the picture emblazoned across the front. "He's one of these guys."

"He looks human," someone suggested.

"Yeah," agreed another. "Sort of Chinese."

"'Chinese' and 'human' are mutually exclusive," the Master of Sinanju said flatly.

There was an abrupt commotion at the edge of the crowd. An M-16 barrel suddenly battled its way through the excited throng. At the far end of the weapon was Beta RAM. He aimed the barrel at Chiun's chest.

"Are you people crazy!" he screamed at the other Camp Earthers. He glanced around, eyes wild. Many of the men and women had discarded their weapons. "Pick up your guns!"

Most of them sheepishly gathered up the rifles they had dropped to the dirt.

"He's okay," Walter assured Beta. "Really. He's an alien."

"He's one of the government guys who chased me from Las Cruces," Beta said, annoyed at Walter.

"Look at him," Walter insisted. "That's no Fed. The head, the eyes, the fingers. Even the robe screams 'alien.'"

Chiun had tucked his hands inside the sleeves of his kimono. He stared blankly at Beta RAM.

Beta looked down at Chiun's wizened form. Flickering light from a dozen fires illuminated his kimono in an eerie glow. On closer inspection, though he hated to admit it, Beta realized the kid might have a point. Even so, he nudged his weapon closer to Chiun.

"If you're an alien, where's your ship?" Beta asked.

"Maybe he's from that UFO the electricity guy shot down," a Camp Earther suggested.

"Let *him* answer," Beta threatened.

Seeing their leader so concerned, some of the others had put their earlier enthusiasm in check.

They aimed their weapons at the Master of Sinanju, as well.

"I have parked my USO in the desert, so as to avoid the prying eyes of your government. See? I am well versed in your paranoid delusions. Now, to the matter at hand. Where is the one who was taken from the military base?"

Beta ignored the question, offering one of his own.

"USO?"

"Yes," Chiun intoned. "I am a great advocate of USOs."

"United Service Organizations?" Beta RAM asked.

"What?" Chiun said.

"That's what USO stands for," Beta explained. "You know, they're the ones who go around entertaining the troops during wartime."

"What are you babbling about?" Chiun asked. "I am not interested in troops. Only a single soldier. The one called Roote."

Some eyes strayed to Beta RAM. They knew that this was the name of the alien they were protecting.

"Roote is a soldier?" Walter asked. "Was he part of the intergalactic militia?"

Chiun did not hesitate an instant. "Yes," he replied. "I seek out this powerful and evil being in order that he might face trial beyond the stars." He waved an ominous hand skyward.

"What did he do?" asked a fascinated voice.

"He is a criminal."

There were shocked gasps. "Like Khan?" Walter asked, referring to the *Star Trek* character.

"Of course not," Chiun replied, thinking they were talking about Genghis Khan, a figure much beloved in Sinanju history. "I tell you this," he intoned, raising an instructive finger, "Khan was not only a great and much maligned ruler, but he always paid on time."

The Master of Sinanju would have gone on to further extol the virtues of the bloodthirsty Mongol leader, but he noticed all at once that the wonder-filled faces of a moment before had been replaced by expressions of cold mistrust.

"I *told* you," Beta barked to his followers. "He's no alien. He's with the government."

All of the weapons were up now. Twenty M-16s were aimed at Chiun's chest.

Remaining as deathly still as the mountain on which they all stood, the Master of Sinanju acknowledged not a single weapon. His hazel eyes were fixed on Beta RAM.

"What do we do with him?" Walter asked nervously.

Beta glanced back across the encampment, toward the lone hut where Arthur Ford's alien was hiding.

Beta turned back to the tiny figure standing before the flickering flames. He didn't hesitate in his response.

"Kill him," Beta said, his voice cold steel.

And the night erupted in automatic-weapons fire.

"THEY'RE HERE!" Arthur Ford whispered hoarsely as he ducked inside the door of Roote's shack.

The private was lounging against one wall. One index finger tapped idly against the top of a spent battery, sparking a single repetitive blue shock of electricity.

"Beta's friends?" he asked with a sick smile.

Ford nodded desperately. Thinking better, he began shaking his head just as frantically.

"Not both of them. Just the old one."

At that moment, gunfire erupted across the camp.

Ford twisted, startled. He was so panicked, he almost dropped his rifle.

"They're coming!" he yelled.

"Calm down," Elizu Roote insisted.

Sighing, Roote glanced up at the corrugated roof of the shed. As the many guns rattled loudly outside, Roote seemed unconcerned. Staring at the ceiling, he continued to tap, bored, against the battery.

Roote's eyes strayed down the tin walls, skipping over to Arthur Ford's intent face. He smiled.

"Well, if he's so eager to meet me, by all means, let's invite him into my parlor," Elizu Roote said with an evil grin.

TWENTY SECONDS before the Camp Earthers started shooting at Chiun, Remo was having his own problems.

He had circled around to a point just above Elizu Roote's shack. Arthur Ford had just ducked inside, and Remo was about to proceed down the hill when he felt the gun barrel in his ribs.

"Get up."

Two men. Perimeter guards.

He should have sensed them. At any other time since his earliest Sinanju training, he would have. But his body had yet to counter the residual effects of Roote's attack. In focusing his senses on the building below he had opened himself up to a nearer opponent.

Remo rose dutifully to his feet, arms raised.

The shack was forgotten. He drew his senses back in tight, focusing on his immediate environment.

Just the two. No more loitering in the brush.

They wore grubby flannel shirts and jeans. Scraggly beards sprouted from their grimy faces.

"Is this the Devil's Tower landing strip?" Remo asked innocently. "I've got to catch a bus to Melmac."

It was at that moment that the gunfire erupted in the camp below.

The men twisted, startled. Looking down into the camp, they were just able to see a flash of silver near the fires. A tiny figure seemed to be dancing among their fellow Camp Earthers. Wherever it went, bodies seemed to fall.

As quickly as their interest in the distant battle was piqued, it evaporated.

Both men felt their guns being yanked from their grimy hands. They spun back to the man they had discovered lurking above the hut of their precious alien.

Remo was tossing the M-16s into the shadows. Soaring unseen, they flew over the side of the cliff, plummeting through the empty space to the Rio Grande far below.

"Hey, what'd you do with my gun?" one man complained.

"This," Remo replied.

Grabbing a handful of grubby shirt, Remo repeated the action he'd performed with the rifle. Screaming all the way, the Camp Earther arced out over the side of the mountain and plunged through the night air. The man's cry for help ended in a distant splash.

After witnessing the fate of his companion, the second man decided to take his chances on land. Without a word to Remo, he turned and flung himself over the edge of the hill, crashing down through rock and brush until he struck the plateau below. Once he hit, he did not move again.

"My life would be a heck of a lot easier if they all did that," Remo commented as he looked down at the body.

In the distant camp, guns still blazed. Chiun could take care of himself.

Senses straining alertness, Remo began picking his careful way down the hill to the shack.

CHIUN SWIRLED through the mob of Camp Earthers, an angry silver dervish.

Guns were wrenched from their owners, tearing arms from sockets in the process. Both rifles and appendages were flung aside.

"You dare!" Chiun raged.

Two Camp Earthers leaned against a pathetic tin shed, thinking that by bracing their backs they could get a steadier shot. But although they tried to track the movements of the tiny figure who flounced and spun within their midst, they failed to score a single hit.

Chiun suddenly whirled on the two men. Framed by campfire, he was like some demon cast up from the very bowels of hell itself.

Panicked, the pair unloaded everything in their magazines. It was not enough. As bullets sang out into the dark night, Chiun flew at the two men.

As he was airborne, nary a bullet kissed a single silk kimono thread.

Sandaled feet caught two brittle sternums, crushing them to splinters. The men exploded backward, crumpling the flimsy shed wall. Even as the dust began to collect on the thin film of blood that gurgled up between their dead lips, the roof of the shack was tumbling downward. It formed a makeshift coffin lid.

Chiun twirled from the collapsed corrugated tin.

The steady pop-pop of automatic-weapons fire had dwindled rapidly since its start mere moments before. The Master of Sinanju spun through the last four firing Camp Earthers.

Toes lashed out; hands were flung in seemingly wild gestures. Fingers clasping guns were shattered to jelly. Blood erupted from throats and chests. The gunmen fell to the dirt.

Chiun wheeled, narrowed eyes searching. He found Beta RAM cowering behind a pile of crates that the residents of Camp Earth had been breaking up for firewood.

Whirling over to the wooden boxes, Chiun brought his hands down in furious slashing movements. The wood shattered to kindling beneath his vengeful fists.

With one hand, Chiun lifted Beta into the air.

"Where is the one called Roote?" the Master of Sinanju demanded hotly.

Beta extended a single, shaking hand. He was like a palsy victim. "There," he gasped, pointing to the far end of the encampment.

With a look of disgust on his wrinkled parchment features, Chiun flung Beta into the ruins of one of the Camp Earth shacks. Spinning on his heel, he marched from the scene of carnage, toward Roote's shack.

Even as Chiun was storming across the camp, Beta was pulling himself to his feet.

He didn't give Chiun's back a second glance.

Heart thudding madly, Beta RAM ran as fast as he could in the opposite direction.

28

Chiun's hooded eyes were knots of vellum mistrust as he watched the familiar figure running toward him.

Arthur Ford ran, stumbling, across the camp, away from the sand-covered promontory on which Elizu Roote's tin shack rested. Eyes wild, he flung himself desperately at the Master of Sinanju. Chiun grabbed the ufologist by the shoulders, holding him at an annoyed distance.

"You've got to save us!" Ford begged. "He's crazy!"

"You aided his escape," Chiun said levelly.

"That's because I didn't know what he was," Ford pleaded desperately. "You've got to believe me. He's dangerous. He has to be stopped."

Chiun released the UFO enthusiast. "This creature. It lurks within?" the old Korean asked.

Ford nodded. "He knows you're here, but he's weak. I don't think he has much power left."

Eyes directed at the shack, the Master of Sinanju nodded crisply. He sensed both truth and deception coming from Ford. Without another word, he turned and crossed the small space to Roote's hut.

Behind him a tiny smile broke out across Ford's face as Chiun ducked through the metal door.

There was a moment of frightening silence.

All at once, a massive thumping noise erupted from the tin shed. And as Ford watched with nervous glee, the entire shack was engulfed in a pulse of electric blue.

HE WAS TOO SLOW!

Halfway up the hill, Remo watched in horror as the massive surge of electrical energy coursed around the exterior of the tiny metal hut. The hum that permeated the night air was that of a million insects' fluttering wings in one horrible instant.

Remo had only seen Chiun at the last moment. Too late to even shout a warning as the old Korean ducked inside the shed.

Now, as he watched the arcs of high voltage leap from one side of the frame to the other at the mouth of the shack, the dreadful truth could not be denied.

Roote was far more powerful than he had been during his encounter with Remo. There was no way Chiun could have survived such a massive burst of electricity.

It was Remo's fault.

This did Remo lament as he scurried the rest of the way down the hill, as he raced over to the shack.

His fault.

If he had been able to stop Roote the first time...

If he had been able to convince Chiun of the seriousness of Roote's abilities...

If, if, if...

At the open door, he couldn't see through the blinding arcs of bluish electrical energy. It didn't matter. His senses already told him the awful truth.

There were no life signs inside.

Chiun was dead.

All of the weakness he had been feeling since his original encounter with the killer drained away. Decades of exacting Sinanju training reasserted itself in one glorious, horrible instant. His heart rate quickened, then leveled.

A world of sensation exploded like a supernova out around the perfectly attuned body of Remo Williams.

Breathing the night air deeply, Remo broadened the focus of his senses to encompass the entire area around the bluff.

He found Roote.

The soldier was behind the shed. Directing his energy toward the rear wall. Frying whoever was hapless enough to step inside the deadly trap.

Remo channeled all of the swirling emotions he was feeling into a single, violent pit of white-hot rage.

Centering himself, he stepped around the side of the shack.

Elizu Roote was leaning casually against a boulder that jutted out of the outcropping of rock above the Rio Grande.

The killer seemed almost bored as he funneled streams of directed electrical energy into the rear of the shack.

A look of great surprise spread across Roote's pale features as Remo stepped around the building. The expression changed to one of satisfaction. He instantly cut the power flowing from his fingertips.

"Old geezer should be barbecued by now, what do you think?" he drawled happily. A smile creased his face.

"I think you're dead," Remo replied coldly. He walked slowly toward the killer.

"Now hold on there, fella," Roote said. "Ain't you forgetting somethin'? I whipped your ass last time."

As a reminder, he held up his hands. Sparks crackled between his metal-tipped fingers.

"You're nothing but a maniac crossbred with a microwave," Remo said. "I'm pulling your plug."

The smile faded from Roote's face. He obviously didn't consider Remo a threat. He stood his ground as Remo strode ever closer to him.

"Are you working for Chesterfield?" the private demanded. "'Cause he's the real maniac. He knew what I was. But he went ahead and made me like this anyway."

"He's next."

Roote nodded. "Yep, I reckon he is. But I'll be the one gettin' him."

And with that, Roote lowered his hands.

Optical targeting sensors locked on Remo's chest. All ten fingers combined their strength, launching a single explosive burst of electricity from Elizu Roote's gold fingertips.

But for the first time since his high-tech hardware was installed, something went wrong. He had a positive target lock, but for some reason, the target wasn't there.

The electrical surge passed harmlessly through the air, pounding into the rear of the shed. The tin roof rattled in angry protest.

Roote scanned the area quickly, looking for Remo once more. He found his target immediately— Remo was several feet to the left of where he had been. He was also much closer to Roote.

At the same time he was locating Remo, Roote's sensors registered another figure in the combat area.

He was coming around the far side of the shed. Racing in Remo's direction.

"Alien killer!" Arthur Ford screamed.

The ufologist was rushing at Remo from behind, brandishing one of the M-16 assault rifles.

When Remo glanced over his shoulder toward Ford, he presented Roote with a perfect target. He was a sitting duck.

The Army private raised his hands, locking on Remo. But at the moment he was about to fire, his autonomic preservation system suddenly kicked in.

Ocular scanners automatically fastened on Arthur Ford's raised gun.

It all happened in an instant.

The blue sparks leapt from Roote's fingers, gathering into a single burst of lightning, but Remo was already falling and rolling even before the bolt of energy popped from the killer's fingers.

The surge leapt over the back of Remo's T-shirt, soaring behind him, connecting with an audible thump with the barrel of Arthur Ford's M-16.

The shock flung Ford backward. He soared high in the air, crashing solidly into the rear of the shed. The metal buckled beneath the deadweight of his lifeless body. Both ufologist and gun dropped to the dirt.

Roote wheeled back to where Remo had been.

He was no longer there.

To his horror, Remo suddenly reappeared, this time standing directly before Roote.

"Time to power down," Remo said flatly.

Roote swung his hand around, trying to get a close-up shot at Remo. He found his arm blocked.

And before he could fire again, he felt a sudden explosive pressure at the center of his chest. In the next instant he felt a push of warm air whistling past his ears, tugging him ever faster to the earth far below. The falling sensation was succeeded by a wet, engulfing blackness.

After that, Elizu Roote felt nothing at all.

ON THE LEDGE HIGH ABOVE, Remo Williams looked down at the limp body of Elizu Roote as it floated down the black strip of the Rio Grande. Desert stars twinkled brightly on the surface of the water.

Remo clenched and unclenched his hand. Something didn't feel right.

The crushing blow he had used against Roote's chest should have felt more solid. Instead, there had been an odd tingling sensation—almost as if the killing blow had failed to make complete contact. Obviously it had worked, however. Otherwise Roote would still be standing there.

Staring down at the limp body, Remo couldn't savor the victory. His success against Elizu Roote had come at a greater cost than he ever wished to pay.

He would have to collect the body of the Master of Sinanju. The old Korean would want to be buried in his native village, along with his ancestors. Although Remo tried to brace himself for what he would find inside the tiny shed, he knew that it would be impossible to do.

Heart heavy, Remo turned slowly back to the shack...

And nearly tripped over Chiun.

"Watch where you drop your fat white feet," the Master of Sinanju complained. He was observing the body as it washed slowly down the river. His face settled into lines of satisfaction as the current carried Elizu Roote around a bend and out of sight.

Remo no longer cared about Roote. He was staring in shock at the wizened form of the Master of Sinanju.

"You're alive!" Remo said, elated.

"And you are a lazybones," Chiun charged. "*Now* you get better. After *I* have done all the work."

"How?" Remo asked, dumbfounded. For the first time he noticed the film of dirt on Chiun's silver kimono.

Chiun shrugged. "The ground here is softer than it is back at the encampment of idiots," he said. He patted the sleeves of his kimono with his slender fingers. Thin clouds of dust escaped into the night air.

"So what?" Remo asked. Even as he said it, a light seemed to dawn in his eyes.

"Now you see." Chiun smiled. "You are not as uneducable as people say."

"You burrowed into the ground the second Roote started zapping the hut," Remo said, nodding in appreciation. "Like a prairie dog."

"Aside from the insulting rodent reference, you are essentially correct," Chiun agreed. "I will overlook the slur in consideration for all that you have been through."

Remo smiled. "So you finally believe me?" he asked.

Chiun was blandly surprised. "Did I ever doubt you?" he said.

All Remo could do was laugh.

As they walked away from the ledge, Chiun continued to flap his silver kimono sleeves against his skirts. Plumes of dust rose into the black desert night.

29

In the paneled study of an anonymous ivy-covered townhouse in Arlington, Virginia, General Delbert Xavier Chesterfield was reviewing his Shock Troops notes. He was scheduled to make a presentation at the Pentagon in just under two hours, and he wanted to make certain that every shred of his involvement with the development of the project was purged from the records.

It was easy enough to do. He controlled the only remaining notes and schematics. The essential scientific staff was dead. The others only knew him as some kind of military liaison to the project. He had always played his cards right with the braniacs on the team. Good thing, too. Even though the shit had already hit the fan at Fort Joy, so far Chesterfield had been able to fob it all off on the CIA. He'd reinforce that impression this afternoon at the briefing.

The big leather sofa on which he sat creaked in protest as he adjusted his massive frame. A small pen gripped awkwardly in his huge fingers underlined important sections in his notes.

Harold Jones. Central Intelligence operative.

The man was an idiot. His arrival on the scene had handed Chesterfield the scapegoat he was looking for.

When the investigations started, it would be a pleasure to watch Jones, the persnickety would-be autocrat, sweating before some congressional oversight committee, trying to explain that he had nothing to do with Shock Troops. No one ever believed the CIA. This would certainly not be the exception to that rule.

Maybe they'd even televise the hearings. The whole nation would learn of the CIA perfidy. Chesterfield would enjoy that.

Remo H. and Chiun, last name unknown.

Jones's CIA hit squad. Remo was the muscle. Chiun was probably some kind of Chinese commie hireling.

It was beautiful. So much so that Chesterfield put an extra squiggle beneath both their names. He would be sure to mention them repeatedly during the briefing. It would lend credibility to his own story.

Of course, there was the one big loose end.

Elizu Roote.

Chesterfield wasn't all that concerned. Left to his own devices, Roote would most likely self-destruct eventually. Psychos like him always did. In fact, Chesterfield wouldn't be a bit surprised if Roote was dead already.

He could picture the deranged, pathetic private

lying facedown in the desert somewhere. Sun beating down. Buzzards picking at his crazed carcass.

Chesterfield smiled at the image.

No, Elizu Roote wouldn't be a problem. Nothing would be a problem. By day's end General Delbert Xavier Chesterfield would have a few extra stars on his shoulders and a rosy red future with the United States Army's Advanced Applications and Development branch. He would ask for more funding for the research. Of course, this time it would be done under the more critical and safety-conscious auspices of the Army.

The Shock Troops data he had brought with him from Fort Joy would be used to create a whole army of Elizu Rootes. Except this time the subjects would be sane and—most importantly—this time Chesterfield would take all the credit.

There was no doubt about it. For this particular general, the world was a big, beautiful place.

Chesterfield struggled to pull his girth from the sofa. The general stepped out of the study and over into the small kitchen. He rummaged around in a cupboard for a while, finally pulling out a bag of Oreos he'd had delivered.

When he returned to the study, Chesterfield was stunned to find someone sitting in his seat. He was even more shocked to see who it was.

"Interesting piece of fiction you've crafted here," Remo Williams commented.

With Chesterfield's notebook balanced on one knee, Remo passed a bored eye over the handwritten notes. He held the general's riding crop in his free hand and was tapping the leather end lazily against the arm of the sofa.

"How—?" the general began, black eyes astonished.

"The gravest insult is that he claims I am Chinese," a squeaky voice announced from the general's elbow.

Chesterfield nearly jumped out of his skin, so startled was he by the closeness of the voice.

When he glanced to his right, he realized that the old one had been standing near his elbow the entire time. He had been so still, the wallpaper seemed to move more.

With the tip of his tongue, Chesterfield picked nervously at the chunks of chocolate between his teeth.

"You boys had best skedaddle," he said, trying to sound threatening. "Your cover's blown. Everyone at the Pentagon knows your boss Jones cooked up the whole Shock Troops thing. I was misled. Typical of you CIA types. I thought he had authorization."

"*Smith,*" Remo corrected.

Chesterfield grew puzzled. "What's that, boy?"

"His name is Smith, not Jones. And he is definitely not CIA. Neither are we, for that matter."

"A fact for which my surviving brain cells are eternally grateful," said the Master of Sinanju.

Chesterfield glanced at Chiun, then slowly back at Remo.

"An obvious falsehood," he said. "I've dished out a few of them in my day. Now toddle along, fellas. My people at the Pentagon—"

"Person," Remo interjected. "You had one contact at the Pentagon," Remo said. "One. An old college buddy." He stifled a yawn as he tossed the notebook onto an end table. "A guy just as anxious as you for advancement. He's the one who sent the extra dough to Fort Joy."

"How—?" Chesterfield began once more. He stopped himself abruptly, trying to gather his wits once more. "How could you know that?"

"Jones is a bright guy," Remo said, standing. "Now, aside from the notes and that stack of records there—" he indicated the printouts next to a computer in the corner of the room "—is there any other Roote-related junk here?"

Chesterfield was already doing rapid calculations.

"Okay," he said hopefully. "You've got me over a barrel here, boys. Tell you what. I cooperate, and you forget I was ever involved in this whole Shock Troops thing. It's all over anyway. What's the harm in lettin' a little two-star general off the hook?"

Remo considered the offer for a moment. Finally he nodded his agreement. "Okay, what the hell," he said. "I just want to get this all behind us. You've got a deal."

Chesterfield's chest puffed out in relief. "Great," he enthused. "Everything is in this room.

The computer is from Joy. There's Shock Troops stuff on the hard drive, plus on any of the floppies around here. That's about it.''

Remo glanced at the items as the general pointed them out. There didn't seem to be much.

"Chiun?" Remo asked, turning back to the others.

"He is telling the truth," the Master of Sinanju said.

"What?" Chesterfield said. He sounded insulted. "Of course I am, boy."

Remo smiled. "That's too bad. Because I wasn't."

Still grinning, Remo nodded to the Master of Sinanju.

A familiar sensation abruptly took hold of General Chesterfield. It was the same weightless feeling he had gotten back at Fort Joy when the old Korean had thrown him through the wall of his own HQ.

But it was different this time. He knew it wasn't the same as the ceiling whipped around and his beefy body made a sudden, rapid beeline for the exterior wall.

This time the velocity was far greater. This time he felt the flat of his meaty back slam with bone-shattering force against the solid interior wall.

The pain was horrific, excruciating. And as quickly as it had come, it was over. As was the general.

General Delbert Xavier Chesterfield's spinal column was crushed to jelly even before the carefully assembled brick wall of his expensive rented town house exploded out into the bright Virginia sunlight.

As the body settled like a rapidly flattening tire to the hard sidewalk, a hail of stone fragments and mortar dust settled gently on the two meager stars on his otherwise bare shoulder boards.

30

Hours later Remo and Chiun stood before the desk of Harold W. Smith at Folcroft Sanitarium in Rye, New York.

"Are you certain this is everything?" Smith asked. He was examining the paperwork Remo had brought with them from Virginia. The general's computer sat atop Smith's desk.

"That's all Chesterfield had," Remo said. "As long as you took care of everything at Fort Joy, we should be all set."

"There is no data left on the base," Smith assured him.

"Great," Remo said. "Then it's over."

"What about the general?"

"Your deceitful centurion will plague you no more, Emperor," the Master of Sinanju announced.

Remo smiled. "My only regret is that he had but one life to give to his country," he added.

Smith nodded his approval. "His Pentagon connection was weak, at best. There should not be much interest among his superiors concerning his death. Chesterfield was not very well liked in military circles.''

"I don't see why," Remo commented dryly. "You'd think they'd love having a walking megaphone like that around just in case the sound system goes down during the Army-Navy game."

"Then that is that," Smith said, satisfied. He pushed the papers to one side for later disposal in the Folcroft furnace. "With Roote and Chesterfield both gone, we can put this episode behind us."

"Um, Smitty..." Remo interjected.

The Master of Sinanju tugged angrily at the back of Remo's T-shirt. He knew what his pupil was going to say. Remo had already mentioned it in the car on their way up from Virginia.

"The Emperor has important business to conduct," Chiun hissed. "We should leave."

"What is it, Remo?" Smith asked, curious.

Exasperated, the Master of Sinanju rolled his eyes ceilingward.

"About Roote," Remo hesitated, glancing at Chiun. "You know how I told you I crushed his chest. It's a pretty standard Sinanju move."

"Yes." Smith's voice had taken on a concerned edge.

"It's nothing to worry about. Honest. It's just that there was a strange tingling in my arm when I took him out. It wasn't a shock or anything. It just felt weird."

Smith nodded. "Superconductivity," he explained. "In reading the schematics of the system incorporated into him, I saw that solenoids were used for his relays. These are electromechanical devices that produce mechanical motions when energized by an electric current.''

"So?"

"The type used in Roote is significant. The scientists utilized magnetic solenoids.''

Remo glanced at Chiun. The Master of Sinanju only frowned. To the old Korean, this was merely more white madness. Akin to admitting possible failure to an emperor. Remo turned back to Smith.

"At the risk of sounding repetitive—so?" he said.

"Magnetic solenoids generate high fields in large volumes of material with virtually no power dissipation. The type used by the Fort Joy doctors in Roote was particularly advanced. Some of the earliest data they collected on him after the procedure indicates that the hardware with which they equipped him altered him on the cellular level. In effect, he became superconductive when his capacitors were charged.''

"I know what that is," Remo said. "Superconductivity is what makes those Japanese trains float above their rails.''

"That is a crude explanation, but essentially correct.''

Remo followed the logical thread, even though he didn't like where it was leading him. "So you're saying that I could have *thought* I gave

Roote the whammy, but never actually hit him. I might have just hit some kind of magnetic field."

Smith sat up more straightly in his leather chair. "You assured me that he was dead," he said levelly. He placed his palms calmly on his desk.

Remo's face was clouded. "I thought he was," he said. "I mean, he is," he added more firmly. "Of course he is. After all, he fell into water."

Smith shook his head. "That means nothing."

"What do you mean?" Remo challenged. "Of course it does. Doesn't water blow up electrical stuff? People kill themselves by taking toasters into the bathtub with them, don't they?"

Smith closed his eyes. "Yes, that is true," he said patiently. "But if an unplugged toaster is dropped into a bathtub, it can be dried out and reused."

"We are wasting the Emperor's precious time," the Master of Sinanju whispered loudly.

Remo didn't hear. "You mean that nutcase could still be out there?" he said to Smith.

Opening his eyes, the CURE director sighed. "Possibly," he admitted. "How far did you say he fell?"

"Far enough to make this speculation pointless," Chiun interjected.

"About a hundred feet. Maybe more. And I think there were rocks in the water."

Smith looked up at them. His eyes were bloodshot from lack of sleep.

"In that case, Chiun is right. Elizu Roote is dead."

But even as Smith said it, there was doubt in his voice.

EPILOGUE

Behind him the dying New Mexico sky was painted in streaks of rusty gray. Before was complete darkness as the battered old truck made its way along the rocky shore of the Rio Grande.

He had survived by the grace of Salvion. Beta RAM knew that there was no other explanation. Few had been left alive after the massacre at Camp Earth.

There was a new purpose to his life. He had been looking to the sky, when he should have been looking right here on Earth. It was so obvious to him now, he was embarrassed by his earlier naïveté.

Salvion and his followers were already here.

As he rode up out of the path at the river's bumpy shoreline, a small bluff rose steadily in the distance, framed on all sides by the panorama of the upended bowl that was the desert sky.

Beyond the bluff, angry black storm clouds rolled in from the south. Streaks of jagged lightning connected the ground to the heavens in violent spurts. Thunder rumbled loudly across the vacant expanse.

Above the flat-topped hill, still far ahead, a flock of buzzards flew in endless lazy circles. The huge birds were waiting patiently for something to die.

All at once, a streak of lightning seemed to explode from the surface of the bluff. Catching one of the circling birds in the breast, it appeared to hold it for a moment, suspending the hapless creature in midair.

Just as suddenly as it had appeared, the lightning vanished. The bird plummeted to the ground amid a mass of gently floating black feathers.

A moment later, it was as if it had never happened. The storm continued to rage on the far side of the bluff, moving ever closer with each passing minute. The wind before the rain pushed swirls of dust into Beta's windshield.

Beta stopped his truck.

He wasn't quite sure what he had just witnessed. After all, the desert sometimes had a habit of playing tricks on one's eyes.

As he sat unmoving on the path, engine idling, the first fat uncertain raindrops began to splatter mud against his windshield. Slowly he put the truck into drive.

Beta RAM drove into the gathering storm.

Political ambitions...

DON PENDLETON's
MACK BOLAN®
EXECUTIVE ACTION

When a bigoted civilian militia targets a group of
Montagnard refugees living on a North Carolina
commune, Hal Brognola asks Mack Bolan to intervene.
But what Bolan uncovers is a plot by a high ranking
Pentagon official to use hate-mongers to propel him
into the White House.

Available in January 2000 at your favorite retail outlet.

The ultimate weapon of terror...

JAMES AXLER

DEATH LANDS®

Dark Reckoning

A secret community of scientists gains control of an orbiting transformer that could become the ultimate weapon of terror—and it's up to Ryan Cawdor to halt the evil mastermind before he can incinerate Front Royal.

Book 3 in the Baronies Trilogy, three books that chronicle the strange attempts to unify the East Coast baronies. Who (or what) is behind this coercive process?

James Axler

OUTLANDERS™

WREATH OF FIRE

Ambika, an amazon female, has been gathering groups of
Outlanders in the Western Isles in an attempt to overthrow
the Barons. But are her motives just a ploy to satisfy her
own ambition?

Follow Remo and Chiun on more of their extraordinary adventures....

THE Destroyer™